Truelove Trail

MARY SHOTWELL

CITY OWL
PRESS

TRUELOVE TRAIL
Waverly Lake, Book 2

CITY OWL PRESS
www.cityowlpress.com

Cover Design by Tina Moss. All stock photos licensed appropriately.

Edited by Tee Tate.

For information on subsidiary rights, please contact the publisher at info@cityowlpress.com.

Print Edition ISBN: 978-1-64898-218-7

Digital Edition ISBN: 978-1-64898-217-0

Printed in the United States of America

To my hiking, AT-loving husband

Chapter One

Monday, October 3

Some would say October was the most beautiful month in Waverly Lake. The westerly breeze off the Appalachian Mountains vanished any remnants of heat the lake held from the summer sun. The aspens and oaks sprinkled their golden and burnt sienna branches in leaf confetti, threatening to cover the roads traversing the miles of coastline and hills in this nook, North Carolina's Hidden Gem of the West.

Tracy Bennett found herself riding along one such road, winding the western edge of the lake and turning east. She, however, had not taken in the breeze, or continuously changing color palette of autumn. She had been lucky enough to stumble out of bed after the late nights of the weekend, taking in every ounce of fun she could have with her visiting Floridian friends before starting her endeavor.

"Do you at least get weekends off?" Sebastian kept one hand on the steering wheel, the other tucking the free locks behind his ear. His side shave of the summer had grown out considerably, yet he refused to cut the longer half of hair to match it.

"It's not exactly a nine-to-five job," Tracy managed through a yawn. "It's an as-needed kind of thing. There will be times I'm busy and times when I can come into town." *The best kind of job.* Working was something Tracy did to get by—to make enough to cover her next adventure. Unlike her parents, she didn't believe everyone had a single purpose in life, nor should they limit themselves to one single goal to achieve.

They remained on the road closest to the lake, at the lowest elevation along the northern banks. It still put them well above lake level, with Sebastian's driving around bends and turns displacing her organs.

She couldn't complain, though. Her lifestyle didn't afford her a car, nor did she want to deal with one and its upkeep.

"Kind of reminds me of our little road trip." Sebastian grinned, keeping his eyes on the road.

"Little? You mean, thousands of miles to California and back?"

"You weren't the best at winding through the Rockies."

Tracy recalled gripping the steering wheel tightly for hours, a rainstorm slicking the pavement and blurring the windshield.

Sebastian turned his gaze to her. "I'm still glad we did it. Even if it meant you didn't get that internship."

Tracy smiled, though the injury of rejection from Biltmore Estate was still tender. Never mind it was four years ago, when she thought she wanted to be an event planner. The four-week, looping trip across the U.S. proved that she was both excellent at planning and not ready to align herself with a stationary career.

"Here we go." The sign to Woodsman's Lodge had simple brown lettering atop a cream background, with a large brown arrow at the bottom. Sebastian turned onto the access road, at spots a steep decline on the eastward side of the property. He did his best to avoid the growing potholes as they passed raised garden beds and a near-empty woodpile before leveling off around the side of the lodge. He parked perpendicular to a handful of parking spots in front of Woodsman's Lodge. "Gosh, it's been years since I've been here. Tell Aunt Dee hello for me."

"I will." Tracy grabbed her backpack and suitcase out of the backseat. She leaned to the front passenger door for a brief smile at Sebastian. "Thanks for the ride."

"Any time. Come visit when you get a break."

"You know it." She closed the door, and Sebastian circled around the lot, leaves rolling in the car's faint smoky exhaust.

Tracy paused a moment, examining the eight wooden stairs leading to the front porch. The lodge, by no means an architectural dream, conjured warm memories for her—of playing, of not caring about the world outside its realm. Its simple two-story structure, with covered front and back porches, four dormer windows along the metal roof, and never-ending cedar walls still looked reminiscent of the homestead that had stood before it nearly a century and a half ago. She only knew that to be true because of the framed picture Aunt Dee kept in her office.

Tracy walked up the stairs, the second step creaking the same as it did years ago, as if it purposely sounded a greeting to guests. The front door swung open before she landed a foot on the porch.

"Tracy!" Aunt Dee opened her arms, ready to catch Tracy's hug.

"Hello, Aunt Dee." She welcomed her great aunt's embrace. At nearly eighty-two, Aunt Dee was the eldest on either side of Tracy's lineage. She had the wrinkles and gray-streaked hair to show for it, but her physical fitness and go-getter attitude defied her age. Perhaps it had something to do with the fresh mountain air and living away from the busyness of the city. Not that Waverly Lake compared to Charlotte, or even Asheville in its population or bustle.

"It's so good to have you here." Aunt Dee examined Tracy's face as if she counted the summer freckles fading with the diminishing daylight hours of fall. "Oh, and that hair." She ran her hand along the brunette curls spiraling around Tracy's face. "I've always been jealous of that head of hair."

Tracy gave up on trying to tame or style her hair long ago. Instead, she let the curls do their own thing, and she took pride in her hair reflecting her life's philosophy. Aunt Dee was one of the few who truly accepted her for it too.

"Come on in, let's get you settled."

Tracy followed Aunt Dee into the lodge and set down her backpack and suitcase on the floor to the right, by the front desk. "It still looks as I remembered it." Tracy smiled, unbuttoning her sweater, the heat of the fireplace on the east wall warming the first floor. Two worn tufted armchairs sat in the front corner by a bookshelf of aged books, while four rectangular tables sat in the back corner near the fire, ready for the afternoon's coffee and tea break. A mural covered the back wall, a depiction of the forest and yellow-brick road from *The Wizard of Oz*, where the Tinman was found. Aunt Dee was short for Dorothy, a name most people associated with the tale. It was how she came up with the name Woodsman's Lodge.

"I hope that doesn't mean it's looking as old as me," Aunt Dee said.

"One can only hope to age like you." Tracy touched Aunt Dee's wrinkled hand on the desk. Her silvered hair was fashioned in a low ponytail, the tail part not quite all the way pulled through the hair tie. While she could probably outrun people twenty years younger, her frame was more skin and bones than the muscular tone it had once been.

"I take it you're still hiking? Is that your secret to looking great?"

"Oh hush. Yes, I get in my early morning walks. I can't say my knees are what they used to be, though."

"No one can say that about their knees." Tracy winked. "So, what all do you have planned for me here, or can we keep chatting and delay all the business stuff? My vote is on delaying."

Aunt Dee pulled out a binder from the bar-height desk.

Tracy laughed to herself. Of course Aunt Dee's vote was business.

"I've got quite a checklist that needs completing," Aunt Dee said. "Now that the summer vacationers are back at home with kids in school, I usually take this time to prepare for the holiday rush. Fall is usually slower around here, except for the hikers, of course."

"They're still passing through here, huh?"

"You know, not as many backpackers as there used to be. Everyone's into their campers and trailers these days. But we still get a few. Thank goodness for the AT."

The Appalachian Trail sliced right by Waverly Lake, more specifically, Woodsman's Lodge. In fact, a side trail split off it and cut across the road she had taken to the lodge. It continued onward east along the lake. For those hiking through, it was a good stop to have a night's sleep under a roof and replenish supplies in town before either heading north through The Smoky Mountain National Park, or south to the trail's end in Georgia. Most hikers this time of year came from the north, heading south. Tracy had enjoyed frequenting a mile or two of it in her youth, hoping to meet hikers. She had never come across a through-hiker that didn't have an entertaining story.

"I hear you've had your share of wandering the past year."

Tracy nodded. "You know me. Before coming back this summer, I was in Australia for three months."

"Oh my, what were you doing there?"

"Exploring. A few of my girlfriends and I took a road trip for about half that time, checking out all the states."

"And the other half?"

"Working to afford the road trip." She chuckled, and Aunt Dee shook her head. Tracy wasn't sure if Aunt Dee took her seriously or thought it was a joke. But it was the truth.

"Well, you're here now and can earn some money for wherever it is your mind takes you."

"That's the plan." A trip to New Zealand after Thanksgiving, to be exact. With the earnings from Aunt Dee, plus what she had saved from odd jobs this summer, and if she limited her spending over the next few weeks, she'd be able to afford the flight. She had assimilated into a group of four girlfriends who called themselves the Aussie Posse earlier this year. They wanted to reunite for a three-month excursion across New Zealand, made possible by half of them working remotely, and the other half living off the grid entirely.

Aunt Dee reached behind the desk and set down a plastic bag.

"Now, in here is your key. You'll be in room one with its own bathroom."

"Are you sure?" Tracy asked. "I'm okay using the shared bathroom if you have guests that want rooms with private baths."

"I'm sure. I will be having an influx of guests soon, but for the time being you can stay in room one."

Tracy pocketed the key. "Thank you."

"I'm also giving you a cell phone." She pulled it out of the bag. "Your mother said you didn't have one, at least not one with a permanent number."

"For as much as she and I don't get along sometimes, she is right on that account." In her travels, Tracy had the habit of buying a cheap phone and phone card to dispose of after her journey. No sense in keeping a permanent one and paying for a plan—an international one at that.

"I only ask that you please use it for business purposes only. It's my way of getting in touch with you, and vice versa."

Tracy crossed an X over her heart. "I promise. Business only. Besides, I've given the lodge's number to my friends anyway, if they need to get in touch."

Aunt Dee gave her a glare, but accepted the indiscretion for now. "Go ahead and put your bags in your room, and I'll meet you down here to go over these tasks."

"Will do." Tracy grabbed her bags and stopped before heading to the stairs. "You said there will be an influx of visitors soon? Is there something special going on?"

Aunt Dee's eyes lit up as she single-clapped her hands together. "Oh yes. It's something new I've arranged this year, to break up the fall lull we have. I'm calling it Lovetoberfest." She stretched out her hands, as if displaying a banner in mid-air.

Tracy blinked slowly, the smile fading on her face. "Do I even want to ask?"

"It's going to be spectacular. Five men and five women will be staying for a long weekend in the hopes of finding love."

"How do you plan on doing that?" *Stop asking.*

"They will go out on five dates with each other, all here locally. Don't worry, you can help pick out what they'll do if you want. I'd love to have your input, seeing as you have expertise in the planning department."

That's why you don't ask, Tracy. "Oh...okay." It sounded like torture. Five blind dates, all in Waverly Lake? Crammed into a long weekend? Who in their right mind would volunteer to do such a thing? Not only volunteer, but *pay* to be a part of it and stay at the inn.

Aunt Dee's expectation for Tracy's positive reaction waned via raised eyebrows and disappearing glee in her cheeks.

"Hey, if it brings in more people for you in the slower season, I'm happy for you." It came out overly canned. Hopefully, Aunt Dee couldn't read through her as easily as the worn edition of Robert Frost's *Mountain Interval* that no doubt still graced the bookshelf in the corner. "Whatever you think is best for business."

Aunt Dee stood a little straighter. "I do think it'll be good for business. Not just for the lodge. I have potential dates set up with local business owners who jumped at the chance to showcase their business on a date."

Tracy softened her skepticism. Not so much skepticism as it was her own discomfort at the idea. "You're right. I can see how that would be great for Waverly Lake in general. More tourists means more local spending. And I bet they'll be sold on the lodge and come back. Maybe even with their significant other they had met here."

"That would be wonderful, wouldn't it? Someone's love story could originate right here at the lodge. It's all very romantic, isn't it?"

Tracy opted for a smile and nod. How she longed to walk into room one and stay there for the rest of the morning.

The rest of fall.

But Aunt Dee needed her and was paying her, and Tracy needed the money if she ever wanted to get out of Waverly Lake soon.

Out of here and onward, to her next adventure.

Chapter Two

Saturday, October 8

THE IDEA OF BACKPACKING HAD A FUNNY WAY OF NOT matching up with reality. No matter how many times Ben convinced himself he missed feeling the soil beneath his hiking boots or waking in the crisp morning to the quiet of nature, or the pride of knowing he could carry all he needed to survive, reality eventually caught up with him.

It had done so two days ago some twenty miles back. Granted, it took over two hundred miles and three weeks to get to that point. But there was a finite number of worn socks, toe blisters, and rainy nights in a tent before even the most seasoned hiker would crack.

It was partly why he had called Dorothy Bennett. Something about knowing how close he was to a hot shower and a meal that didn't contain peanut butter made him hypersensitive to the aches and weariness of backpacking. He longed for the convenient. For the comfortable.

But it had been his plan all along, to visit Woodsman's Lodge. It wasn't just for a break off the AT. After five years of convincing Frank Letts to continue to manage his parents' estate, Ben had a choice to make. One that had to be made in less than two weeks.

He sipped the few remnants of water left in his hydration bladder, eyeing the sign with the arrow pointing to the right. *Truelove Trail*. Below that, *Woodsman's Lodge 0.6mi.*

Truelove Trail was one of hundreds of side trails off the Appalachian Trail. According to his *Trails of Western North Carolina* map, Truelove Trail was a measly six miles of east-west footpath along the north side of Waverly Lake. It promised a wide view of the lake at its highest elevation, but more importantly, especially to Ben at this moment, it led to Woodsman's Lodge.

As he had started out north of here weeks ago, the trees had already peaked, shedding their leaves along the trail. Sometimes covering it completely. As he moved further south, the foliage on the branches lingered, the hues vibrant as he walked the trail to the lodge.

A brown building appeared around the bend, the lake visible here and there between the lower trunks of trees. He crossed a road and continued along the downhill path winding around the two-story building to the front. Each step starkly reminded him of the thirty pounds he carried, the frame of the pack digging at his back. He considered flinging it off and chucking it into the woods. Good riddance. But then when he left he'd have to buy a new one, and take the next hundred miles getting used to that one until it made marks of its own on his back and psyche.

After bouncing an extra time on the second step to hear its classic creaking under pressure, he willed himself to the top of the stairs and let down his pack. It met the front porch with a thud, as annoyed with Ben as he was with it. He brushed his boots on the wiry welcome mat and entered the lodge.

The aroma of fresh bread from the kitchen to the left weakened his knees. He leaned an elbow on the front counter, the mural of forest in front of him mocking. It showed the pristine, perfect picture he had in his head of the woods before starting his trip. Before the forest and mountains gnawed at his tendons and joints and his will to carry on.

The ironic part was that he'd be ready to go back out there in no time.

"Can I help you?" A young woman approached, placing the poker in its stand by the fireplace. Her head sprung forth curly, dusky hair that she'd tied in a thick ponytail. The tool belt around her waist looked fit for a man twice her size.

"Yes. I called Dorothy about visiting."

"You made a reservation?"

"Not exactly. At least, I'm not sure if that's how Dorothy treated it."

The woman sighed. "Are you planning on staying in a room?"

"Yes, I believe she has me staying in a room."

"So, you want to book a room, but don't have a reservation. I'll have to open up her availability here. I don't think it'll be a problem getting a room." The woman stared at the computer monitor atop the counter, typing away.

"No, I'm not—" None of this was coming out right. "I don't want to book a room."

The woman stopped typing and stared him right in the face. She paused, her milk chocolate eyes strikingly familiar. Like smelling grass being mowed—he may not have ever been in that person's lawn, but the smell reminded him of early childhood summers spent bruising himself on the Slip-N-Slide. He had never seen this woman, but an underlying happiness washed over him.

"You will be staying here, but have no reservation, nor do you want to book a room. Does that mean you're going to sleep in the lobby?" She thumbed toward one of the chairs behind her by the bookshelf.

Perhaps he had been away from people too long. Yet another night in the trees, away from communication, didn't sound so bad right now.

"Is it really you?" Dorothy Bennett entered from the kitchen, arms spread.

The young woman stood, hands on hips and perplexed.

"I can't believe it." Dorothy gave him a bear hug before eyeing him head to toe. "Look at that beard of yours. And your hair."

Admittedly his hair had grown out of control. He'd meant to start the hike with it short, but the September air had been cooler than expected. He'd rather grow out his hair and beard to keep warm than to have to lug another item of clothing.

"Care to introduce me?" The woman crossed her arms, eyes curious at Dorothy.

"Oh, Tracy, this is—"

"Ben." He outstretched a hand. "Ben Walker."

Dorothy hesitated then followed through. "Yes, Tracy, this is...a friend of mine, Ben. Ben, this is my great-niece, Tracy."

"Tracy Bennett?" He had said it out loud. *Right? It had come out of his mouth and not just his head?* He froze, either from hearing the name out loud or being the one who'd said it out loud. Probably both.

Tracy obliged with the handshake. "Do I know you?"

"Oh, I—" He fidgeted with his beard. Dorothy was right. It was embarrassingly long. Some men could get away with long beards just fine, even more than fine. But not the case with Ben. He was graced with beard genes that aged him fifteen years, and to put it bluntly, gave him a creepy look. "I assumed, since you were related to Dorothy."

"Please," Dorothy said. "You can call me Aunt Dee. It's what you—" She shook her head. "It's what my closest relatives and friends call me."

"Okay. Aunt Dee it is." He had called her that as a kid, but thought adulthood meant formality.

Tracy looked through the front windows to the porch, catching a glimpse of his backpack. "Did you just come off the AT?"

"Sure did."

"Are you a thru-hiker?"

"Not entirely. I actually started south of Blacksburg, Virginia."

"Ben is going to be staying with us for a while." Aunt Dee

walked around the counter and scrambled for something in the cabinet below.

"So you're a guest, then?" Tracy threw her arms up in defeat.

Ben opened his mouth, prepared to talk his way around the situation. Fortunately, Aunt Dee took the reins.

"Not quite," she said. "Ben will be staying here, but has agreed to help out."

Tracy stepped back, eyebrows raised. "Help out? In what way?"

Aunt Dee smiled at Ben. "I should've told you I have Tracy here helping me out for the season. But there's plenty enough to do for the both of you. We can make sure to leave the heavier lifting to you."

Tracy scoffed. She may have a small frame, but something in her attitude told Ben she was much stronger than she looked.

"Here's the key to your room, room two."

"That's across the hall from me." Tracy glared at Aunt Dee.

"That's right, thank you Tracy, for letting Ben know where to find it." Aunt Dee returned the glare. "In fact, Tracy, could you bring up his pack and place it in his room?" She dangled the key over the counter until Tracy reluctantly retrieved it. Tracy stepped outside and hauled the pack in, Ben holding the door for her.

"You don't have to do that."

"Just following Aunt Dee's orders." Tracy grunted, but managed the pack well enough.

"Are you sure you can spare another room?" Ben asked. "I don't want to put any booked guests out."

Tracy cleared her throat and adjusted the pack on her shoulder before hitting the stairs, her shoes thumping at each step.

"You're not putting anyone out," Aunt Dee said. "It's my pleasure that you're here."

"About that." He checked the staircase, all signs signaling Tracy had made it to the second floor. "I was wondering if you could keep my identity under wraps. At least for the time being."

"Yeah, about that. Ben *Walker*?" She smirked as if a salesman had pitched her a timeshare in the forest. "You couldn't come up with a better last name? Might as well have been Ben Hiking Boots."

"It's the first last name I could think of."

"I highly doubt anyone will recognize you. Especially with that terrible beard."

"You bring up a good point. Maybe I should keep the facial hair."

She chuckled. "Lose the facial hair. It's been so long, no one will know, I assure you."

Tracy's footsteps sounded down the stairs. Ben straightened, not realizing how crouched over the counter in whisper-talk he had been standing.

"Whatever I can do to help out." It came out too loud. "I appreciate your hospitality."

"Like I said," Aunt Dee graciously switched subjects along with him, "I'll have to divvy up the projects between you and Tracy. Although, maybe you could help us with Lovetoberfest."

"You don't have to burden him with that." Tracy eyed him. "Unless you're into awkward blind dates, one after the other, you should probably steer clear of the event."

Her skeptical expression was kinda cute. Of course she'd turned out cute. What had he expected?

For one, not to see her here. Aunt Dee could've given him the heads up before he'd stepped foot in the lodge.

To think he'd stay amongst complete strangers was a foolish notion. He was bound to see familiar faces anywhere and everywhere he went in Waverly Lake, even in the outskirts around Woodsman's Lodge. Waverly Lake was tight-knit, a town where everyone knows everyone—*your business is my business.*

It was one of the reasons he had to come back. So many years he had roamed, foster home to foster home, a stranger being taken care of by strangers. Just when he'd surpass a level of familiarity with any one of them, he'd be handed over to the next. No one truly knew him as a kid outside of Waverly Lake. Aunt Dee was perhaps the adult in Waverly he knew best. Thinking of her reminded him of what it felt like to be welcomed into a home as if he belonged there. Of what it felt like to be loved.

It was also one of the reasons he had stayed away for so long. Although his memories had faded, or at least had time to simmer, he doubted the same held true for the folks of Waverly. No, they would know him, know his past, know how he ended up who he was today.

They would expect too much of him. A part of him he wasn't ready to give. A part of him he wasn't ready to relive or reclaim. Yet the window to do just that was rapidly closing.

So what was he doing in Waverly Lake? Why come back, after all this time, if he was too scared to do anything about it?

Whether his answer was the truth, or something Ben convinced himself was true, time would tell. But after all the years of family-hopping, all the miles of road driven and trails hiked, he had seen all the places he had wanted to see. And as he looked at *The Wizard of Oz* mural on the wall, he wondered if the words Dorothy had spoken as she clicked her heels rang true.

He came to Waverly Lake because it was home.

Chapter Three

TRACY SPENT THE LAST WEEK GOING DOWN THE LIST OF chores Aunt Dee prepared for her. She rinsed off the plastic chairs that lined the small lakefront beach, deflated the flotation toys and rafts, and organized them neatly in storage. She started to change out the linens in the rooms from the airy pastel colors to earthier tones, but Miranda the housekeeper insisted she was doing it all wrong and took over the task. She moved on to paint touch-ups throughout the lodge. The touch-ups were a quick fix to the scuffs and bruises the walls endured from swinging luggage, children at play, and wear and tear every building endured.

It was right when she was working on the wall by the fireplace, thinking how she might completely paint the walls if she had enough time left over at the end of the month, when the hiker had entered. Now he stood with her and Aunt Dee, in his army-green, convertible hiking pants and muddy boots, threatening to upend her October plans.

"Aunt Dee, a word?" Tracy nodded toward the reading corner, the faint smell of must a welcoming scent of childhood. Aunt Dee excused herself from Ben's company.

"I think I'm going to freshen up, if you ladies don't mind." Ben pointed to the staircase and awaited their answer.

"You go on ahead," Aunt Dee said.

"Please do," Tracy said. She followed it with a forced smile and waved him off.

Aunt Dee swung around and clasped Tracy's wrist, urging her to put it away like a revealed weapon. "You're going to have to keep your smarminess in check."

Tracy scoffed, most certainly not adhering to the suggestion. "What is going on? Since when do we hire strange hikers from the trail to work here?"

"First of all, we get hikers here all the time. You know that."

"I do know that." Aunt Dee's nonchalance was irritating. Was she not worried about her safety, and the safety of her guests? Not that she had a packed lodge at the moment. But Tracy had hiked enough across the globe to know better. In general, most hikers were friendly, responsible, and respectful. Unfortunately, there were bad apples in every orchard. "They come here for a night's stay. Not for a career."

The subtle eye roll from Aunt Dee must've taken most of her eighty years to perfect. "It's just for a little while. Besides, he didn't spring this on me, I knew he was coming."

"But—"

She shushed her with a raised hand. "I already told you, we know each other. I didn't think it would be a big deal for him to stay for a while."

"If you knew he was coming, and he's to work for his stay, then why ask me here? One person can get that list done well before the holidays." Before mid-November, to be precise. All in time to paint the walls that needed it most, then spend Thanksgiving with family before her trip Down Under.

Aunt Dee's eyes softened as her sternness faded. "Am I not allowed to want to spend time with my grandniece?"

On some level, it probably held true. Aunt Dee had always taken to Tracy, ever since she could remember. Tracy believed she admired her feistiness and sense of adventure. Her brother Danny was the complete opposite. Cool, composed. He calculated and thought through every decision. He'd say he had to in order to be a father to Hannah. But their differences were evident as children. Tracy was the wild-child, and Danny the sensible one. Aunt Dee gravitated toward the one with fire in her veins.

On another level, it was an elderly relative's excuse for her behavior.

"I was wondering if you had any soap I could use? I ran out two mornings ago." Ben stood shirtless in the middle of the room, as if it were okay to roam around the lodge with his muscular, taut-shouldered physique exposed. Tracy naturally followed the chiseled pecs down to the rippled abs before catching herself.

"Yes, we should have some soap and shampoo for the guests in your bathroom." Aunt Dee eyed Tracy. It took a second to process what the heck Aunt Dee had just said.

Soap. For the guests. Checking the rooms for supplies was on her list, a task she had checked off on Wednesday after preparing two rooms for guests to use this weekend. Had she known about Ben, it would've been three rooms.

"I checked, but didn't seem to find them." It sounded innocent enough, but Tracy detected a hint of finger-pointing from this, what, co-employee?

Because you weren't supposed to be here. She checked her attitude, choosing civility over impulse. "There should be extra in the common bathroom at the end of the hall. In the tall cabinet."

"Tracy." Aunt Dee used a certain tone in the name at times like these. It wasn't yelling. Rather its two syllables carried thick disappointment.

"I mean...Let me get that for you." The words came through her clenched teeth.

"Great." He smiled, one she might have found pleasant were it not for the patchy bushy beard thrown on his face.

Be nice. The man has done nothing to invoke such a rise out of her. No, this was all Tracy. She enjoyed her freedom, and when she did have to work, she liked working on her own terms, her own schedule. In her own way.

She walked up the green stairs, a burgundy runner adding to the padding of the steps. Stairs had a way of eroding faster than any other flooring, and Aunt Dee insisted it was easier to change the runner than to install new carpeting. The same carpeting Aunt Dee wanted replaced in her office sometime this month.

Tracy passed her room on the left, the newfound straggler's room on the right and continued straight down the hallway to the end. The guest bathroom accommodated guests staying in the four rooms that lacked a private bathroom. The rooms rented for a lower price and were the last to fill up. Tourists these days often expected their own bathrooms, as hotels and many bed and breakfasts supplied. Aunt Dee had looked at the cost and feasibility of changing the rooms. Not only would she have to lose one entire bedroom, but the cost of the redo—with it being a historical building, with notoriously finicky plumbing and wiring—wouldn't break even with her profit for ten years. Besides, hikers were perfectly content having a roof over their heads for one night, bathroom or not.

Except for this hiker, apparently. Aunt Dee felt he warranted one of the larger rooms, equal to her own. Was he seen as equal to Tracy?

She needed to stop with the negativity. *Give the guy a chance.*

She knocked on the door before entering, then opened the tall cabinet along the left wall, opposite the shower.

"Here you go." She handed him a plastic bottle of liquid soap and two others for shampoo and conditioner.

He accepted them, but stood still, blinking.

"Is there a problem with those?"

"Oh, no, sorry. I also couldn't find a towel. Or washcloth."

"Ah, those are back in your room." Although she hadn't set them out.

He followed her back to his room, opening the door for her. She spotted his backpack on the bed, cringing at the thought of the dirt on the bedspread as she moved straight to the bathroom.

"We keep the linens and towels in the locked cabinet when the room's not in use."

"I wondered what you kept in there."

"Easier for the housekeeping to have them in each room. Plus, Aunt Dee doesn't like having a wheeled cart running back and forth on the carpet."

"She keeps a tight ship."

Tracy's eyes widened as she looked at him. "If you don't already know, you'll find out soon enough."

She crouched low and grabbed a towel, washcloth, and hand towel. She rose, spinning on her feet to hand them over, and lost her balance.

"Careful now." Ben held her shoulders and she outstretched a hand to his chest, preventing her from falling onto the sink. She stared at her hand on his solid chest for a second too long before retracting it, as if she had touched fire itself. His rough fingers held a gentle grip on her arm. Hands that had seen their share of mileage on the trail. She could appreciate that, in the sense this man wasn't like many of those in Waverly Lake, never having stepped foot in another county.

He let go and grabbed the towels out of her hands. "Thank you. I think that's everything."

Suddenly she felt out of place, standing in the bathroom with this half-naked man. It was an invasion of privacy; a moment in life someone else wasn't supposed to be a part of. She scurried past him for the door.

"I'm sorry," he said.

She turned around, pausing in the doorway. "For what?"

"I didn't know Aunt Dee had someone else working on the lodge right now." He looked down at the stack of towels, then placed them on the counter by the sink. "I probably would've come at another time."

She inhaled deeply. "I'm sure you just did what was best for your schedule on the trail. Not many people would want to hike come December or later in the winter." Although people hiked year-round along parts of the AT, thru-hikers tended to hike the warmest six months or so out of the year. October hit the tail-end for the long-haulers. But then again, he wasn't a thru-hiker if he had started out in Virginia. Was that what bothered her about him? That it was unusual to backpack for that long and not do the whole trail, to end up here in Waverly Lake, on purpose?

"Besides, I'm her great-niece." *Blood ran thicker than friendship.* "If being here means it helps out Aunt Dee, then okay." She turned to go, then thought against it. *No holiday travels if no holiday money.* If he did all of her work, what did that leave her with? "I guess just let me do my thing, you do yours. As long as we don't get in each other's way, it should be fine. Plus, knowing Aunt Dee, I can see her tallying up the other jobs she wants done now that she has another pair of hands." Hands that had saved her from humiliating herself a minute ago. Fingers that left a lingering touch on her wrist. She blushed at the thought.

He grabbed the door, readying to close it. "I fully intend to earn my stay here, however long that may be. But I promise to stay out of your way, as much as that is possible."

She gave a strong nod. "Good. All right then."

"Tracy?" Aunt Dee's voice carried up the stairs and across the room. For such a small frame, she really had the bravado to command an army.

"I'd better go."

"Right. Don't want to keep her waiting."

"Nope."

"Plus, I'm going to shower."

"Right again." Tracy turned around, astounded by her feet not having moved from the doorway. She should've been running in the opposite direction by now.

"Coming, Aunt Dee!" Her voice broke in its shout, not nearly as strong as her great-aunt's.

She quickly took the stairs and awaited Aunt Dee's instructions. Although there was a list of to-dos to accomplish this season, Aunt Dee liked to pepper in errands throughout the week, sometimes daily to keep Tracy on her toes. It was more likely that Aunt Dee couldn't foresee every little thing that needed to be done ahead of time, but sometimes it felt like Aunt Dee didn't want Tracy to stay in the same spot for more than five minutes.

"I need a few items from Bleary Hardware, if you don't mind making a trip into town."

With her chores set out for the day, a trip to town was the last thing she needed. To get to downtown Waverly Lake, she either had to use the lodge's boat to cross the lake, or take the winding road around, either direction being quite a drive, at least for a simple errand like picking up screws and paint.

But...leaving would give her time to process the new arrival. Reset her mind. She had been incredibly rude to him, hadn't she? How many times had she arrived at a new place, not knowing a single soul? It was hard to do such a thing and stay positive, hoping to be accepted or at least not looked down upon as the foreigner. Yes, going to town would be a good distraction.

"That's fine," Tracy said. "Make sure you have everything you need written down. Do you need any groceries or anything like that?"

"No, Bleary's will do. And you know what?"

Aunt Dee walked to the bottom of the stairs and looked up, listening. "Maybe I'll have Ben go with you. It'll be good for him to see the town and find his way around ag—" She straightened her shirt. "Find his way around."

"That's okay, I don't mind going by myself." *Prefer it.*

"Don't be silly. You're the perfect person to show him around town."

"He's busy showering, don't worry about it. I can leave now and be back in time for lunch."

"Look, if you're going to both be working here, the quicker you get to know each other, the better. Just sit tight and I'll let him know."

Tracy pressed her lips in a neutral line. It was the closest she could get to a polite smile. So much for staying out of each other's way.

"Okay then. Sitting tight."

Chapter Four

HOT WATER NEVER FELT BETTER THAN AFTER backpacking for a considerable amount of time. As it flowed over his face and hair, Ben closed his eyes. The house appeared, its columns and wrought iron fence equal parts menacing and awe-inspiring. To a child, the building was a castle, a giant play area where imagination took flight. To him, it had been simply home.

His mind roamed back to the lodge, the shower itself lined with clean, white tile so outdated it almost was back in fashion. He hadn't spent much time upstairs as a child. Most of his memories were of the roaring fireplace, the painted wall mural, or wandering the grounds. Playing hide and seek, or looking for bugs under logs, or sitting at the kitchen counter splitting a fudgesicle, all with the girl with the freckles and curly hair. All with Tracy.

For a second, he had thought she'd recognized him. She had met his eyes, boring a hole through his facade. What were the chances she knew who he was? She was younger than he, by a year or two. How well do children remember being four or five? The good news was that he hadn't recognized her at first. Maybe Aunt Dee was right. No one would know his true identity at this age. He hadn't been in Waverly Lake in almost twenty years. Many of the people who did know him could have moved away or simply forgotten his name altogether.

He dried himself off and wiped the steam off the mirror with the washcloth. It made streaks of tiny water droplets, but he could look past those to his reflection. Aunt Dee was right. The beard didn't suit his face much at all. The way he looked now, people who knew him as an adult would have a tough time pinpointing his identity. While it may be a good disguise, it felt uneasy not recognizing his own face.

He stopped at a dull sound. He opened the bathroom door and poked his head out. Someone knocked on the room's door.

Tracy checking up on him? She didn't seem the type, considering Aunt Dee had to indirectly ask her to grab him some soap. Why did his mind immediately go back to Tracy?

"Hello? It's Aunt Dee."

"I'll be right there." He fumbled for a pair of boxers, T-shirt, and the other pair of hiking pants from his backpack. He unlocked the door and cracked it open.

"Hi there, Ben." Aunt Dee winked at his name. "I'm sorry to disturb you."

"It's okay, I was just finishing up."

"Oh, good. Then you may be able to accompany Tracy to town? I have a list of items needed from the hardware store. I thought it'd be a good idea to go with her, have her show you around?"

He opened the door wider, inviting her in. He sat on the corner of the queen bed. "I appreciate you thinking of me, but I'm not so sure I'm ready to see the town yet. I mean, this is the first time I've set foot in the limits of Waverly Lake since my parents died."

"I know." She stepped in and clasped her hands on his cheeks. "I'm so glad to see you, really. I still see that little boy in your face. Your eyes haven't changed a bit."

He smiled, a mix of delight for being around a familiar face from his youth, and strain, for the same reason.

"Hopefully that doesn't give me away," he said.

"Nonsense. I already told you, no one will know. And your

secret is safe with me. I promise. But you shouldn't avoid going into town on the off-chance I am wrong."

"It's not that." He rocked his head back and forth. "Okay, it's not *all* that. I just don't want the attention. You know, before I left, everyone looked at me like I was the saddest thing alive. The looks of pity were unbearable. If it wasn't the sorry eyes I was getting, it was the people who wanted me, a six-year-old, to somehow have a say in what would happen to the house. As if I had the cognitive development to know what to do with the property and continue with the legacy my parents had left."

Aunt Dee sat beside him. "I'm not going to force you to do anything. Unless it's work around here to pay your way."

He smiled, genuinely out of contentment this time.

"I do think it'd do you some good to see the house." Aunt Dee had her own way of asking without asking.

"I take it it's still all right? The last time I spoke with Mr. Letts, he sounded overwhelmed by the upkeep, but I wrote it off. That was almost a year ago. If only he had told me about the cancer. I didn't even know he was sick, let alone dying. I would've come sooner."

"You're here now." She patted his knee and he put his hand on hers. Despite the discomfort and looming dread hanging on his shoulders, it did his heart some good to have someone he loved from his past support him now.

"Besides, I hope you don't mind," Aunt Dee stood, smoothing her outfit as if she had crumbled cookies all over it, "I took the liberty to make you an appointment to clean yourself up."

"I just had a shower."

"No, properly clean yourself up. I had figured you'd be a bit disheveled from hiking and looks to me I figured correctly."

"It's not that bad, is it?"

She chuckled, shaking her head. "It looks like you've been living off the grid for years. And off the razor's edge."

"Well, I have. Not for years, but sometimes it feels that way."

Before setting out from Virginia, he had returned to his last foster family for half a year. Although more like grandparents in age, Grace and Roger Dornan were the closest people he had to parents. They treated him like a son, a hard position to accept as a teenager, but one he grew to appreciate into adulthood. It was why he called with every move he made, so at least one pair of souls knew his whereabouts. Before that, he toyed with a semester at Roanoke College and a handful of odd jobs. Prior to that he had switched foster homes four times. Nothing he tried and nowhere he found himself had established roots. He couldn't shake the feeling his roots tangled deep into Waverly Lake's soil.

"I didn't give them your real name. I just told them it's for Ben, and that I have it all covered. If they try to charge you, tell Carly to call me."

"Carly?"

"Carly Fletcher. She runs Dye Happy Salon in town."

"You set up a salon appointment for me?" He pictured a handful of people doting on him, blow drying his hair and painting his nails, like the cowardly lion and companions.

"For a shave and haircut. Nothing fancy."

He closed his eyes and took in a breath. She was going above and beyond to accommodate him. How could he say no?

"Okay," he said.

Aunt Dee stood, face beaming. "Good."

"Under one condition."

"What's that?" Her fists rested on her waist.

"You be the one to tell Tracy I'm coming along." She wasn't going to like this. Not especially since he'd promised to keep his duties to himself, free from hers.

Aunt Dee laughed, a pitch higher than her voice, but still hearty from the gut. "Don't tell me you're afraid of Tracy."

"She's...formidable."

"Honey, Tracy is a firecracker. I'll give you that much. But underneath all that bravado is an insecure, soft woman who has no idea what she really needs in her life."

"What do you really think of her?" A scathing review from Aunt Dee, but one he trusted due to its source.

"She's my great-niece, and I love her dearly, but it's true. Now if only the right man came along to see that."

Based on their brief encounter, he wouldn't be any kind of man to Tracy, let alone the right man. Aunt Dee must've caught his bumbling shock.

"Don't you worry. Tracy already knows. She's waiting downstairs for you to finish up."

"I—" No sense in arguing. Aunt Dee had it planned, and she had twisted it around to make him feel like he'd agreed to it. Did it only take three weeks of no adults around to be so easily manipulated? Or was it Aunt Dee's special talent? He suspected the latter.

"I'll see you downstairs?"

He nodded, a clear defeat against Aunt Dee's persuasion, and the door closed behind her. The red flannel shirt that had been crumpled into a ball in his backpack was a wrinkled mess, but at least it was clean. Fairly clean. He did the nose test and it passed, which was better than how his other two shirts had fared. Never mind that his smoothing of the fabric did not replace a proper ironing in any capacity.

If he was going to stay here for a week or even longer, it was probably best he went to town anyway for a few more clothing items. The last thing he wanted to do was slip his boots back on, but they were the only footgear he had with him, other than three knee-length pairs of socks. He shoved his thin wallet into his back pocket along with his room key and headed downstairs.

Tracy was nowhere in sight, and Aunt Dee stood behind the counter typing something into the computer.

"Do you think Tracy would mind stopping at a clothing store? I could use another shirt or two, and a pair of pants."

"I'm sure she could swing by a store. You'll be getting your hands dirty, working for me. I thought you particularly could help me out with landscaping issues."

"If you'd rather I start working I can—"

"No, no, you go with Tracy."

As she said the name, Tracy walked in from the back office. "I'm taking the boat." She jangled a key hanging off a red and white floating keychain the shape of a fishing bobber.

"You recorded the trip in the log?"

"Yes, ma'am. Wrote it down in the book in your office before I even touched the key."

"Good. Safety first."

Tracy nodded. "Of course, Auntie."

"The boat?" Ben swallowed the word in a dry gulp.

Tracy eyed him. "Yeah, it's the quickest way to get into town."

"I thought there was a road..." A winding one if he recalled correctly. One that afforded a peek at the lake in certain bends. A road his parents used to drop him off here in the summer. "I mean, isn't there a road?"

"Of course," Tracy said. "But you're looking at twice the time, one way." She stared at him, reading his fear. That's what she was doing. Scanning him because she smelled his fear. She knew he couldn't swim. Or maybe she remembered after all.

"Are you okay?" Tracy looked at Aunt Dee for guidance, or reassurance, or some -ance that he wasn't giving her.

"No, it's fine. I'm just, not used to boats, that's all."

"Don't worry," Aunt Dee said. "She's a great driver."

He nodded, wanting to take her word for it, but many things could cause drowning, not just poor driving.

"Yeah, trust me." Tracy smiled politely. "Shouldn't get too wet."

Chapter Five

"THAT SHOULD SERVE YOU WELL ENOUGH." TRACY tucked in the loose ends of the cords of Ben's lifejacket. Although rated appropriately, it stiffened his upper body, as if turning his head required turning his entire torso.

"Are you sure?" Ben checked the buckles along the middle.

"Don't worry. No one has fallen off the boat on my watch." Not that she ever had passengers on *Tin Can*. It was true she had never thrown herself overboard. He didn't need to know the finer details.

"It's a short jaunt to town. Just have a seat beside me." The thirty-five foot outboard motorboat could hold a handful of passengers, but Aunt Dee mainly used it to make trips to and from town. The bench seats in front had enough storage space for a grocery haul.

Tracy stood behind the cockpit, just shy of the center of the boat. Ben sat in the seat next to her, clinging to the railing with one hand and cupholder-armrest with the other. She lowered the motor and started it up. The dock wasn't much of one; a few boards running along the edge of the lake nearest the lodge. Although the lodge did not have a sweeping view of Waverly Lake, its beachfront did. The western mountains, eastern meadows, and town to the south, competed for which direction was the most awe-inspiring. Enough guests had trampled down the hill over the years to take in the beauty, leaving a worn path. Aunt Dee had a wooden staircase built on the steepest part, and brush and roots cleared along the rest of the footpath. Eventually she invested in chairs and beach toys for guests in summer. Tracy suspected she did it to divert guests from fishing off the dock.

Tracy cast off the two lines keeping her in place portside, flipping the fenders into the boat. She kicked off the deck, setting *Tin Can* adrift, its reflection on water's surface barely visible with the overhead sun buried beneath clouds. The name amused her, as it fit in line with *The Wizard of Oz* theme. However, it would've been perfect had the boat been metal, or at least a silver color. Instead the fiberglass fit somewhere between butter and mayonnaise in color. She pushed on the throttle lever and started the journey.

Ben jerked back at the initial acceleration, clasping tighter to the rail. How did someone Ben's age never learn to swim? But then again, not everyone grew up next to a lake. If she hadn't, who knew where or when else she would've learned.

Guilt rose at taking any pleasure from Ben's discomfort, even if she had kept it to herself. He obviously was terrified to be out on the water, but he didn't refuse. He faced it and dealt with it. Would she be able to say the same, with her claustrophobia? How would she feel if someone insisted she ride an elevator? Granted it wasn't the same thing. If anything, his fear of drowning made more sense than her fear of suffocation. Just how many people died a year from panicking in an elevator?

"Would you mind slowing it down a little?" Ben shouted over the noise of the motor.

The wind sloshed her hair around and made her eyes water. She cut back on the throttle, the hum of the motor lowering while their bow sat high.

"We're not going to be planing if we go this slow."

"What?" He shifted on the seat, just enough to face her better.

"You see the front? It'll stick up like that the rest of the way if we go this slow. If you don't mind us leaning back..."

"It's okay. That is, if you don't mind."

Tracy nodded. She minded a little. Although they moved slower, they left behind a choppier wake, not to mention how silly they looked crossing the lake as if an elephant sat at the stern.

She had wanted to get to Pearson's Wharf as quickly as possible. The lake formed an L shape, the longer stem running east-west, as if water had trickled down the Appalachians from the west and north and pooled into the aspen-laden meadow below. Aunt Dee's property sat a few miles west of the crook in the L on the northern banks, with town nearly straight across the lake. It made boating the most direct way to get across. But perhaps Tracy had been looking at this all wrong, though. Maybe now, with the slower pace, was her chance to get Ben to talk.

"You know, I've known Aunt Dee all my life. There isn't much I wouldn't do for her."

Ben looked at her with uncertainty, most likely unsure of where she was going with this.

"I'd hate to have a squatter at the lodge, or someone who took advantage of an old lady's charity."

Ben nodded, understanding her angle. He even broke a smile. "I assure you I'm not taking advantage. I promised I'd work for my stay, and I intend to do so, for as long as that is."

"You don't know how long that will be?" She steered clear of one of the tiny islands dotting the center of the lake. In the summer they filled with picnickers and partying teens. But the October air lost too much warmth to make the cool water of the lake bearable.

"I have a few things to take care of."

She averted her eyes from the water long enough to meet his, her curiosity unsatiated.

"It's personal," he said.

"Can I ask if it has to do with Waverly Lake specifically? Or you just need time in general?"

"You can ask." He smirked and loosened his grip on the rail, obviously enjoying stringing her along in his mystery.

She pushed the throttle and swerved. Ben clenched the rail tightly again, holding his breath until she resumed course.

"What was that?" he shouted.

"Something in the water." She held back the smile. It was cruel, admittedly. But his secrecy didn't sit well with her.

"Look, I don't know what I have done to you, or what you think I might do to Aunt Dee. I have no intentions on taking Aunt Dee's generosity for granted. And if it's okay with you—I don't know why I'm asking you this, because it seems like something that should be done anyways—I'd like to keep my personal affairs personal. It's nothing malicious or harmful. We can stick with the plan we agreed to. You stick to your business, and I'll stick to my business. You're just going to have to trust me on this. Although from what I have seen thus far, I can't imagine you to be a very trusting person."

He was right on the personal aspect. She didn't have the right to interrogate him on his business. Although with Aunt Dee involved, it became her business. She'd have to let that slide. As far as trusting people...

"I trust people. At least those that are trustworthy."

"Oh really? I'd love to hear the list of people you trust."

"Not that you know most of them, anyway." She held her chin higher, scanning the water's surface. She didn't need to justify herself to this man. Yet she couldn't hold her tongue. "I trust my brother, Danny. And his daughter. And Aunt Dee especially."

He crossed his right ankle over his left knee, the conversation apparently easing his tension. "Anyone outside of your family?"

Her breathing quickened and she pressed her lips together. What did this guy know? "The point is, I trust people."

They approached Pearson's Wharf, the largest dock in all the hundred-plus miles of lake coastline. It sat at the eastern edge of downtown Waverly Lake, just beyond the main copse of cute shops and boutiques that drew in tourists nearly year-round. While Aunt

Dee didn't have a paid slip for *Tin Can*, the wharf had a filling station with open slots for temporary berths.

Tracy maneuvered past the sailing vessels and pontoon boats. Waverly Lake wasn't known for its large yachts like those seen on larger Lake Norman further east, or in saltwater towns along North Carolina's coast. But it did have a substantial community of sailors stretching from the western Smoky Mountains past Asheville.

She tied up *Tin Can* and stretched out a hand to help Ben off after he ditched the life jacket. She didn't feel much like speaking to him. Secrets were not something she tolerated in people. She had no trouble sharing any part of her life with just about anyone. There was nothing mysterious or hidden in her life. If someone wanted to know about it, she'd tell them, plain and simple. Aunt Dee would say it was one of her flaws. The truth can be a slap in the face, even if right.

Hopefully Danny wasn't working today, or if he was, he was down in the hull of some vessel on the other side of the wharf. All she needed was her brother to spot her out with this stranger. He would assume she was friends with Ben. Some saw her as a social butterfly, in that she occupied most evenings and weekends spending time with friends. However, she wasn't friends with everybody. Quite the opposite. Tracy befriended a few, devoting her energy to fierce loyalty. Her friends were her second family.

"Hey, Tracy!" Danny waved off a pontoon boat near the main building of Pearson's Wharf.

Great.

She marched down the dock, Ben two steps behind her. The faint smell of freshwater fish—bass, catfish, bluegill—lurked beneath the fumes of boat fuel.

"A friend of yours?" he asked.

She didn't bother to turn around, but stopped at the boat. Danny slicked back his black ringlets and closed a toolbox. "What are you doing in town? Aunt Dee sick of you already?"

"Never." She sneered.

Danny smiled, a *GQ* smile that annoyed Tracy in its perfection.

How did the son of the family inherit all the good looks? "Who's this? You running a water taxi business?"

"That's not a bad idea, actually. We'd just need people who wanted to get across. And who didn't mind paying an outrageous price."

"You could always sail them over."

"Are you offering up *Kare Bear*?" Danny's team placed second in the summer's regatta, not only affirming his sailing skills, but helping Kara's Dad grow a business of selling handcrafted sailing vessels. *Kare Bear* was the first.

"Does it look like I lost my mind?" Danny read Tracy's face. "Don't answer that."

Tracy chuckled. "Danny, this is Ben. Ben, this is my old brother, Danny."

"Old*er*." Danny leant out a hand. Ben scrambled to the edge of the planks to reach it, shaking it abruptly and backing away. "What brings you to Waverly Lake? Looks like you're fresh off the trail."

Tracy folded her arms. "Go on, Ben, tell him why you're here."

Ben feigned a smile. "I'm just sorting out some personal stuff. Earning my stay at the lodge."

"Hmm." Danny nodded.

"Tell me about it," Tracy said.

"You're the brother with a daughter?" Ben said.

Danny nodded. "I'm her only brother. And yes, I have a daughter, Hannah. She's seven. How long have you been here, and how much has Tracy told you?"

"Not a whole lot. But she said she trusts you and Hannah."

"Oh, did she? I guess that's good to know, Tracy." Danny's white teeth sparkled, even with the growing overcast sky. Where the heck did the light come from?

"All right, that's enough." Could he have embarrassed her more? "We're off to Bleary's for an impromptu supply run. See you tomorrow at Mom and Dad's?"

"As usual. Good to meet you, Ben."

"You too." Ben put his hands in his pockets and followed Tracy to the parking lot.

"What was that all about?"

"What was what?"

"Telling him that I trust him."

Ben stopped and shrugged. "What? You don't think a brother would like to know his sister trusts him? I think it's endearing."

"I think it's embarrassing." She marched on, down the north sidewalk of Dowager Street. The main thoroughfare cut across the south side of the lake, with the center of town opening into a square.

"I didn't mean to embarrass you," he said. "I don't have any siblings. I always thought it would be nice to have a brother or sister."

She didn't know much about this Ben, but he certainly had a way of making her feel guilty. "It's okay." They had stopped at the east entrance to the square, a courtyard of yellowing grass ready to lie dormant for the oncoming winter.

"That's me over there." Ben pointed across the square to the other side of the street. "Dye Happy Salon. Aunt Dee made me an appointment that I couldn't refuse."

Tracy chuckled. "She'll do that." Like coming into town today and bringing this stranger along with her. "I'll be at Bleary's. It's just a few more buildings down the road. I'll hang out around there until you're finished."

"I was wondering if I could also, maybe, shop for some clothes." He held up his hands. "Just a few items, nothing major. A pair of pants, two shirts or so."

Tracy closed her eyes. Best leave the eye rolling to herself. "How about you go to your appointment, and I'll pick up some shirts and pants at Bleary's."

"At the hardware store?"

"They have durable work pants and basic shirts. What size?"

"Oh, um, well—"

She turned him around and grabbed his collar, reading the tag on his shirt. "Large."

"I could've told you that."

"Seemed quicker to find out myself. Pants?"

He flattened his hands around his waist. "Thirty-two, thirty-four. Take my word for it."

Tracy giggled. "You want me to trust you an awful lot, you know that?"

"And you really like to get personal quickly, don't you?"

Tracy smirked. She was well-aware not many people could handle her abruptness and openness. Danny had said so, as well as Mom, Dad, Aunt Dee. Even Hannah would get in a jibe now and then. But Ben seemed to hold his own with her.

Maybe he wasn't so bad after all.

Chapter Six

WAVERLY LAKE WAS BOTH FAMILIAR AND NEW TO BEN Walker. He remembered the bones of the town—shops along Dowager Street, the courtyard square, and even the flag poles adorning the buildings. He remembered the smattering of red, white, and blue during Fourth of July, the poles now holding brown flags with a simple orange leaf. Garlands of fake leaves colored buttery-yellow and rusty-orange wrapped around the lampposts of the courtyard that he now traversed. Only one of the benches in the courtyard was occupied, an older gentleman cradling a cup of coffee.

The air itself brought him back to being a kid. It wasn't the same as sea air. There was no salty taste or seafood smell. Rather, it was like the air held a cool freshness to it; a warm, minty moisture that grazed his skin with the steady wind off the water. It was the same breeze that had brought him relief in his childhood summers and reddened his cheeks in winter.

While he recollected the skeleton of the town, the flesh—the fine details—were all new. A flower shop, bakery, souvenir store, and pharmacy. He had been to a drugstore with Mom, scanning the candies while waiting for whatever medicine he'd needed. But he didn't remember the name was Nichols and Dimes, or where it sat along the main street.

The same could be said for Dye Happy Salon. He certainly had been inside before. The fuzzy memory melded the sound of the buzzer with visions of pink. That's all that showed up in his head. Even though the inside of the salon was decorated in gray and black tones, with ergonomic chairs and silvery mirrors on the walls, there was no question Mom had taken him here too. Back when the room was pink, ceiling to floor.

"Welcome." A pale woman with deep-red hair slicked back in a ponytail greeted him from behind the long, black front desk. She stared at the matted mess of hair on both ends of his head long enough for him to feel embarrassed. "Walk-in or appointment?"

"Appointment. For Ben."

She scanned her computer, scrolling the wheel on the mouse.

"Aunt Dee—Dorothy Bennett, made it for me."

"That's mine!" A high-pitched voice rang, through the sound of hair dryers and gossip and the running faucet of a client being shampooed in the row of sinks in the back. Ben was wrong about the pink—it did exist in the salon, in the form of this bleach-blond woman's capri pants and floral blouse.

"I've got him, Kristy." The woman had a southern accent, one like his second foster mom, from when he was stuck in the middle of Nowhere, Georgia, had. But her actual voice—the pitch, the tone—rang familiar. What were the chances he had known her in his past life?

"I'm Carly." She grinned bigger than any Barbie could and reached out her hand. He shook it, surprised at the assertiveness she put behind it.

"Right. Filcher?"

"Fletcher."

"Sorry, Fletcher. Aunt Dee mentioned you to me."

"I'm sure only the greatest of things." He caught the faintest eye roll before she motioned him to follow her.

"So you're Ben?" She dusted off the seat and swiveled the chair around for him to take a seat. She motioned to Kristy, who picked up a broom and swept around Carly's station.

"Yeah." He sat, rubbing his palms on his quads. Something about her made him nervous, sweat building up under his shirt.

Carly draped a black cape around his neck. "Any last name?"

"Um, yeah. Walker."

"Ben Walker." She paused, holding a comb mid-air. He could almost see her mind rifling through the index of names she had acquired over the years. "Hmm, what brings you to Waverly Lake?"

His nerves calmed down as she combed through the mess of overgrowth on his head. "Apparently a haircut and shave. At least, that was Aunt Dee's priority."

She chuckled. "I've seen worse. In fact, I think if you reshaped and trimmed the beard it would look all right. Did you want to keep it?"

Kristy's sweeping stopped long enough to give a head shake before minding her own business.

Was it that bad? He examined himself in the mirror and recalled the four or five days of itchiness he had gone through as it grew out, somewhere in the southern mountains of Virginia. "No, I think it's time to let go of it."

"Very well. Better to see that handsome face anyways." Carly winked and began work on cutting his hair.

He began to enjoy the fingers rifling through it, shedding the load of the past weeks onto the floor.

"You have gorgeous eyes." Carly smiled. "It was the first thing I noticed about you. Besides the beard. Such a lovely combination of brown and green."

"I never know what box to check when filling out forms. I think my license says hazel."

"Vale."

"What?"

"I believe they're called vale." She set the scissors down and grabbed her phone. "Hold on. Here." She showed him her screen, an eye color chart. "I know my colors. It's my job to know my colors."

"Of eyes?"

"Eyes, skin, your natural hair. It all plays into the tone and hue of hair color. If you match a warm color with a cool-skin tone, or vice-versa, it's going to look like I plopped a wig on you, or you tried to dye your hair with Jell-O like the kids used to do back in the day."

"Oh."

"Are you sure you haven't been here before?"

Ben swallowed hard. "Why do you ask?"

"I feel like I've seen those eyes before. I can't pinpoint when or who, though." She shook her head. "I'm sorry, I don't mean to freak you out. I swear I don't catalogue every customer who comes in here."

"She does." Kristy worked the broom by them again. "Just not on paper."

"Oh, get out of here." Carly waved her off playfully and plugged in the buzzer. The sound oddly calmed him, and he closed his eyes while she worked on creating the shortest bits and trimming around the ears. She finished up with the scissors, keeping the top longer than the sides in a side part. "I think a slightly longer version of the ivy league suits you."

Ben shrugged, having no idea what she meant. He looked in the mirror. If this was an ivy league, then she was right. It did suit him.

"Now for that beard." She tipped the chair back at a slight angle and clipped off the bulk of his beard. She added towels around his shoulders and laid a hot towel across his jaw. "So just where did you come from?"

Ben cleared his throat. It was a question he could answer without revealing too much. "Virginia." The wet cloth muffled his voice. "I've been backpacking on the AT for almost a month."

"It shows." Carly winked. "I've always been...in awe I guess, maybe more like never understood how anyone could just go out in the woods and survive."

"It's not exactly *Survivorman*. I get the hesitancy though. It's not for everyone."

"So, you hiked down from Virginia, and you're staying at Dorothy's place?"

"That's right."

She removed the hot towel and foamed up his face. She worked quickly, guiding the straight razor with as much confidence as if clearing crumbs off a tablecloth, all while accommodating his moving jaw. "How do you know Dorothy?"

A trickier question to answer. "Oh, you know. You see other hikers along the way. Sometimes you stay overnight in the same area and get to talking. They share their experiences, where to avoid, and what to check out. The lodge was one of those places I heard more than once as a good spot to rest."

Carly raised an eyebrow. "Hm, that's funny. Dee told me you and her are old friends."

Damn it. From now on he'd better ask Aunt Dee what exactly she had told anyone he'd be around. "Yeah, there's that too. I wouldn't say we are close. Acquaintances, really. My family has a history with her."

He closed his eyes. *Should've left that last part out.* "What can you tell me about Tracy Bennett?" It was all he could do to change the subject. Carly seemed one for gossip, and if it were true, she had a robust rolodex of people in that memory of hers; she'd know the locals to a tee.

Carly's face lit up, as if she were injected with a jolt of happy juice. "Ha! What can't I tell you about Tracy? I don't know if you want to get mixed up with that one."

"I sort of don't have a choice in the matter." He looked back at her, delighted not only to have successfully changed the subject, but to also learn more about his bold co-worker. "She's also staying at Aunt Dee's and helping out this season."

"That's right! I had almost forgotten. Well, I just say, don't get too close. She's like the cicadas. Gone for a year or two, then back in Waverly in everyone's business for a month, then gone again."

"A bit of a nomad, then?"

"I see it more as Waverly Lake is her homebase, yet her tether runs rather long. I just don't think she knows what she wants in life, but I blame that on Beverly and James."

Ben raised his eyebrows.

"Her parents. It's amazing Danny came out so sensible. How do I put this?" She stood still, straight razor in hand, mulling over her words. "They're more from the well-to-do side of folks in this town. Folks like the Bennetts, they have their own ideas of what success looks like, do you know what I'm saying? They had hoped their son and daughter would carry on that legacy."

He knew all too well the pressure of legacy. All he needed to do was visit the Phillips Medical Wing of the library in Waverly Lake.

"Danny came into his own, with his beautiful daughter, bless their hearts, and Tracy, well, I think she just needs time."

"She seems..." *Formidable? Tenacious?* Those words had a negative connotation, like the honesty and confidence behind them were weaknesses rather than strengths.

"Like a bulldozer driven by a drunk guy who knew it was his last day on Earth?"

He choked in laughter. "Well, I guess that's one way to put it."

"Why do you ask? You haven't got a thing for her, do you?"

"For Tracy? I just met her." *False.* He had only just met *adult* Tracy. For how long it had been, wasn't it sort of true? Being away from someone without any contact for years then reuniting was like a first meeting, especially when that time spanned them growing up.

"I just wanted to know what to expect in working with her." Not that she wanted him working *with* her. They were supposed to work together for Aunt Dee, separately.

"Now see, that's where you'll get yourself in trouble." Carly wiped the residual shaving cream off with a wet cloth. She placed a cold wet towel on his face for a few seconds, the cool soothing his freshly exposed skin. "Don't have any expectations with Tracy. The more you do, the more you're setting yourself up for a world of hurt."

She laughed, shaking her head. "The stories I could tell with her. By some miracle, or perhaps it was all planned, she made prom court her senior year of high school. Now, I don't know how they do it where you're from, but around here, everyone on the court takes part in the parade in the football stadium. There they were, all the nominees, sitting in their cars waving to the crowd as they were supposed to do. But no Tracy."

"She ditched?"

"Oh, no. That's not her style. No, Tracy showed up on the back of Mitch Caleb's motorcycle, holding a majorette's flag she to this day claims she borrowed, racing up the line of cars. She riled up that crowd before Mitch blasted the stadium with noise on their way out."

"She's an attention grabber, then?"

"That's the thing. A lot of people would think so from that night, or countless other Tracy doings. But I know her better than that. It's not about the attention. It's about being different from the status quo. About doing something new, shaking things up. That girl is allergic to tradition."

Ben smiled. Carly articulated the Tracy he'd known as his best friend, the young girl who got him in all sorts of situations his parents were none too happy with. Maybe growing up hadn't changed her.

Carly straightened the chairback. "There you go."

Ben processed the face before him. The cut atop of the clean face took years off, back down to the twenty-six-year-old he was.

"You could almost pass for a college student." Carly smiled, then shook her head. "I don't know what it is, but I get the sense we've met before. I know, you think I'm crazy. But I'll figure it out soon enough."

Could she possibly have been his hairdresser two decades ago? And if so, would she be that astute to know it was him? Or even remember him as a kid?

Then again, her distinct voice had triggered a connection. A familiarity.

He could only hope that Carly Fletcher wouldn't figure it out too soon. Or at all.

Chapter Seven

Tracy stood in the corner of Bleary's Hardware, scanning the folded shirts aligned on the shelves. She set the handbasket on the floor, its plastic weighed down by door hinges, bathroom hooks, and various other items Aunt Dee had on her list of supplies. The two bottles of cleaner were enough to give Tracy's arms a workout.

When she'd said Bleary's had a limited amount of work clothing, she wasn't kidding. Her choices ranged from a red and black plaid shirt to a blue and black plaid shirt, with a blue denim shirt in for the wildcard.

Ben would look better in blue. She picked up the stack of blue plaid, checking the tags for a large, and threw it in the basket. She stared at the other shirts. What was she thinking? Who cared what color looked best on him? It wasn't her job to dress the man, nor was it in her interest to even care what he wore. She picked one of each of the other shirts and added them to the basket.

The pants were easier, with one style to choose from—a durable khaki-colored pair. Luckily they had his size. She chuckled, thinking how Ben had shooed her away when she'd checked his tag. For being thrown together on this jaunt into town, he was a good sport about it.

She plonked her basket down at the register.

"Dee sending you on a run, I see." Richard Bleary stood in his hickory-brown collared shirt, the Bleary Hardware name embroidered over the chest pocket. A wrench stood in place of the 'l' in the name. As a child, Tracy rarely stepped into the store, but when she did, she was greeted by Richard's dad, who always let her get a gumball from the machine. Nowadays his son ran the place, but he carried on knowing the customers by name.

Although she had to pay for her own gumball. *Adulthood*.

"The second one this week," she said. "I'm sure not the last, either."

"I won't complain about her loyalty. Appreciate the business."

Tracy nodded and grabbed the bags, the heavier hardware in a brown paper bag. It seemed a silly thought, but such bags were hard to come by these days. Not many stores provided them. There was a sense of nostalgia, but also a tinge of sadness over time's changes.

"Have a great day."

"You too." She backed into the front door and exited. No knowing how long it would take Ben to finish up at Dye Happy Salon. If he was with Carly, he could be there all day. That woman loved to chat about anyone and everyone. Probably telling him all about her.

The thought was irritating. If someone wanted to know about her, she'd rather it come from her mouth. Most of Waverly didn't understand her. They couldn't understand why someone would want to leave so often, and go a million miles away. *To be a single woman out there traveling like that.* Carly had said as much, according to Sebastian.

As if being a woman made it much worse. Wanting mutual respect and equal opportunity made her a feminist, so she'd accept the label. But a piece of her did appreciate male chivalry. Not that she wanted someone to carry her groceries or hold her door open for her when she was perfectly capable. She only wanted someone *to want* to do those things for her, and understand why she might turn down his offer of doing those things.

Anyway, folks around here had a warped view of her, one that Carly Fletcher probably shared with Ben right now. *And they wonder why I don't stay.*

Tracy carried the bags down Dowager Street, through the square and over to Pearson's Wharf. She successfully dodged Danny this time as she placed the bags in *Tin Can* and moseyed back to the square. For a Saturday, the shops were fairly empty. Many folks spent fall weekends in the mountains RVing or tenting before the campgrounds closed for winter. A few stragglers perused the shops, buying cinnamon and pumpkin spice candles from Nichols and Dimes, or colorful fall wreaths from Weeping Wares. The air had a chill, the autumn sun veiled by a thin layer of gray clouds. More sweaters and scarves adorned the passersby each day, and Tracy found herself crossing her arms, warming her chest as she eyed Dye Happy Salon.

Carly Fletcher could be seen through the front windows, talking to an employee at the front desk. She couldn't see Ben further in, but if Carly was chatting with someone else, he was probably finished. One thing about Carly—if she was working on a client, her focus was one hundred percent on the client.

But where would Ben go? Check on her at Bleary's?

She paced back to Bleary's, the street parking busier on this side of the courtyard. Most of the locals lived west or south of downtown, while the tourists generally arrived from the east, making the square serve as a natural barrier—or connector— between the two .

A few customers rummaged through Bleary's, but no sign of Ben. Tracy walked back outside and scanned the street. She almost missed him, with the short hair and clean face. He stood two blocks down, staring south. She caught up to him, breaking his trance.

"Your clothes and Aunt Dee's supplies are in the boat already."

"Okay." He kept his gaze ahead.

You're welcome. She stared at the brick house, its four white columns in need of paint. It was a sight to see, even in its current state. "That's Phillips Manor," she said. "Used to be one of the prettiest houses in all of Waverly Lake."

He turned to her, his greenish hazel eyes more piercing than before. They were striking now that she had a better look at his face. Solid jaw. Perfect lips. His smooth shaven skin almost begged to be touched. "And now?"

She turned back to the property. Beyond the iron gates, the stalwart oaks stood untrimmed and the hedges had overgrown. Leaves rustled across the stairs, vines of Virginia creeper strangling the corners and crevices of the house. "The owners died in a car crash. Their only child was to inherit the property, but he..." She could picture him, the young brown-haired boy two fingers taller than her. Laughing with her as they anxiously awaited Aunt Dee to discover the fake spider in her salad or digging a tunnel between their properties so they could freely play in each other's backyards. Her crying as he got in the black car, one suitcase in hand, Mom telling her to say goodbye. For good.

"No one knows where he is these days, but for a while there was a custodian taking care of it. After he passed away, the city is slated to deal with it."

"It's owned by the city now?" He stuffed his hands in his pant pockets. "It's just such a unique-looking property, right here on the main street."

"They don't own it yet. Apparently, they have sixty days to find the son, or for him to come forward, which is at its tail end. But after that, they'll take it. Honestly, I don't think the city cares much about the building as a home. It's more about what the property could be, or even the land."

He pressed his lips together. "Why am I sensing that you care, though?"

"It's not the house so much. It's more a reminder of..." She saw the giggling face of Hunter, fair skin against the blond-streaked hair. She reached out to tag him, her socks and shoes full of mud, ringlets a tangled mess.

Tracy abandoned the memory. "Well, that's none of your business."

"What? Now you're keeping secrets from me?"

How'd he get her talking so much? "If you really want to know, it's a reminder of how money isn't as important as people make it out to be."

"How so? Tell me, please." He must've seen her hesitation. "Aunt Dee has nothing but pleasant things to say about Waverly Lake. You'd think it was an ideal place to live. Are you saying status is important here?"

"Waverly Lake has its rich and poor, like most places. In this case, the Phillips were rich. At least in Waverly Lake standards. Perhaps outside too. I couldn't really say because I was just a kid. But however much was in their bank account, it didn't matter, because they died. Too young. Money comes and goes. Living life, experiencing it all, is more important."

"Aren't you working for Aunt Dee for money?"

She put her arms on her hips. "Ever hear of working to live, not living to work? That's my philosophy. And you bring up a good point."

"What's that?"

"We should get back to Aunt Dee's, so I can continue working to live."

He nodded and felt his jaw, undoubtedly not used to the lack of beard.

She headed east, and he followed behind. "You don't look half-bad, by the way." She didn't bother turning around. It was enough to pay a compliment. He didn't have to see her blushing face as she did it. Just because she was honest didn't mean she fully owned up to it sometimes.

"Thanks." His footsteps halted, and she turned around. "What's that house over there? The one behind the Phillips house?"

She bit her lip in hesitation. Why did it matter if he knew? He'd find out eventually if he stayed in Waverly Lake long enough. Heck, he had already met Danny in his first few hours.

She cleared her throat, the sudden onset of dryness aggravating. "That would be my parents' house."

"Oh." His eyes opened wide. "Your...parents are wealthy as well?"

"Keyword parents," she said and continued walking. "I can't say my parents, God bless them, share the same life perspective that I do."

"Ah, I see." He smiled.

"Oh, do you?" What was he getting at? That she was a spoiled rich girl? She hated people thinking that sentiment in middle and high school. She thought she had overshadowed that cloud as she'd grown older, so hearing it now sounded worse.

He caught up to her, walking side-by-side. "I'm just saying that I can see how you would've developed your outlook on life growing up in that kind of environment."

She eyed him, looking for signs of sarcasm on his face. She found none. "Oh. Okay."

"Certain expectations of you?"

"To say the least." It was answer enough for them both to be content moving on.

They walked in silence past Nichols and Dimes and Dye Happy Salon. It was a wonder how empty it was on an October weekend. Maybe Aunt Dee's idea of Lovetoberfest wasn't so bad. It would breathe some fresh life to the town in its autumnal lull.

"What was that sign I saw, on the gate of that manor? Phillips Manor, you said." Ben really had a curiosity for the property. Or was he trying to get more at her wealthy upbringing in a roundabout way? "It said something about a hall?"

"Oh, right. There's a town hall forum on Tuesday night about what to do with the property."

"What do they want to do?"

She shrugged. "I've heard all sorts of theories. Turn it to a museum, make it into the mayor's house. I think the most likely theory is to sell it to an out-of-towner."

"Why someone out of town?"

"Someone who can afford to restore it. Investors are buying up properties left and right in western North Carolina, turning properties into daily rentals online." She'd seen it in other places, and it was a shame. It drove property values up, and that hurt the locals who wanted to stay in town, but couldn't afford the taxes.

They rounded Pearson's Wharf and walked the dock. Danny chatted with Mr. Pearson himself, a middle-aged balding man whose heart was bigger than his growing waistline. He gave Danny a job as a marine mechanic shortly after his ex–wife left him and Hannah high and dry. His understanding in accommodating Danny's schedule, especially with Hannah's special needs with autism spectrum disorder, ranked him mighty high in Tracy's respectable people book.

Danny caught them walking by and waved, Tracy waving back.

"How is it you know so much of the goings on in Waverly Lake?" Ben asked.

Tracy stopped at *Tin Can*, letting Ben on board first. "I may be cooped up most of the month at the lodge, but I still know what goes on around town. Plus, it helps to have a father on the Town Council. Most of the town will be there."

"Are you going?"

"If I do, I already have a date." The words felt out of place and embarrassed her. "My friends Sebastian and George. They invited me to come along. They're a couple." She internally shook her head, as if she needed to explain herself or her friends. "If you're curious, maybe you should go too."

He nodded as he suited up with his lifejacket. "Maybe I will."

Chapter Eight

BEN GRABBED A HOLD OF THE RAILING ON *TIN CAN*. HE couldn't help but picture the ramshackle house that had once been his home. Really his only true home. Even though when he was young, he hadn't grasped just how well-to-do his parents had been, he still could remember the grandness of it all. The crystal chandelier in the foyer. The sweet tea breaks on the pillared porch. Squeaking his sneakers on the shiny marble floor.

Maybe coming back here had been wrong. Seeing the house left him confused, agitated even. His stomach tensed in a knot, the breeze on the boat hardly enough to settle his rising fever. He hadn't anticipated feeling so angry—at the lack of care for the property, over adults he barely knew fighting over his future, all those years in foster care, for his parents not being more careful during that fateful drive back from the county's community center that night.

He didn't have a right to feel angry though. He had ignored the letters, and the phone calls to foster parents, and Frank Letts pressuring him to claim the property once he turned twenty-one. He abandoned the property along with his past, so how could he justify being angry? The only one to be angry with was himself.

"Are you okay?" Tracy called out from behind the cockpit. She took the return trip easier, more steadily. Unless he was so caught up in his confusion he hadn't noticed. "You kind of lost your color. You feeling nauseous?"

He shook his head.

"It's okay if you are. It's common if you're not used to boats. I can slow it down, but I find the steady pace and breeze to help."

"No, it's not that."

Tracy nodded once, not pressing it further.

There was a sense of obligation to explain himself. Aunt Dee was one of the few people he had remembered fondly and missed while away. The other stood right here at the helm.

Aunt Dee doubted he'd be recognized, and so far so good, although Carly Fletcher left him uneasy. But heck, he was only six when they took him away from Waverly Lake. He had wondered what happened to Tracy, the little girl he'd considered his best childhood friend. To realize she still hung around Waverly Lake was shocking in and of itself, although apparently, she never stuck around for long. He had pictured her moving on to a bigger city, perhaps a collegiate swimmer or a star on stage, destined to spread her wings elsewhere. Destined to forget him. But to hear her memories, to hear the hint of fondness in her voice as she spoke of him, the Phillips' son, was more than what he could've hoped for.

He felt obligated to be as open with her as he could be. The problem was that he couldn't sacrifice another person discovering who he truly was. It would send the town in a tailspin and put him back in the position of having to decide the fate of his parents' legacy. Especially since the estate would revert to the town soon.

As much as he wished to be, he wasn't ready.

Tracy slowed the boat as they approached the dock on the north side of the lake. It truly was beautiful, the leaves changing, trees framing the lodge up on the hill. He almost enjoyed the vantage point from the water.

Almost.

Tracy tied the last knots around the dock cleats, and Ben unsnapped his life vest.

"You know, you really ought to invest in swim lessons." Tracy held out her arms to receive the bags from the hardware store. "It's a good life skill to have."

"Maybe if I stay long enough in Waverly, you can teach me."

She grinned. "It's awfully cold to be learning this time of year. Although I have experience teaching."

She most certainly did. It was the only experience he did have with swimming, the summer before the accident, right here at the lodge. Tracy maneuvered in the water like she was born a mermaid. She'd hold his hands in hers and convince him to go underwater and blow bubbles. That's about as far as he got with it before his idyllic life shattered into pieces.

He followed her up the hill, her pace fast and determined. "Here, let me carry at least one of those."

"I'm capable, thanks."

"I didn't mean to imply you weren't. But I get the feeling Aunt Dee is old-fashioned enough to think negatively of me if you walked in there with both bags while I'm empty handed."

"You make a valid point, although she did make me carry your loaded backpack." Tracy looked at him, her breathing a tad heavier with the strain of the hill's climb, but he caught a faint hint of a smirk.

"That's because she thought the host should accommodate the guest. Although I did get a sense she got enjoyment out of irritating you."

"I'm not the only one who thought that, then?"

He smiled. "So...? Give me one?"

"And not have the chance to hear what Aunt Dee would say?" She handed him the one not making the jingling noises with her steps. "That's your stuff anyways."

He unrolled the top and peered into the bag, the clothing neatly folded and stacked. "Thank you for doing that."

"No problem. I do what's best for Aunt Dee, even if it means buying the strange hiker clothing."

They reached the stairs of the lodge leading to the front porch. "Buying these clothes was a favor to Aunt Dee, then?"

"Of course." She paused at the front door. "Aunt Dee is keeping you around to work for her. You needed a larger wardrobe to better do your job."

"I see." He smiled and reached for the door, but Tracy beat him to it.

She held it open with her foot, the heavier bag in her hands. "Good. Then the best thanks you can give me is to perform your job even better with your new work clothes."

He smiled and nodded. "Okay, Tracy. Will do." He walked into the lodge, and she followed him, swinging the door closed behind her.

"Is that you, Tracy?" Aunt Dee called from somewhere in the back of the lodge.

"Yeah, we're back." Tracy placed the bag of supplies on one of the breakfast tables across the room, then laid out the items on the table.

Aunt Dee appeared from the room by the stairs. Ben knew the downstairs private room behind the mural wall was her bedroom, a common hiding spot when he and Tracy had played hide-and-seek. That left the one closer to the stairs to be Aunt Dee's office, tucked away from the sometimes-busy front desk.

Aunt Dee carried a clipboard that she set on a table next to Tracy.

"Oh good, they had the right towel hangers." She grabbed the rods out of Tracy's hand.

"I managed to get everything on the list."

"Including some clothes." Ben raised his bag and felt foolish once the two women stared at him.

Tracy stepped out of Aunt Dee's way, who examined the items as if inspecting them for OSHA compliance.

"What's this?" Tracy held the clipboard, a list of items in blue ink too far away for Ben to read.

"Oh, those are the ideas for dates for Lovetoberfest. I still have a few vendors to speak with about participating."

Tracy examined the lines, shaking her head. "Trip to the

pumpkin patch?" She released the pen from the snapping closure at the top and crossed out the item.

Ben neared, looking over her shoulder. "What are you writing?" He interpreted the quick handwriting. "Punkin' chunkin'." He stood back, Tracy tipping the clipboard away from him. "What the heck is punkin' chunkin'?"

"You know, when you have a catapult and hurl pumpkins in the air."

"That's your idea for a date?"

"Yeah. The pumpkin patch is a bit juvenile, don't you think? You need something more exciting, with a little more oomph. Something more fun than walking a pumpkin patch."

"Don't you think it's easier to connect with someone you don't know if you could talk over a calmer setting? You know, being out in nature, getting to know each other through conversation. Not cheap thrills."

Tracy's mouth hung agape. "Um, no. If you're giving someone the chance to win you over, to sell you on being with them for the rest of your life, then he'd better pull out all the fun stops up front, else there'd be zero chance of fun in a marriage."

"Wow." Ben stood, bewildered. "So many things to say to that."

Tracy hugged the clipboard like a high schooler hugging their textbook in the hallway, free hand resting on her hip. "Oh yeah? Why don't you go ahead and say them, then?"

"Okay." Ben folded his arms across his chest. "For one, a date is not something to win the other person over. It's not a sales pitch."

"Please, enlighten me on what it is then."

"It's a way to see if you are compatible with each other. And second, shouldn't you see what the other person is like day-to-day, doing something calmer, more routine? Then you'd have a better idea of what a marriage would be like with that person. Because a marriage isn't all pumpkin throwing."

"Maybe that's what my marriage would be."

He shook his head, trying not to smile at her fire and naivety.

"That's enough, you two." Aunt Dee snatched the clipboard

out of Tracy's arm. She stared at them, Ben feeling her eyes boring into his psyche. Why did he get the sense she was up to something?

"You know, I think I know just the way to settle this."

Tracy stepped back. "Aunt Dee, whatever it is you're thinking—"

"Consider it part of working for me."

"What exactly are we considering?" Ben asked.

Aunt Dee smiled, not a friendly, nice lady smile, but a I-caught-you-two-in-a-trap smile. "The two of you will try out these ideas."

"What do you mean?" Tracy cocked her head. "Like, as in, go out on the dates?"

"Exactly. A trial run."

"That's a terrible idea," Tracy said.

"No, thank you." The words slipped out of Ben's mouth as he thought them. He didn't even regret saying them.

"Yes, it's perfect. The two of you can go out on these three here." She circled the top three in her list. "And you each add one of your choice. Then at the end, you pick the top three dates for our guests to go on during Lovetoberfest."

"Aunt Dee, with all due respect, I said I'd help you out, but I didn't sign up for this."

"You signed up to help me, period." Her voice grew firm and strong, a sternness behind it. "I need people to stay at Woodsman's Lodge in the fall, and Lovetoberfest is a way to draw in guests. Now, let me know what you want to add, and I'll arrange it with whatever vendor can help us out."

"But—"

Aunt Dee shoved the clipboard in front of Tracy. It was a showdown of wills, and Aunt Dee stood perfectly still while Tracy's gaze caught Ben's stare. She was cracking. He wanted to help her, defend her stance in that this was a bad idea—even though the prospect of proving Tracy wrong about dating had its appeal. But did it really have *that* much appeal? To push them on not one but five dates?

Don't cave, Tracy. He had no idea how Aunt Dee would carry on with them if Tracy won, but he was willing to find out.

Tracy's shoulders dropped.

No!

She reluctantly took the clipboard, refusing to make eye contact with Ben or Aunt Dee.

"Good. Now I suggest you two start planning with your additions." Aunt Dee replaced the items from the hardware store back into the bag, the clink and clang of the metal parts the only noise out of the three of them. She rolled down the top of the paper bag and moseyed back to her office.

The silence was torture, standing in front of Tracy.

"I uh, I guess we walked into that one."

"I don't know what to say." Tracy shook her head. "Maybe if we apologize for arguing? Maybe she'll change her mind."

But Tracy had to have known, perhaps better than he did, that Aunt Dee wasn't one to go back on a decision. Even six-year-old Ben knew that.

She sighed. "I guess I'd better get to searching for more things to do around here."

"Well, I already know what I've got to do now."

Tracy's confusion read clearly across her face. "What's that?"

He lifted the paper bag in the air again. "If we're going on five dates, I'm going to need more clothes."

As hard as Tracy tried to hide it, he caught her muted smile.

Chapter Nine

Sunday, October 9

As much as Tracy didn't want to be back at her parents' house a day after her downtown tour of Waverly Lake with Ben, she couldn't say no to Sunday brunch. Technically she could say no, and she had before. Once. The rest of the week, she had to dodge Mom's phone calls and persistent guilt trip about not spending time with her family. *You're in town rarely enough as it is,* Beverly Bennett would say. *It's a shame you don't want to spend that time with your family.*

Spending time with Danny was enjoyable. Even fun, sometimes. Time with Beverly and James Bennett? Not so much. It was a love-hate relationship. Okay, hate was a strong word. Love-irritated relationship?

Tracy had docked *Tin Can* at Pearson's Wharf and hurried west along Dowager Street. The square remained empty Sunday mornings, outside of the trail of parked cars of churchgoers along the side streets. After the services, many hit the town for lunch and families enjoyed shopping or picnics in the park in the afternoon. Mom and Dad opted for family brunch time. This required Mom to skip out on the post-church chit-chat over donuts and coffee in the gathering hall. She got her fill of gossip with her volunteering throughout the rest of the week. Tracy wouldn't doubt it was a prime motivator to volunteer.

She paused at Phillips Manor, gazing through the iron gate. Just about every weekend over the summer had her visiting the Bennett residence, yet she hadn't fully taken in just how severely time had stricken the neighboring property with melancholy. Ben's curiosity had been contagious and got her wondering about the fate of the house and its only survivor, her lost friend.

The sound of mingling on the back porch of her childhood home overshadowed her thoughts. The morning was brisk, but the rising sun left pockets of warm spots in its wake.

"There she is!" Beverly Bennett's voice rang across the yard.

"Coming, mother." She moaned it more to herself than out loud.

Hannah, her niece, ran to the backyard's gate, latching open the side door leading out to the street. Her raspberry-red sweater hugged her slight belly, the sleeves reaching an inch or two above her wrists.

"Why, thank you Hannah."

"You're late."

"Good morning to you too." She patted Hannah's sandy brown hair, pulled into two pigtails. Ever since Danny had started dating Kara Carter, Hannah had slightly more kept hairdos. Recently she seemed to be shooting up in height, and Tracy couldn't blame Danny for not being able to keep up with the wardrobe. Plus, Hannah's autism manifested in specific ways, one of them being her insistence on wearing certain clothing over and over until the very fabric disintegrated or refused to give to her growth spurt.

Tracy walked through the grass to the back of the house. The sizable two-story home had a creamy-gray stucco exterior, the kind that showed wear and tear in the form of chips on the walls and cracks in the corners of the double-pane windows. Two cement stairs led up to the covered porch, a later addition that didn't quite blend in as flawlessly as her mother would've liked.

Mom kissed her on the cheek. "Glad you could make it." It was Beverly's way of saying what Hannah had said directly, with the addition of an adult passive-aggressive filter.

"I know, I'm late. Morning, Dad."

James Bennett sat in one of the all-weather hemp-colored wicker chairs. The set of pieces had cream-colored cushions—a color Tracy wouldn't choose based on Mom's red wine collection alone. Not to mention having kids over. Hannah may have been past her toddler years of spills and tears, but she generally occupied her time by coloring with markers and not wanting to put the caps back on.

"Here you go." Kara handed her a thick mug filled with black coffee.

"Thank goodness. Don't ever leave Danny." Tracy winked at Kara, who shook her head and smiled. Kara really was a breath of fresh air to the family. Even if she wasn't officially family. But Tracy couldn't imagine Danny finding a better partner, or a better woman to be a stepmom to Hannah. Tracy wasn't one to believe in a particular higher being, or in miracles. Kara returning to Waverly and rekindling a relationship with Danny was the closest thing Tracy had ever seen to a miracle.

"You look nice this morning," Kara smiled.

Tracy examined her sweater, the color blocks matching the fall flags coming into town, all the way down to the boots over her jeans as if she had forgotten what she wore.

"Big date?"

Tracy choked on the sip of coffee and reached for a napkin. While it held true she prided herself in speaking her mind, being an open book with her family was another story.

"Does this mean we can eat now?" Danny stood next to the table that ran along the back wall of the brick house. Mom had covered it in a mocha-brown tablecloth and an apricot table runner.

"Hold on one second." Mom took off the aluminum foil over

the dishes—fruit salad, macaroni and cheese, spinach and artichoke dip with pita chips, honey ham sandwiches made with yeast rolls.

Tracy's stomach gurgled at the sight. She had skipped breakfast to get here on time. Aunt Dee insisted she take *Tin Can* instead of the lodge's truck, since Ben would need the vehicle to meet up with her for their "date" this afternoon. More like a work event.

"How's it going with Aunt Dee?" Kara scooped a spoonful of mac and cheese on her plate as Tracy picked up two sandwiches for hers.

"It's...fine." She contemplated how much to reveal.

"That bad?"

Kara had a knack for knowing how people felt. Then again, Tracy had a knack of showing how she felt, with her face.

"I'm sure it's just Tracy hating to actually do physical labor," Danny said. He jabbed Tracy with his elbow as he snuck in line to reach for a peanut butter cookie.

"It's not that at all, but thanks for the commentary, brother." Tracy all but stuck her tongue out at him. "In fact, I'd be pleased if that was all that Aunt Dee has asked of me."

"What else is she having you do?" Dad perked up. "I can speak with her if she's working you too hard."

Tracy shook her head. It was one thing to have parents who provided you with everything you needed in life and more. While Tracy appreciated the privilege that Beverly and James had bestowed up on her in growing up, she didn't like them interfering with her life. It wasn't uncommon for them to control their children's lives, even if they saw it as helping.

"No, Dad. I can be a hard worker, and I don't need any of you to speak with Aunt Dee."

"Then what's the issue, honey?" Mom sat on one end of the wicker sofa, gnawing on a cracker with dip.

It was one of the reasons she didn't want to come out here today. Her family had a way of getting information out of her, and if not her, they'd find a way to get it out of anyone in town who knew anything about it. Lovetoberfest and Ben Walker were the two things she did *not* want to talk about.

She sighed, accepting defeat. Well, accepting was a strong word. "Aunt Dee is planning an event near the end of the month, called Lovetoberfest."

"Oh boy," Danny said.

Tracy eyed him. *Exactly.* She didn't have to say the word. It was that brother-sister connection.

"What is that all about?" Kara asked. "And does she need a photographer?"

Tracy smiled briefly. Ever since Kara had worked her way into taking over Portside Portraits, she jumped at the opportunity to photograph a community event. "Five women and five men will be staying at Woodsman's Lodge for a long weekend. They will go out on three dates with the top three most compatible partners, as planned by Aunt Dee. Or I should say, as planned by me through a questionnaire I have to devise." She examined her audience—Mom, Dad, Danny, and Kara hanging on to her words. Hannah sat on the floor of the porch eating grapes and coloring her paper plate.

"Do I want to ask what your role in this is?" Danny sat in a chair near Hannah.

Mom's eyes grew big. "Are you one of the five women? Oh Tracy, that would be marvelous!"

Tracy flung her head back, eyes closed. "No, Mother. I'm not." *Almost worse.* "Aunt Dee wants me to 'try out' the dates to see which ones would be the most fun, or romantic, or whatever."

Danny snorted, nearly choking on his food. Kara elbowed him in the arm, glaring at him to stop.

"What do these dates entail?" Mom asked. "Are they at the lodge?"

"All around town," Tracy said. "It's also Aunt Dee's way of increasing local business, using local vendors for the outings."

"I think that's a great idea," Mom said. "It sounds like a great experience to have in event planning. And to have you check them out! I think it's long overdue that you spend some time in town, appreciating what Waverly Lake has to offer, instead of gallivanting here and there."

"Yeah, Tracy. Enough of that gallivanting," Danny jibed.

"There's a reason why I spend more of my time away from here."

Kara raised a hand, as if necessary to get a word in during a Bennett family discussion. "Coming from someone who's lived in New York, there is a certain charm to being here you can't get in the big city."

In no way had she meant to admonish anyone who would choose to stay. Just because it wasn't her thing didn't mean that everyone felt the same way. If anything, she was the odd person out. "That's the thing. I'm not looking for charm. I'm looking to be alive." Her non-plate-holding hand waved about, her eyes opening large. "Wind in my hair as I'm paragliding, legs aching until I reach the crest of the mountain, or sand whipping my face."

"We have sand." Hannah stated the fact without looking up from her plate. Tracy never knew how much Hannah listened in on their conversations, but she suspected it was close to all the time.

"I know, sweetie. But the shores of Waverly Lake don't exactly scream sandboarding."

This time Hannah put down her marker and turned around. "Daddy, what is sandboarding?"

"It's like surfing, but on sand dunes. And much more painful." He eyed Tracy. *Thanks a lot.*

Tracy sometimes forgot how much influence she had on her growing niece. She pictured Danny having to sit by the lake on a wakeboard to convince Hannah that was close enough to Aunt Tracy's sandboarding.

"Are these things that you'll check out by yourself? Or are you inviting a friend to go along with you?" Kara had gotten to the crux of the situation in no time.

"I really don't want to talk about this. You've heard enough."

"Hardly," Danny said. He read her face, as if seeing her thoughts, and he stood, folding his arms. The grin foreshadowed the words coming out of his mouth. "Would this have anything to do with that Bob I met yesterday?"

"Ben." She wasn't going to tell any of them about Ben, but Danny got it out of her anyway.

"It does!" Danny got way too much entertainment out of this. "You have to go on these dates with him, don't you?"

"Who is Ben?" Mom asked.

"Ben is nobody."

"A handsome guy, for sure," Danny joked, as if he ever judged a man's looks before now.

"If you like scraggly beards. I bet he has quite the array of tattoos too." Tracy didn't care about any of those things. It was all to get the repulsive reaction Mom had on her face right now. A sure-fire way to end the conversation about Ben.

"Oh, that's not true. I saw you two when you left town yesterday. He had quite the respectable haircut and a clean-shaven face." Danny turned to Mom. "He was nothing but a gentleman in speaking with me."

"Is that so?" Mom said.

Tracy laser-eyed Danny. *I hate you.* "He's a hiker off the trail that Aunt Dee seems to know somehow. He's working for her too, to pay for his stay at the lodge."

"Now Aunt Dee wants you to date him?" Kara asked.

"No." Tracy closed her eyes. Did Aunt Dee truly realize the ask she was making on this whole Lovetoberfest? "We're supposed to check out the venues and give our opinions on what the guests should and shouldn't do."

"Maybe you should give the guy a chance," Mom said. "It wouldn't hurt to at least be nice and presentable."

Tracy scanned her jeans and sweater. "I am presentable." She looked at Kara, who nodded in support.

"You're going on one today?" Danny asked.

"Oh, bless his heart." Mom clutched her chest.

Tracy's back pocket buzzed.

"Since when did you get a cell phone?" Mom asked.

"Aunt Dee provided it." Tracy pulled it out of her pocket.

"That stubborn woman. I told her I'd buy one for you, and she wouldn't have it."

Thank goodness. "It's strictly for business." If Aunt Dee had left it to Mom, that would've crossed the line again from helping to controlling. She'd be called at all hours of the day and night for who knew what. But it would be 'justified' because Mom had paid for it.

Tracy opened the message. *Meet Ben at the lodge at 1:30. Don't be late.*

"I need to get going soon." Tracy finished her sandwich and popped the little bit of fruit left into her mouth.

Kara took Tracy's plate off to the kitchen, and Danny rose, stepping aside with Tracy. He leaned closer, talking low. "I know it's not your thing. But maybe go easy on the guy. Get to know him."

"Are you serious? Since when do you take Mom's side?"

"It's not about sides."

"You hated when I took Mom's side about dating when Kara came back to town."

"Yeah and look how that turned out." He glanced back at his girlfriend, who returned and sat on the floor next to Hannah.

Tracy sighed. "Forget I said that."

"Okay," he said. "I'll forget you mentioned it when you admit that there's a piece of you that is curious about Ben."

"What?" She laughed it off.

"I know you." Danny pointed his finger.

"Oh, is that right?"

"Yes. You put on the whole 'I'm irritated with this person' act when really it bothers you *not* knowing them."

She scoffed, one that sounded fake, even to her. "I don't know what you're talking about."

Danny nodded, smiling. "If I'm wrong, I'll own up to it. You enjoy your date in the meantime."

"It's not a date. It's...an assessment of a date."

"Whatever you want to call it." He waved before retreating to Hannah and Kara.

Kara waved to Mom and Dad and crossed the backyard to the gate. The good news was that Aunt Dee's text saved her from any more family scrutiny.

The bad news is that she had to go on the first date with Ben Walker.

Chapter Ten

BEN WALKER SAT IN THE BROWN AND SILVER CHEVY C/K. He had never even heard of a C/K before entering the rusted heavy-duty clunker. But the red, velvety interior with its musty smell had been seen before. He closed his eyes and felt the worn bucket seat fabric and remembered sitting atop someone's knee, riding the curves of some mountainous road, Tracy riding in the middle. She squealed with each turn, setting them both off into a giggle fit. A memory that in today's safety-conscious society would be shunned by parents across the country.

He ran the heater, the vents blowing air colder than outside. After a few minutes, he turned the knob lower, the heat a hot combination of warmed air and the fumes and swelter of the old engine.

Through the trees he had seen *Tin Can* arrive and now awaited going on this obligatory date. The first of several. He couldn't complain. Aunt Dee let him stay at the lodge, and if she needed someone to help her out with Lovetoberfest, he'd do it without blinking.

Except he wished it was helping in any way but this. Dating was not his forte. He had the occasional flirtation with women at bars or over a fire at a larger shelter. Admittedly he had a few flings, if he were being honest. The closest he had to a relationship was in the eighth grade. He had just switched foster families and enrolled in a new school. New schools either meant kids wanted to bully him, or fought to be the new kid's friend. Eloise Barrister was one of the latter types and held his hand in the hallways for a whole week. Until he got in a fight with John Myers and lost. He hadn't even wanted to fight in the first place.

But that's the way it was, town and school hopping. Not so hard making friends as it was keeping them. Heck, Tracy Bennett may have been the longest friendship of his life. Unfortunately, it didn't seem like she wanted anything to do with him now that they were adults. Granted she didn't know who he really was. But if she did? Would her behavior, her reaction to him, change? He did want to get to know her again, to see how she had changed, how she hadn't. In the form of a date, though?

The pull on the passenger door startled him. Tracy knocked on the window, pointing to the handle.

"It's unlocked," he said.

She tried again, pulling back, her brown ringlets shaken by the tug. She shook her head.

He shifted in his seat, lifting his leg over the passenger side. He kicked the door, and Tracy yanked it loose. It whined in revolt as she opened it wider. She sat in the passenger seat and slammed the door closed. "Well, that was something else."

Aunt Dee crossed in front of the truck and waved, making her way to the lodge. Ben waved back.

"Yeah, Aunt Dee said the passenger door sticks sometimes."

Tracy put on her belt. "I'm surprised the door is still on this thing to begin with."

He put the truck in drive and pulled out of the parking lot, up the hill to the main road.

"Where exactly are we going?"

"Honeysuckle Farm. It's on the east side of the lake."

"Yeah, I know it. I guess we're doing one of Aunt Dee's picks first?" She looked at him and he turned away, her brown eyes the color of the darkest strands of her curls.

"Wasn't my pick, if that's what you were asking. Not after knowing your opinion on pumpkin patches." He flicked on the radio and played with the dial. After hearing static in both directions, he returned it to its original position, a country classics station that went in and out depending upon the car's orientation on the hills.

"I'm surprised Aunt Dee still has this thing." Tracy pet the dashboard, then examined the glovebox.

Ben eyed the handgun lying atop papers inside the box.

"Don't worry," Tracy said. "It's not loaded. In fact, I don't think it fires even if it were loaded." She closed the glovebox. "Aunt Dee likes to have it for looks, just in case. She said if the sight of one doesn't scare off whoever is coming after her, then she'd have no hope anyways."

"That's a pleasant thought." Ben shook his head. "I don't know who'd be crazy enough to go after Aunt Dee, though." He glanced at Tracy. "She's scary enough."

Tracy smiled before resting her head on her hand, elbow on the door.

He pictured that young girl giggling as he swerved along with the curve in the road. "So, Aunt Dee has had this truck for a while?"

Tracy kept her eyes ahead. "As far as I can remember."

"Then that is amazing it runs."

"Aunt Dee is pretty good at making sure things are well taken care of." She felt the seat between him and her. "She used to take me riding sometimes. We'd go into town for an ice cream, and she'd let me sit in the middle between her and my dad. I couldn't see over the dash, which kinda made it more fun along the windy roads."

"Sounds dangerous."

"You don't realize it so much as a kid."

"I guess not." He dropped further discussion of the memory. He wanted her to mention him, to remember the times they had like he did. But he'd be heartbroken if she didn't remember, if she didn't cherish their friendship as he had, even after all this time.

They rode in silence for the last seven or eight miles, which took a good fifteen minutes. Few roads around the lake were flat or straight. On this side, although the lake was obscured most of the time outside of winter, the various oaks, maples, and hickory trees offered an autumnal menagerie, an ombre of coffee colors at the top of the mountainside down to soft yellows by the lake.

The farm's sign had a pig in overalls standing upright between two ears of corn. Ben pulled into Honeysuckle Farm and a handful of teenagers at strategic posts guided him through the gravel parking lot. He parked and opened the door. Tracy hesitated.

"What are we supposed to do?" she asked.

He paused, half out of the truck. "I guess, see what all there is to see here?" He shrugged. "At least show proof to Aunt Dee we checked it out."

Tracy nodded and grumbled something. All he caught was the clearer last word. "Okay."

The gravel turned to muddy grass as they walked to the entrance. Kids with their faces painted ran around, screaming with delight. Parents carried pumpkins and tuckered out toddlers on their way out. Hay bales stacked by a wooden sign served as a photo-op for families waiting in line for their turn.

"Not sure how romantic this place would be for a date." Tracy walked with her hands in her jean pockets. Her sweater, with its own splash of pumpkin-and-chocolate bands, brought out the highlights in her hair. She had wild curls, curls she didn't bother to slick down or tie back. For a second he wanted to reach over and run his fingers through them. "You agree?"

"Huh?" Ben blinked hard and returned to reality. "I don't know. It looks like everybody's having fun at least."

Tracy led the way to the ticket booth. The twenty-something guy behind the counter gave the family in front of them their tickets, and Tracy moved up.

"Hey, Trace! What are you doing here? I thought you'd be gone after summer."

She opened her mouth for a reply and paused for a second, as if rethinking her original retort. "Long story. Did a woman named Dorothy call about us coming?"

"Let me see. I just got here myself not too long ago." He rifled through some papers and found two armbands paper-clipped to a sheet of paper. "Here we go. Two tickets. And I'm supposed to tell you," he flipped the paper over, "find your way through the maze and feel free to do anything extra."

"Thank you." Tracy handed an armband over to Ben.

"A friend of yours?"

She wrapped the band around her wrist. "An acquaintance."

Ben held down one end of the band and wrapped the loose end around his wrist, losing grip on the first end. "Some help here?"

"You can survive for weeks in the wilderness, but an armband bested you?" Tracy chuckled and rolled up the sleeve of the blue flannel she'd bought him. Seemed appropriate enough for a date on a farm. She attached the two ends of the armband. "There you go." She stared him right in the eyes and paused. It was a second. A split second. A millisecond. But he felt it. More than just a stare.

"The blue looks good on you." She started walking further along the path, and he caught up. "The shirt."

"Oh, thanks."

"Tracy?" A woman with light blond hair to her shoulders held a little girl's hand. The girl yawned and rubbed her eyes while the woman reached for a hug from Tracy.

"Oh, hi." Tracy kept her face a good distance from the woman's body in the awkward hug, lightly tapping the woman's shoulders as if tapping out of the deal.

"So good to see you. I heard you were going to stay for the fall, but I didn't believe it, and here I am proven wrong."

"Yep." Tracy feigned a happy face.

"I'd love to stay and chat, but Annie here is ready for her nap."

"No problem. You go ahead." Tracy waved at Annie as the two walked off.

Ben stood in front of Tracy, grinning.

"What?"

"Is there anyone you don't know?"

She rolled her eyes. "It's more like they know my family." She pointed to the woman, now carrying little Annie. "That's Lynn, she graduated with Danny and sings in the choir at my mom's church."

"And ticket booth guy?" He meant it innocently, but his voice cracked.

Tracy's mouth grew into a grin. "Does it bother you, Ben Walker, that people know me?"

"No." He shook his head. "I just—for someone who wasn't so... I mean, when we first met..."

"I wasn't so friendly? Is that what you mean to say?"

His mouth remained open, yet the words lagged.

"You're surprised people like my company?"

"I didn't mean that, I—" This time he cut himself off before she could. *What am I saying?*

"I'm just kidding." She laughed. "That's the curse of living in this town. Although my mother would say that's the blessing. Everyone knows everyone. And for the record, ticket booth guy was in my graduating class. We took drivers ed together."

He didn't know what to say. To any of it.

"Look, I know I haven't been all roses and sunshine to you. But this is important to Aunt Dee, and obviously you know her from somewhere, so I trust she wouldn't be sending me off to get lost in a corn maze with a serial killer."

"I appreciate that. I think."

"All right then. New start?"

He nodded. "Sure, new start."

She smiled. "Now that's behind us, what do you say we do this thing?"

The farm extended for acres eastward along the flat valley landscape. The public access portion was divided in half, a main pathway carved through the center. On one side was the maze and vendors selling pumpkin spiced drinks, pretzels with dipping sauces, and corndogs. The other side had a playground of plastic sides along hay bales and stacked tractor tires to climb, and farm animals anxiously awaiting human hands to release food pellets.

They walked to the entrance of the maze, an opening in the cornfield to the left. Tracy paused at the start. "Where's the exit?"

Ben examined the rows of ears. "I think on the other side?" He sidestepped around the corner. "Over there, I see people coming out." He stared at Tracy. "You scared?"

"No way." She rushed through the entrance and made a left turn.

"Wait up!" Ben ran after her.

Tracy walked briskly, pausing at the next branch. "Which way?"

"Try right?"

They walked through, passing up a family of four coming from the other direction. "Should we be concerned they're going the other way?" Tracy asked.

"I was thinking the same thing." They carried on, twisting, turning, backtracking through the rows of corn. They stopped for a break, Ben completely clueless as to which direction they had already come from, the cornstalks too tall to see over.

"I think I hear the tractor for the hayride." Tracy turned her head, listening.

"I can't hear much over my stomach growling. The smell of kettle corn is killing me."

The crunch of feet over the flattened stalks made them both turn the same direction.

"Walking toward us?" Ben asked.

"I think away." Tracy met his eyes, and they laughed.

"We should be corn maze tour guides, we're so good at this." Ben shook his head in amusement.

"You know, this would be pretty cool to do after sunset," Tracy said. "In the dark, with flashlights. Imagine then how lost we'd get."

"That'd be pretty spooky."

"Yeah, and with zombies." Her face lit up as if she won money through a scratch-off lottery ticket.

"Zombies?" Ben laughed it off.

"People dressed as zombies, hiding in corners and coming after you." She wiggled her fingers at him. "Don't worry, my date pick will more than make up for the lack of zombies here."

"Wonderful. Can't wait to see what that is." For what he knew of adult Tracy, they were probably going skydiving. "Can't you at least appreciate the effort that goes into making this?" He touched a cornstalk. "The farmers had to plant and grow these crops, harvest them, then design the maze. It's pretty amazing."

Her shoulders dropped, and the smile erased. "You're right." Her tone turned serious. Maybe she did have the ability to appreciate the things in life seen as mundane and didn't have to take wild risks or be on crazy adventures to have a good time.

They walked together in who knew what direction. He was having a good time. He'd have to let Aunt Dee know that the corn maze wasn't entirely a bust.

"It would still be cooler at night." Tracy giggled, her smirk twitching again.

He shook his head. "Come on, zombie lover. Let's find our way out of this."

Chapter Eleven

"AND VOILA!" TRACY JUMPED THE LAST STEP OUT OF THE corn maze, her brown knee-high boot crunching on straw. "I wonder what the record is for completing that on the first try."

Ben rested his hands on his head, stretching his chest. "Would've been faster if we hadn't gone that dead-end way somewhere in the middle."

Tracy forced back the giggle. They had completed a set of twists and turns only to find themselves at a dead end. Ben had slightly freaked out, fanning his shirt and wiping his brow in his sleeve, until she reminded him they were in a corn maze, not amongst walls of cinderblock.

"Well, what now?" Tracy gazed at Ben. Admittedly the maze had been better than she imagined. Daresay even enjoyable.

"Should we head back? Tell Aunt Dee what we thought of the maze?"

Tracy heard the questions, but focused on the activity across the pathway. "I have just the thing."

Ben stepped back. "Should I be scared?"

"Come on." She grabbed his wrist and got him moving down the path to the corner of the roped-off property. She couldn't believe her eyes when she'd seen the sign.

"You've got to be kidding me." Ben stood by the giant pumpkin painted to look like it flung off the sign, shaking his head. "Pumpkin Pitch?"

"I hoped it meant what I'd thought it meant." Tracy perused the pumpkins assembled on the ground. They weren't like the ones in the pumpkin patch near the front of the farm, ones nearly perfect in round plumpness, uniform color and organized by size. These were misshapen and splotchy. They would make fine jack-o-lanterns all the same, but most people didn't want the imperfect ones to stack on their front porches. She picked one up, drawing it near her ear and knocking with her knuckles.

"What exactly are you doing?" Ben awaited in the path of pumpkins, hands in his pockets.

"Picking the best pumpkin to hurl in the air." She grinned.

"Oh yeah? How can you tell which one is best?"

She placed the pumpkin back on the ground. "I have no idea." She shrugged sheepishly and Ben laughed. His laugh was crisp and hearty, like genuine joy emanating from his body.

"Okay. You use your method, and I'll use mine." He picked up a pumpkin, turning it over.

Tracy stopped, hand on hip. "And what's your method?"

"It's all about the shape." He rubbed his hand on the pumpkin. "You want the most aerodynamic."

"Is that right?" She settled on a pumpkin with a short stem, a little squat but robust. "Here I didn't think you were into pumpkin chucking."

"If we're going to do it, I'm not going to just stand by and let you win."

"It's a competition now?" Tracy's eyebrows flared. Did he realize competitiveness could've been her middle name? Heck, it could've been her first name. Granted, a really long and silly one.

He walked by her, choice of pumpkin in hand, heading for the launch area. "I'll even give you first choice of weapon."

"How generous of you." Tracy examined the row of launchers. A father and son operated the pneumatic cannon, a long tube that hissed loudly as it launched the pumpkin in the air. "Hmm, tempting. But I like to keep it old school."

"Old school?"

"Yeah, medieval times. I'm gonna go with the catapult." She placed her pumpkin in the contraption and awaited Ben's choice.

"Very well. If we're keeping it medieval, then I think I'll take the sling shot." He stood next to his launcher. "Ladies first."

Tracy nodded, her pulse pounding in her neck, in her temples, all over. She had talked up pumpkin chucking at the lodge as if she had done it before, but this was her first time. The excitement was hard to contain, but she remained as outwardly calm as possible.

"Here goes nothing." She pushed the wooden lever, and the catapult arm swung upward, launching the pumpkin across the field and slightly to the right. She squealed in delight as the gourd slightly surpassed the red painted wooden scarecrow serving as a distance marker.

Ben turned to her, a hesitant smile across his face. He looked around, a crowd of eight or ten people now watching their mini competition.

"No pressure."

Tracy smiled and winked at him. "You got this." Poor guy, being watched. At least she hadn't been, as far as she knew. She probably would've choked. When she had bungee jumped, she'd insisted on going first, not because she'd lose her courage, but because she didn't want any of the others in the group to see her reaction at the bottom.

Ben placed his pumpkin in the sling and pulled the handle back. He dug his heels in the muddy ground, pulling the bands taut. His arms shook with the tension. As he let go, his feet slipped, and he fell on his bottom into the muck. Tracy was torn between the shock of him falling, and the trajectory of the pumpkin flying in the sky. She eyed the pumpkin as it landed, a good fifteen feet past hers. The crowd clapped at the landing.

She reached an arm out to help Ben up.

"How'd I do?"

"You won." She stepped closer, tugging at his arm. Her boot lost grip, and she fell with a shout, hands and knees catching mud. "Ugh."

Ben stared at her in shock, then his lips curled up, and he laughed. He laughed and laughed, losing all care about the mud, and rolled over in it.

"You think it's funny?"

He put his hands up in surrender. "Hey, at least you don't have mud on your butt."

Her facade of concern broke, and she chuckled. The crowd had stuck around, standing around them, as if watching this couple who had lost their minds in laughter, in the mud.

"Let me help you up." Ben gripped above her elbow, locking arms with her.

Her knee sucked out of the mud, and she managed to plant a foot, which squished a little too much for comfort in the muck. "Are you sure you can?" She giggled as they played a balancing act of pushing and pulling to work their way upwards.

When they both stood upright, Ben spread his arms up in the air as if in a touchdown victory. "We did it!"

Tracy laughed, picking the larger chunks off her hands. "Now tell me you didn't get a thrill out of that."

"All right, I admit it. I had fun." Ben wiped the back of his jeans. "The real question is, what do I win?"

"Win? For what?"

"My pumpkin went farther."

"Oh, right." She spun around, scanning the farm. "How about a drink, on me?"

"Can't argue with that."

They walked over to the petting and feeding area where a large plastic basin was set up. They pumped the water with a foot pedal and washed their hands. Tracy opted to wet the knees of her jeans to clear off most of the mud, and Ben did the same with the back of his pants.

They walked to the rows of vendors, the aromas changing every few feet—fresh baked pretzels, corn dogs, sausages with peppers. Tracy veered off to the cider station and Ben caught up with her a few minutes later... "Here you go." He handed her a plastic bag filled with kettle corn.

"You couldn't resist, could ya?"

"Honestly, it's all my brain—and stomach—were thinking about since I caught the first whiff."

She chuckled and handed him a cup filled with cider.

They strolled along the main pathway cutting through the vendors, leading out to open farmland. The earthy smell of dried crops rose as the din of the crowd gradually faded.

"That's really good," Ben said. The dark, nutty liquid was cold but refreshing, a good mix of tart and bitter. It complemented the salty sugariness of the popcorn.

Tracy nodded and took another sip. "Almost worth coming out here just for that."

He stared at her, a second too long, or whatever length long enough for her to feel looked at. Not stared at, but really seen.

"I may be assuming here, but I get the feeling you enjoyed this outing more than you thought you would."

She sipped the cider, not giving in easily to his assumption. Although it was correct. "And I think it's safe to say there is a bit of an adventurer in you after all."

He stopped walking and turned to her, face in disbelief. "What do you mean? I've hiked a good portion of the AT. It takes quite a sense of adventure to do that."

"I guess you're right." She accepted the minor defeat.

"All right, Miss Adventure. Just how much of the world have *you* seen?"

She shrugged, continuing the slow walk. "Europe after high school, a semester in Chile as an exchange student. Most recently a stint in Australia." She stared off into space, feeling his eyes of surprise on her.

"Wow, I had heard you had traveled, but had no idea."

"No idea I left the state?" She broke the sarcasm as quickly as it had left her mouth. "I've been fortunate. Not many people make it out of Waverly Lake, let alone the country."

"How do you manage to go to all these places, if you don't mind me asking?" He offered up the kettle corn, and she politely declined.

"I don't mind." She held her cup in one hand, the other in her pocket. Her palms felt sweaty, despite the chilly afternoon air, wet jeans at the knees, and cold cider coursing through her veins. "I have friends from all over. College helped with that. When I decide on the next place I want to be, I figure what it will cost and what I have to do to get there."

She looked at him, catching his greenish eyes. The blue flannel really did work well with his complexion. "Then I find whatever jobs I can to save up the money to make it happen."

"Like one that has you going out on five dates with a stranger off the trail?"

"Exactly. If trudging through five outings is what I have to do, then..." She grinned.

"Hey now. It hasn't been that bad, has it?"

No. The opposite. "I'd say it's been tolerable." She elbowed him with her chuckle.

"Well, I know we didn't get off to the best of starts, meeting each other." Ben's smile faded. "But I'm impressed, with all the traveling, the self-sufficiency you have for yourself. And—" He rocked his head back and forth, as if contemplating the next words. "Perhaps I should consider myself lucky you were here when I arrived. It doesn't sound like you stay in Waverly Lake very long."

"You got that right." She took another sip of cider.

"About staying in Waverly?"

"About considering yourself lucky." She laughed and he tapped her shoulder. A simple, playful tap between two people who had grown comfortable with each other over a corn maze and some pumpkins. But as she took in this man, this handsome stranger who was quickly working his way into her life as more than a stranger, she couldn't shake the feeling that maybe she was the lucky one.

Chapter Twelve

Monday, October 10

WIND RUSTLED THE LEAVES IN THE TREES OUTSIDE Woodsman's Lodge. Ben dodged a few pinecones dropping to the forest floor as he worked on clearing a trail. He reminisced about running to the rocky outcropping, more like a smoothened boulder bulging out of the mountain. The forest opened to a clearing, where the lake could be seen with a nice view of one of the islands ahead, a tuft of orange-tinged maples atop a rocky crag like candles in a birthday cake.

Aunt Dee didn't have a pathway to the spot, something Ben thought she could use as it lie on her property. Maybe she could affix Adirondack chairs there permanently, or at least provide guests with a private view of the lake, even if it was a little hike from the lodge.

The work was laborious. Raking didn't suffice since the tines caught on tree roots and rocks. He had to painstakingly move the rocks, creating an uneven, muddy path in his wake. There wasn't much he could do with the tree roots. They didn't prevent passage, but forced the hiker to pay more attention to each step.

He wiped the sweat from his forehead and headed back to the

lodge. He scraped his muddy boots on the scratch pad at the back door and made a beeline for the kitchen. For how chilly the morning air was, he had worked up a sweat, which meant he needed water. Dehydration was the most frequent injury in cold weather. Most people didn't realize how much water they lost huffing and puffing in the cold air, especially if it was dry air.

The kitchen reflected the lodge in that it was nothing fancy, but practical. Oak cabinets lined three of the walls, and an island sat in the middle of the floor space. There were no tables in the kitchen, only cooking space and food storage. The sink had a large basin, and the black freezer-fridge had to be ancient, but served its purpose. When he joked to Aunt Dee about it, she said the newer fridges with all the "techy stuff" just couldn't outlast the one she had. He couldn't argue, nor did he want to. With Aunt Dee it was wise to nod and go about the day.

Aunt Dee walked in as he filled a glass with water. He sipped the cold liquid, no need for ice with the morning's low temp. The ground had to be getting cooler by the day, as the hot water took longer to arrive out of the shower tap. Plus, his hands had frozen, making headway with the muddy trail.

"Oh good. I was going to go outside to find you, but you're here." Aunt Dee cradled a folder in her arm.

She grabbed the free hand of Ben's and examined it. "You're a mess." Dirt had found its way into the fine lines of his rough hands and under his fingernails.

He shrugged. "Just means I've been working hard for you."

"I'm gonna need you to switch gears for me."

He set down his water on the counter, noticing the smudged fingerprints on the outside of the glass. "What is it?"

"I need you to go into town." She held up a hand. "You can take the truck."

It hadn't taken Aunt Dee long to realize *Tin Can* was not an option if she wanted him to go anywhere without Tracy. Presumably his co-worker was busy. He had briefly passed her this morning on her way out of the kitchen. She had been carrying a cardboard box in her arms and a pastry in her mouth. She'd attempted a hello, and he'd smiled, giving her a "good morning." He had heard some banging near the roof of the lodge as he cleared the pathway, a reminder that she was around. They had a good—no, great—day yesterday. Tracy still didn't want to call it a date. But it certainly felt like one.

"I need you to take these to Steve Albertson. His law firm is along the town square."

Ben reached for the folder, and Aunt Dee pulled it away, eyeing his hands. He washed them in the sink with lemon dish soap before she surrendered the file.

"He'll be one of the guests for Lovetoberfest. As such, he helped draw up the official documents—waivers and such—for participants to sign. I've made some notes on these by hand and need you to deliver them."

"Can't you just email him your comments?" Or scan them or take photos on her phone and send them? Anything not to encounter the most recent attorney who took over the legal aspects of his parents' estate. He probably now dealt with the city, waiting for the clock to run out.

Aunt Dee continued staring at him. "It's quicker to print it out and write what I need. Besides, they're legal documents, which I believe are safer traveling by hand if it's all the same to you."

It wasn't the same to him. It required a trip to town. But Aunt Dee had her ways, and she wasn't going to change now.

"He's expecting you, so you'd better get going."

"Yes, ma'am." He exited the kitchen and picked up the truck keys from behind the desk on his way out of the lodge.

He started the truck, the engine reluctant but yielding, and headed east. Either direction took about the same amount of time to reach downtown from the lodge, having to go halfway around the lake. The half hour drive was still preferrable over the alternative.

He managed a parking spot in the street behind Nichols and Dimes Pharmacy, with the Law Firm of Steven Albertson, J. D.

around the corner. He eyed the black BMW up front, wondering if the status symbol belonged to the attorney inside. He opened the door, the deep mahogany wood of the front desk and basil carpet absorbing the contrasting brightness from canned ceiling lights. If he had to imagine an attorney's office, this was it.

"I'll be right with you." A voice rang out of the door behind the front desk.

"No problem." Ben stood, examining the framed degrees on the wall. He moved to the desk, catching a picture of a black woman in graduation garb, and another of the same woman in sunglasses at the beach holding a child on her hip.

"Sorry to keep you waiting. My paralegal Margaret is out serving papers this morning. You must be Ben Walker."

Ben turned around and shook the hand of the young man, not much older than himself. His hair lie neatly parted on the side, and he adjusted his gray suit jacket as if he had just put it on over the white collared shirt and striped tie. "Steven Albertson. You can call me Steve." His white teeth were as orderly as every item in the room., and Ben felt extremely tan compared to the man's fair complexion.

"Okay, Steve. Well, I have the papers Aunt—Dorothy—wanted me to hand over."

"It's okay, I call her Aunt Dee too." He accepted the folder and waved his hand. "Come on back."

Ben had hoped for a quick transaction, anxious to get back to the lodge to continue his work. He still felt uneasy about being seen around town, but at least Steve wasn't someone he remembered ever seeing before.

He followed the attorney back to his private office, the door remaining open. Steve walked around his desk, shuffling papers around and making a spot for the folder. He inspected the papers inside.

Ben caught a yellow flyer on the corner of the desk, atop a pile of papers. It was the same notice he'd seen on the gates of his former house this past weekend, advertising the town hall forum.

Steve looked up, reading what caught Ben's attention. "Interested in attending that?"

"Oh, I uh...I don't know."

"If you have any ideas on what to do with the property, I'd suggest going. The town could certainly use some smart suggestions."

"I don't think I could say." He caught Steve's stare, making him uncomfortable. "I just arrived in town this weekend."

"Yes, how are you settling in with Aunt Dee?"

"Fine. She's been very generous."

"Good." The conversation stopped with the one-word answer. The silence lingered until Ben couldn't take it anymore.

"What do you think they'll do with the property?" He pointed to the flyer. "Phillips Manor?"

"Oh." The attorney closed his eyes and shook his head. "Hard to say. It'd be a heck of a lot easier if the living descendant actually cared about it."

Ben winced, a flinch of hurt he quickly covered up.

Steve seemed not to notice. "I think the majority of people who love this town want to see it restored and taken care of, back into the hands of the Phillips family. It was such a tragic event, but they were so revered in town. Some would say the medical collection of the library stands as testimony for their love of the town. But I say it's that property. I was only a kid at the time, but from what I hear they could've lived anywhere they wanted, but they chose here."

"Their son has not been heard from?"

Steve's forehead wrinkled. "How'd you know the descendant was a son?"

Ben cleared his throat. "Aunt Dee's niece, great-niece rather, Tracy, said as much. We were walking past the property the other day."

"Oh, right. I suppose it only takes a blink to get all the scoop in this town."

"Or a haircut."

Steve laughed. "Dye Happy?"

Ben nodded.

"Say no more." Steve adjusted the flier atop the stack of papers on his desk. "Anyway, I've been doing all I can to find their son within the sixty-day deadline. Last point of contact I have placed him somewhere near Harpers Ferry, but that was months ago. He could be anywhere by now."

Ben shifted his weight from one leg to the other. He wanted to stop talking about it and know more at the same time.

"Once it's in the town's hands, that's it for the son? Can he not claim it back later?"

"If Hunter avoids responsibility by the deadline, then he can't claim it later. It's out of his hands. If he were to return in time, it'd be up to him what happens to it. It gets a little tricky when it comes to property taxes and the fine details, no matter who ends up owning it. But that's part of the job handed down to me with this situation."

Ben nodded, swallowing hard with his dry mouth.

"How impolite of me. Can I get you a glass of water? Margaret is much better than I am at remembering that sort of thing." He walked to a table amid his shelves of books and accolades, and poured water into a glass out of a sweating silver pitcher. "Here we are."

"Thank you." Ben felt embarrassed. The topic of conversation shouldn't have upset a visitor to the town. But he wasn't a random visitor. He was Hunter Phillips, the elusive property dodger who still had no idea what he'd meant to do in Waverly Lake in the first place.

He took another sip, the frigid water calming his nerves and cooling his hot hands. He had almost forgotten why he had been sent here to begin with. "Aunt Dee said you'll be participating in the first ever Lovetoberfest?" Now that he had asked, it sounded too personal. Did everyone in town know about it and who was going?

Steve stuck a finger between his collar and neck, lightly loosening it. "Yes, actually. I'm not going to say I'm looking forward to it, per say." He eyed Ben. "Can I be honest with you?"

"You're a lawyer. I'd hope so."

Steve laughed. "That's a good one."

Ben didn't get the joke. He hadn't much experience with lawyers directly, although if he had owned up to his inherited responsibilities that may have been different.

"I've had my share of dating. I don't mean that as bragging. It's just, I'm hoping to meet some interesting people, and do something different. Not just the usual dinner or drinks or a movie date. I've had enough of those." He placed his hands on his hips, the opening of his suit jacket widening. "You know how the definition of insanity is doing the same thing over again and expecting a different result?"

"Yeah."

"Well, that's my dating life."

He really was being candid. Ben almost felt sorry for the guy. Through all his fancy car, framed degree, mahogany facade, he was just a guy who wanted to find love.

"I can say, at least so far, since Aunt Dee has me working on a Lovetoberfest project..." How else was he supposed to explain it? A Lovetoberfest dry run? "These dates will definitely be different."

Steve nodded. "Do you think they'll get two people together?"

Tracy's smile flashed in his memory, a pretty side of her he got to see falling in the mud. It wasn't that he was thinking of her all the time, it's just...he was more aware of her presence. He liked knowing she was nearby.

And they had plenty more dates left to go on, a thought that made him giddy in his stomach and dizzy in his head.

Ben shrugged, wishing he could give Steve a more definitive answer. "Ask me again at the end of the week."

Chapter Thirteen

Tuesday, October 11

TRACY TURNED LEFT, HEADING DOWN AMBLE WAY, THE main artery dividing the southern half of Waverly Lake's town square. Sandwiched between Nichols and Dimes and Dye Happy Salon, the road held most of the municipal buildings like the library and its wonderful lawn, and the courthouse, to which she found herself joining several other townsfolk to its brick steps.

Sunlight grew scarcer at this time of the evening. It was a quarter to seven, and the streetlights shone while drivers used their headlights. In a few weekends they'd set back the clocks, locking in the darkness by five-thirty.

She hadn't planned on attending the meeting over Phillips Manor. Ever since Ben had inquired about the property, she couldn't shake thinking about it. With her parents living next door, she walked by it every weekend. Yet Saturday was the first time she had let herself think about her old friend and his family since returning this summer. Was it so wrong of her to wonder what had happened to Hunter Phillips?

She walked up the stairs, the double doors propped open. A table with pitchers and plastic cups stood near the entrance, and

Tracy helped herself to a glass of sweet tea. Her day had been spent tearing up old carpet in Aunt Dee's office, which meant moving her solid oak desk and shelving that weighed more like lead than former tree parts. With the padding under the carpet removed, Tracy had about seventeen thousand nails to pull up. To say she was tired was an understatement, and quite frankly she savored the sugar and caffeine coursing through her veins.

Folks chatted around the door and aisleways, some finding seats while others worked the room. Ben had joked about it with her at the farm, but she really did recognize quite a few faces. It was like that in any small town, she supposed. Live there long enough, you get to know the regulars.

"Tracy!" Sebastian waved, rising from the metal folding chair. She approached and gave him a hug, half out of not seeing him since he dropped her off at the lodge and half thankful he had a seat for her.

"George." Tracy touched the shoulder of Sebastian's partner and leaned in for a kiss on the cheek. George was significantly older than Sebastian, at least by Tracy's guesstimate—maybe ten, twelve years—and he held a sense of refinement compared to Sebastian's free-spirited tone. He wore khakis and a green sweater over a collared shirt, while Sebastian sported an unzipped, black hoodie over a skater shirt. Their physical polarity—Sebastian's head of long combed-over locks atop the summer's shave versus George's balding one—played to their balance together, as if they were two unique, interlocking pieces.

"I thought you'd pass on the invite." Sebastian's nasally voice cut through the din of the crowd.

"Me too." She took the seat next to him.

"I told George I'd have to see it to believe it, now here you are. Care to explain?" There was one thing Sebastian may have loved more than George, and that was gossip. Of course that was many folks' first love here.

She shrugged. "I don't know. I had passed the property and noticed the sign, figured I'd come see what the town may do with it.

My parents live right next door, you know." Everything out of her mouth was true, but it didn't encompass the whole story.

"Speaking of, I thought I saw them come in a few minutes ago."

Tracy followed the path from his pointing finger to the front of the room. Dad faced the crowd at the council's table awaiting the start of the meeting, hands folded as if praying tonight would go smoothly. Mom socialized with other spouses of council members in the front row. Even if Dad hadn't been on the council, the Bennetts would've attended. They didn't want an eye sore, or a busy shop for their next-door neighbor.

"That's him." George tapped Sebastian on the arm. "That's who Carly Fletcher was talking about the other day."

Tracy turned around. If she had waited a second to think about, she'd have guessed who he was talking about. But she hadn't waited. She turned around without thinking, and therefore dropped her jaw when she registered Ben Walker standing in the doorway.

"The guy off the trail?" Sebastian asked. "Oh, Tracy, don't you work with him at your aunt's?"

Tracy turned back around, taking a deep breath. "Yeah, I do. What about him?"

George's round eyes grew. "Carly said he stopped here in Waverly Lake, of all places, from trail hiking. And that your aunt knew him somehow."

Tracy grinned. "I think you've been hanging around Sebastian a little too much, George. He's the one who's supposed to spread the gossip."

"Well, is he wrong?" Sebastian awaited an answer.

"No, he's right." She contemplated over how much she wanted to reveal about Ben. She didn't know a whole lot about him, though Sunday's outing at the farm did win her over a bit. He had been charming, respectful, and even fun. Something she hadn't expected at all that afternoon, and out of him. "He's an old acquaintance of Aunt Dee's, and he's working during his stay. That's all." She stared at the two men all too eager to absorb her words. "Just cut him a break, will you? He's an okay guy. The last thing he needs are your talons digging in."

Sebastian sat back, blinking hard. "Hold up. Tracy Bennett is defending the guy who is the latest town mystery? Sounds like there's something more there than you're letting on."

She imagined how Ben looked in the blue flannel shirt, laughing in the mud. Tracy suddenly felt the heat of the room, the crowd thickening and noise building. "I don't know what you're talking about."

The two men's smiles turned into chuckles, their stares shifting from her face to behind her. She turned around, and Ben stood there, also smiling.

"Hi." He wore the red flannel shirt, an even better color that turned his eyes to fiery golden brown.

"Hey." Tracy's voice cracked. She cleared her throat. "Ben, this is Sebastian and George." The men exchanged handshakes.

"I didn't realize you'd come," she said.

"Me neither." Ben tilted his head, eyebrows furled. "Sort of a last-minute decision."

"Have a seat," Sebastian said. He scooted one chair down, leaving a space between him and Tracy.

"Thanks." Ben sat, rubbing his hands on his legs. Was he nervous?

"How are you liking it so far in Waverly Lake?" George sat diagonally in his chair, facing them in the row.

"Oh, just fine. Thank you. Are you both from here?"

"We both live here now, but Sebastian was born and raised here. I wasn't."

"Hasn't Tracy shared anything about her gay friends?" Sebastian reached over Ben and tapped Tracy's knee. "You're hurting my feelings."

"It's okay," Ben said. "Considering she knows everyone in town, I'm sure she'd get to you eventually." He winked at her, smirk on his face.

Sebastian and George froze for a second, the joke absorbing.

Sebastian broke out in a laugh and leaned forward, getting a better view of Tracy's face. He didn't have to say it. They both liked him.

She nudged Ben, and he held his arm, dramatically playing up the non-injury.

"Great," she said. "Now I have three of you to contend with."

"Thank you everyone!" Mayor Halbrook stood at the podium. She tapped the attached microphone, quieting the crowd. Stragglers took the remaining seats left, while others opted for standing room in the periphery.

"I appreciate you all coming out tonight to discuss the property located at 109 Dorset Drive, known as Phillips Manor."

Ben leaned closer, pointing across the room, and whispering in Tracy's ear. "Is she related to the mayor?"

Tracy examined the seated young woman in the front row, closest to the middle aisle. She had the same smooth brown skin, but longer ringlets than the short pixie cut the mayor sported. She leaned to the child next to her, touching her knee to stop her from swaying her legs in the chair. "That's the mayor's daughter, Margaret, and her daughter Simone. Why do you ask?"

"I thought I recognized her from a picture in Steve Albertson's office."

Tracy nodded. "She's a paralegal there."

The mayor continued. "This isn't an official legislative town meeting. I simply wanted to open the floor up for ideas regarding the future role the property will play in Waverly Lake, if it should end up in our hands. With ten days left in the sixty-day grace period, it is looking more like a certainty it will be."

Tracy turned, Ben's face close to hers. What business could a newbie to town have with a lawyer? Was there a chance Ben had fled legal trouble from wherever he came from? "What were you doing at Steve's office?"

Ben backed up, crossing his arms. "I was on an errand for Aunt Dee. Apparently, he's participating in Lovetoberfest."

The uptight attorney, blind dating in Lovetoberfest? Tracy

couldn't help but giggle. It made sense now, sending Ben. Steve would've been mortified if he had to talk to Tracy about it.

Ben winced. "I don't think you're supposed to know that yet, though."

"I can keep a secret," Tracy said.

Sebastian and George whispered to Ben as the mayor opened the floor to suggestions. Probably best Tracy couldn't hear what stories about her they were telling him.

A microphone was placed at the front of the aisleway, and three people approached, the latter two waiting in line for the first to finish.

"I would like to see the property used as office spaces."

"That's Nora Jean," Tracy whispered to Ben. "She works at Waverly Dental."

"There are several rooms in the house that could be rented for private practices or independent contractors and use the entranceway as a lobby."

"You'd have to use the yard for parking," a man shouted from the crowd.

"Wouldn't it be more valuable as retail space?" The next man waiting in line for the microphone spoke up.

The crowd rose in clammer.

"That's Mr. Cavidge, who runs the two largest souvenir shops downtown. He's always looking for commercial property to buy up to expand his business."

"The town vulture?" Ben smiled, his face so close she could smell the clean soap on his skin.

"Either way," Mayor Halbrook said, "we'd have to discuss rezoning the property to allow for commercial potential and sell it."

An older man Tracy recognized from Mom and Dad's church stood. "If you're going to destroy the lawn for parking, might as well tear down the property all together. Make the whole lot for parking. We all know that parking along the street is limited, especially on Sunday mornings. That way the city can still own it, and even charge for parking with meters to make some money."

A few in the crowd cheered and clapped at the thought.

A woman booed. "What local wants to pay for parking? Make it free!"

"No!"

Tracy's heart stopped. Ben had bolted out of his seat, mouth still open from the shout.

"Who are you?" the older man asked.

Even though Ben's appearance had nothing remarkable to signify he was from out of town, he was unfortunate enough to be in a town hall meeting where everyone knew everyone else.

"I—" Ben fumbled, clearing his throat. "My name is Ben Walker. I'm sure most of you know by now that I'm new to the area."

"Sit down," someone cried out.

"Hear him out." Carly Fletcher's voice flung across the room. Tracy didn't even have to find her in the crowd to know it was her.

"I know I don't necessarily deserve a say in this. But I walked by the property, on my first day ba—in town." He swallowed hard. "I was struck by the beauty of the house, even if though the property hasn't been kept up so well the past few months."

"The past few decades," Mr. Cavidge said.

"Tracy Bennett told me about the Phillips family."

Tracy's heart raced at her name. Mom had fully turned around and eyed her, as if it was her fault the town stranger now spoke.

"I heard of both their tragedy and legacy. I hear there's a dedicated medical wing just down the street at the library with their namesake. Don't you think they would've wanted something better for their house? Something better for the town?"

Tracy was speechless. She had no idea that sharing what she knew of Hunter Phillips' story would have such an effect on Ben. What did he care? He wasn't planning on staying in Waverly Lake, was he? Yet he spoke with a passion that was hard to find in even some of the locals, as if he grasped who the Phillips were to this town.

"I just think turning it into a parking lot would go against everything they stood for."

"Here, here!" Carly shouted and clapped.

Another man rushed the microphone. "What do you know of the Phillips? What they really wanted was their son to manage the property, but he outright refused to step up. I say it's all fair game."

The crowd broke out in argument. Tracy caught someone behind her complaining about parking during Christmas and another supporting Ben's sentiments.

Mayor Halbrook tapped the microphone on the podium. "Quiet down, quiet down." The discussion calmed. "I propose, for those of you with ideas on how the town could use the property, write them down on one of these slips of paper, and submit them in this idea box. The council will look over all ideas and assess feasibility. However, if it's better all-around for it to be out of the town's hands, we do have the right to hold an auction. In doing so, we may not get to say what happens to the property, but the profits could be put to good use to improve other parts of town. Thanks again for coming, and the council members and I will be around for questions."

The discussion blew up again as the mayor stepped down from the podium.

George approached Ben with a grin. "That was amazing! Anyone who stands up against paving over any of the history in this town deserves a handshake."

Ben turned red in the face. "It was nothing. I hadn't really planned on saying anything at all."

"It was like the holy spirit moved you," Sebastian said. "You flung up out of pure passion."

Ben rubbed the back of his neck, sheepishly accepting the compliments.

"Hey, how about you come out with us on our boat Saturday?" George asked.

Tracy eyed George. She had been invited to go out, just the three of them.

"It'd be great to have you come."

"He doesn't like boats," Tracy said. *That'll stop all of this in its tracks.* Ben was a nice guy, and they had a good time Sunday, but that didn't mean she wanted him getting chummy with her friends.

"Tracy's coming too." Sebastian smirked, catching Tracy's stop-what-you're-doing eyes.

"In that case," Ben looked at Tracy, who gave her hardest decline-the-offer look. "I'd love to join you."

"Great. It's a date." Sebastian winked at Tracy and hugged her.

"You're a terrible person," Tracy muttered.

"Love you too." Sebastian grabbed George's hand in his, and they headed off to the drink table.

Ben shrugged as Tracy fumbled with her purse.

"I guess I'll see you back at the lodge." His face was so innocent, a combination of bashfulness at his outburst and delight at the invite. It'd be a heck of a lot easier to be upset with him if he hadn't been so handsome.

"Sure." Tracy stepped toward the exit. "Although, I'll probably get there before you, being on the boat and all. Unless you want to leave Aunt Dee's truck here and come along with me?"

She had him. He didn't want to go out on *Tin Can* in the middle of the day. No way was he going to survive a sunset cruise.

"Unfortunately, I came to town a little early to pick up some things for Aunt Dee, which are back in the truck."

She nodded. "Okay, then." By Saturday, it'll be the three of them, sans Ben, just as she had planned.

No sense in complicating matters. Five dates with Ben were enough.

Any more time with him and he'd dominate her thoughts.

Chapter Fourteen

Wednesday, October 12

BEN SAVORED THE WARM WATER ROLLING DOWN HIS neck and shoulders. It seemed like every task Aunt Dee asked of him increased in physicality. Today she had him tearing up the raised garden beds, a set of rectangular patches further up the hill from the lodge. It made sense to have them there, since they collected water running down the hill, but allowed for drainage to the bottom. It also was one of the few clearings on her land, south-facing, that welcomed the sunshine.

He wasn't sore yet, but fully expected to be tomorrow. His hands were tender in places he had gripped the garden tools, but that only added to the menagerie of roughness transforming his palms over the years. While he didn't hold a steady job in any one place, when he did work his way for what he needed, it was physical labor—lifting furniture for local movers, shoveling snow-ridden driveways, hauling landscaping materials.

In that way, he and Tracy weren't so different. He also worked to live. But what sorts of things did she do for work? If the jobs were anything like the locations she had been to, she'd probably found more exciting and rewarding work.

He slipped on the new pair of jeans, and gray sweater over the red flannel shirt. Yesterday Aunt Dee had given him time to shop for a few more clothing items before attending the town meeting.

Ugh. The town meeting. He had awakened this morning, still in disbelief that he had interjected, throwing himself into the center of the discussion about his parents' property. He merely wanted to observe and not be noticed.

Yeah, that had worked out well.

He answered the knock at the door, patting his hair down one last time. Aunt Dee stood in the hallway, dangling keys. "You two can use the truck again tonight."

"Thank you." Tracy appeared behind Aunt Dee, grabbing the keys out of her hand before Ben had the inclination to accept them. "My turn to drive."

"I'll let you two work that out." Aunt Dee patted Tracy on the shoulder. "Enjoy your evening and bring my baby back safely. She's got quite a few years left in her." She retreated down the stairs.

"Someone should tell the truck that," Ben said.

"For real. It had a few years left back in 1990." Tracy stood in the doorway. Her brown boots came up to the knees of her skinny jeans, her oversized beige sweater exposing the thick strap of a tank on her shoulder underneath. She knocked the wind out of him.

"You ready to go?" She tucked a bouncy curl behind her ear, Ben noticing the hoop earrings for the first time. In fact, he couldn't recall seeing her wear earrings before.

"Ready." Ben shoved his wallet in his back pocket. "You clean up nicely."

"Who said this was cleaning up?" Tracy winked.

Ben closed the door to his room, and they walked down the stairs. "You know, sometimes it doesn't hurt to accept a compliment."

Tracy crinkled her nose, probably coming up with another quick retort. Instead, she stopped him on the landing halfway down the stairs and looked him right in the eyes. "You're right. Thank you."

They continued downstairs, past Aunt Dee's office which awaited new carpeting. Aunt Dee didn't seem to mind working with the subfloor exposed. At the front door, Tracy paused, shouting off to space. "See you later, Aunt Dee! No craziness while I'm gone!"

They trotted down the porch stairs and, after wrestling with the passenger door, sat in the truck. Tracy started it up and buckled.

"What do you think Aunt Dee does when we're not around?" Were it not for his and Tracy's presence, she'd have spent most of her days and evenings alone. "Do you think she had a wild side, back in the day? Sometimes it's hard to picture older people being our age once."

Tracy gleefully smiled. "I think she has a whole history she wouldn't dare tell us. I would not be surprised if she has another life now she keeps secret from us."

Ben shrugged. *She wouldn't be the only one.* "Hey, you never know. I wouldn't put anything past her."

"That's for sure. Speaking of secret lives, where have you been all day?" Tracy had a knack for keeping an eye on the road and the other on the passenger.

He swallowed the irony. "Tending garden."

"Ah. She got you to do that, did she?" Tracy turned the radio on and lowered the volume, keeping it as background noise more than as entertainment. "She'd been asking me to do it, but I purposely found literally anything else on her list to occupy my time."

He chuckled. "What do you have against gardening? Don't like getting your hands dirty?" He grinned. "You seemed okay at the farm the other day."

Tracy shook her head. "It's not that. Let's just say I've had enough experience at a Chilean asparagus farm to know why the phrase *back-breaking work* exists. Mad respect to the families depending on it for their livelihood."

"That must be amazing, traveling the world, seeing different cultures. It sounds like you're the type to immerse yourself rather than observe as a tourist."

Her mood shifted, her voice carrying a calmer tone. "It's easy to stay in one place. People get comfortable in their bubble, and they either don't realize what else is out there or don't try to care."

He hesitated with his question, wondering if it bordered on too personal. Not for her, but for him. "Does it ever make you appreciate the world you do live in?"

"You mean Planet Earth, the United States? Or are we talking Waverly Lake?"

"The latter." He hadn't decided anything on his future. The status of Phillips Manor and the meeting last night ignited a passion in him he hadn't fully accepted yet. But what about Tracy's future, after Aunt Dee's work? Where was she headed? Was there any chance she'd stick around in Waverly Lake? Or was reconnecting with her the same as trying to touch a ghost?

She stared at the winding road, so long that Ben considered asking the question again or changing the subject. "It's starting to." The words came out gentle, like an admission that exposed something in her she dared not want anyone else to hear.

Throughout the last three or four days, Ben had felt compelled to blurt out his true identity to Tracy a number of times. Right now, it had been almost more than he could bear. But his fear of the repercussions of people knowing was confirmed last night. He'd be attacked for having stayed hidden for so long, for not responding to inquiries. They'd pick at him for answers on what to do with the property, like turkey vultures picked at a deer carcass along the trail.

What would Tracy think of the truth? She was slowly letting him into her world, into her head and feelings. Being with her was the most fun he'd had in a long time, even if she wouldn't admit as much. Would she close herself off if he confessed his true name? What if she figured it out herself? His outburst at the town meeting certainly would raise suspicion. Would it be worse if she concluded before he told her?

"Are you okay?" Tracy glared at him then back at the road.

"Oh, just got lost in thought." He dusted off his doubts. "Do you ever think of one thing, and then it leads you down a chain of thoughts until you forget what got you there in the first place?"

"You mean, like searching for flooring options online for Aunt Dee, and thirty minutes later she catches you watching K-pop videos?"

Ben chuckled. "Do I want to ask?"

"Let's just say I'm not allowed to internet browse while on the job anytime soon."

They rounded the southeast corner of the lake, heading into town. Vehicles occupied the street side parking, while the cafes and restaurants were a flurry of activity on the weekday evening.

"Do you know what we're going to be doing?" Ben knew the date was indoors, but that was about it.

"I'm assuming something with paint? I mean, it's at the art studio." She pulled up to Breakwater Art Studio, a retail space two stores west of Steve Albertson's law firm. The row of parking spaces were occupied, and Tracy slowed to a crawl. A sedan's reverse lights shone, and Tracy awaited its space.

"We got lucky with the spot," she said. "Maybe we do need a parking lot."

The thought churned Ben's stomach. How could townspeople suggest doing such a thing?

Tracy shook her head, giggling. "It's the last thing my parents would ever agree to."

"Do they have a say in it?" That changed things, if the Bennett's had some say in the property. Her father was on the other side of the table last night, after all. It'd be easier to stay out of it if the Bennetts would do it justice.

"None at all, legally speaking. My father is on the council, but they exist to follow procedure, not do whatever they want. However, my parents do have financial influence in this town. They'd sooner sell their house and the whole town with it before turning Phillips Manor into a parking lot."

They exited the truck and walked into Breakwater Art Studio. In the front window, under a spotlight, sat a watercolor painting of a sailboat at sea, sitting on a wooden easel. The greige walls held mainly paintings of boats and freshwater life, with the occasional mountain setting thrown in. Most had ornate golden frames, a bit too gaudy and old-fashioned for Ben's taste.

A sign stood near the entrance with black lettering over a blue arrow. *StArt Night meeting in classroom.*

"StArt night?"

Tracy shrugged and they followed the arrow to the back of the studio. The classroom had six tables, arranged in three rows and two columns. A trio of women sipped on wine and chatted at the table in the back left, in front of the beverage table. An older couple sat up front, analyzing the supplies laid out.

"Welcome, Tracy." A fifty-something man greeted them. With his balding head and rounded figure, he looked like Tracy's friend, George, that he had met last night, only fifteen years older. "This must be Ben." He shook hands. "I've heard you caused quite a stir at the town meeting last night."

Ben retracted his hand after the shake, wanting to continue the retreat out of the studio.

"I think you'd be proud of our newest resident, Mr. Kemper, the way he stood up for the Bennetts and their property."

Mr. Kemper responded with a warm smile. "Good to have you here. Help yourself to a glass of wine and find a seat, wherever is empty."

Tracy turned to the beverage table, and Ben followed. She grabbed the white wine and poured a glass while Ben opted for red.

"I suppose Mr. Kemper was also a high school classmate?"

Tracy scrunched her face at the tease. "Very funny." She took a sip of wine. "He knows my parents more than me. He is, dare I say, the only art curator in these parts, and my parents have an affinity for art." She winced at that. "Or an affinity to look like they know art, at least." She leaned in closer. "Have you seen the art he sells in here?"

Ben returned the whisper. "I thought maybe I was the only one who found it to be...awful." A better, less-harsh sounding word failed him.

Tracy giggled, covering her mouth. "Who would've pictured, Tracy and Ben, as two art snobs?"

He smiled. Not so much that they were acting like art snobs. He couldn't care less about what art was sold here. If people liked it, and that's what kept the art studio alive, all the better. Art was subjective.

No, what had him smiling was the fact that Tracy had paired the two of them together. Like some dynamic duo, a team that the town should know by now and probably did know by now.

Tracy and Ben.

He loved the sound of it.

Chapter Fifteen

"You're making a right mess of it." Tracy chuckled at Ben's fingertips, paint increasingly covering them.

He paused, stealing a glance at Tracy. "A right mess?"

Tracy shrugged. "So, I picked up some sayings in my travels. And yes, a right mess."

"I'm sorry, have you painted acorns before?" He dipped his brush in the blue paint and continued his work, inevitably getting paint on the top rough part of the nut, which they learned in class was called the cupule.

"First timer here." She placed down a red one next to her collection.

Mr. Kemper came around, investigating their artwork. He scanned Tracy's and nodded. He moved on to Ben's. "Well, not everyone is meant to be a painter."

Tracy looked at Ben, both of their mouths agape.

"Hey, he's making an effort." Tracy made a face as Mr. Kemper walked away to the ladies' table. "Only friends can make fun of friends' acorns." She winked at Ben.

They both reached for the green paint, hands bumping briefly.

"You go ahead," she said.

"Don't mind if I do." He placed his brush in the small bowl, slowly swirling the bristles in the paint while humming, dragging it out.

She shifted weight to one foot, mocking impatience. "It's okay. I'll just fix one of your acorns over here."

"You wouldn't dare."

She accepted the challenge and painted a happy face in red over his blue acorn. "There we go. Much better."

"Very well. We can't have yours looking all perfect now, can we?" He aimed for a yellow one of hers, and she reached for it. The brush swirled over her hand instead of the acorn.

Ben's eyes grew big, mouth open. "I—I'm sorry, I didn't mean—"

She dipped the brush in the green and quickly stroked his cheek. Her straight face lasted a second before breaking out into laughter.

"Oh, it's on now."

"No!" Tracy squealed and Ben got her forehead. She used an arm to stop him and managed to get his chin.

"If you can't control yourselves—" Mr. Kemper shouted from the corner of the room.

Tracy ceased fire and locked eyes with Ben. "Truce."

"Truce," he said, tugging his sweater down. "This is serious work, Tracy."

"Yes. Very serious."

They turned back to their painted acorns. Ben lost it a second before Tracy, both giggling like they were caught passing notes in grade school.

"Sorry, Mr. Kemper," Tracy said.

Ben nudged her in the arm, and she nudged him back. "You're getting us in trouble," she whispered.

"I believe you started it."

They looked at each other. His strong jawline had the beginnings of a beard again, the kind of days-old scruff that was Tracy's weakness. She wanted to clutch his sweater, pull him in closer, and taste his lips. This man had walked into her life days ago, yet he got her. He understood her quirky humor and way of seeing the world. How was it possible someone could do that so quickly?

A light flashed, the brightness inducing her to blink before registering what happened. A dark-haired woman hid behind the lens of a camera.

"Kara?" Tracy said. "What are you doing here?"

Danny's girlfriend Kara stood by them, camera around her neck. Her long locks were in a high ponytail, her bangs reaching over her eyebrows.

"Mr. Kemper hired me to take pictures of the event for advertising and what-not." Kara looked at Ben and smiled. "Hi, I'm Kara."

Ben put up his hands, displaying the multi-colored paintings along his fingers. "I'll save you from the mess. I'm Ben."

Kara gasped, eyes big. "So, this is one of your dates then!"

Tracy felt the stares from three pairs of eyes of the ladies group. The women had grown tipsier by the minute, enjoying the wine a little too much. Not that she could judge their behavior when she'd just had a paint fight with Ben.

"This is one of the assignments Aunt Dee sent us on, yes." *Date* still didn't sit right with her. Although she was having a great time with Ben. And it honestly did feel like a date, but not the kind of uncomfortable blind date that it could've been. The kind of date she'd hope to have if going on a date. Just like the last one...

Her heart raced. Who was she kidding? This *was* a date. Not only was she having a great time, but a second ago she had wanted to kiss Ben. This was not how things were supposed to be.

Kara tapped on her phone, and Tracy snapped out of her date shock. "What are you doing now?"

"Oh nothing." Kara put the phone in the pocket of her jeans. "How are you liking Waverly Lake, Ben?"

"You don't have to make small talk with her," Tracy said. "She's on the job." She turned to Kara. "Which you need to get back to, right?" She said it with a closed jaw and forced smile.

"I don't mind," Ben said. "It's been great so far. Aunt Dee has me working hard, and Tracy here keeps me on my toes."

"Had a little fun with the paint?" Danny stood, arms on his hips, catching his breath.

What an opportune time for a little family reunion. "What the heck are you doing here?" Tracy asked, but she realized the answer and stared down Kara.

"He was just outside, waiting around for me to finish the job. No sense in him waiting in the cold and missing out on saying hello to his sister."

"Yeah, Tracy. Can't a brother want to say hello to his sister?" Danny reached a hand out to Ben, who looked at Tracy. It was one thing to be mindful of the mess with Kara. Danny was another story. Tracy nodded, holding back the smirk. Ben squeezed Danny's hand in a shake, transferring paint to his palm.

"Oh dear," Tracy said, faking concern. "That's a shame. You should probably wash that up."

Danny examined his hand. "At least I don't have it all over my face like the two of you."

Ben turned toward Tracy. "Is this not Advanced Face Painting?"

Tracy slapped her hip. "We must've gotten our days confused." She smiled, comfortable in the fuzzy warm vortex of his full attention and sarcasm.

"What are you supposed to do with these?" Danny picked up a purple acorn. "They almost look like Easter eggs."

"They're decorative," Kara said. "You know, put them in a dish, or along a table runner."

"Actually, they'll come in handy on the trail." Ben picked up two in his hands. "Sometimes when I'm backpacking, I'll head out on a side trail to explore. Usually, they're not marked as well as the main trails, and it's easy to get turned around. Before you know it, you've spent two hours of your daylight looking to get back to where you started. With these I can lay them out along my path. That way if the side trail doesn't loop back to the main trail, I can retrace my steps."

Tracy caught the faintest hint of a smirk before he set the acorns down, looking away from her brother and his girlfriend.

Danny examined the acorn in his hand further. "Is that for real?"

Tracy bit her lip, and Ben unveiled the facade with a chuckle.

"You two are terrible," Kara said.

Danny put the acorn back in Ben's pile. "It's bad enough having one Tracy around. Now we must contend with two?"

So Tracy hadn't been the only one to see their connection. Ben did get her, and made her laugh, and even held his own against Danny, who still managed to show his inner rotten-yet-loving teenage brother self every now and then.

Kara shook her head. "I'd better work the room and get more pictures." She leaned to Tracy's ear. "He's cute." She flared her eyebrows in two push-ups.

"I'll just hang out with my sister and her new buddy."

"Come on." Kara pulled on Danny's shirt. "We'll stay out of your hair."

"Which is more than what the paint can say," Danny muttered.

Tracy turned back to her art project with a sigh of relief. Not much embarrassed her, a personality point she was proud to have. But Danny and Kara had come close. Why should she care though if Danny embarrassed her in front of Ben? What did she have to be ashamed of? That was her family, and this was someone she had known for a few days.

A few days in which her resolve had gone from sturdy rigidness to Play-Doh. Ben had an effect of softening her, getting inside that curly head of hers and making it okay to be herself in front of him. She usually didn't have a problem being herself, but Ben not only accepted that, he seemed to enjoy being around her.

Her attachment to him grew, which was not wise. Who knew how long he'd be here, or how long she'd be here? Attachments only made excitement and adventure—what she wanted to do with her life—that much harder.

There still were questions that needed answered. How exactly did Aunt Dee know him, yet Tracy didn't? After last night's town meeting, she had been more curious than ever. He had spoken out as if he belonged in Waverly Lake, in the class of local citizens who appreciated what Waverly Lake stood for. Maybe he was against the general destruction of property in an environmental sense. But the way he spoke, with passion, and off the cuff...it made her think it was more than just a general cause.

Ben had a specific purpose for being in Waverly Lake. A purpose that somehow connected him to Phillips Manor.

And if Aunt Dee or anyone else knew about it, Tracy would soon find out.

Chapter Sixteen

BEN COULDN'T HELP BUT LAUGH AT DANNY AND HIS girlfriend Kara. Part of him was sad to have missed out on growing up with siblings. They were like built-in friends in adulthood. What he wouldn't have given to have a family to celebrate holidays with, to congratulate each other on achievements, or simply have someone trusted to confide in at a moment's notice.

On the other hand, it would've made navigating the foster system that much harder. He had seen a set of three sisters split up to different families, and who knew how easy it was for them to reconnect in the future. Having a brother or sister would've made the inheritance situation more complicated as well.

It was complicated enough already. He hadn't set his mind on stepping up, reaching his neck out to take over Phillips Manor. But the way things were going, with what the townspeople wanted to do with it, he didn't know if he could stand by and watch it disappear.

"Have you had dinner yet?" Tracy held her stomach. "I don't want to drink any more of this wine or else it'll go right to my head."

"You mean it hasn't already?" He winked.

"I do want to drink more of it, to wash out the fact that my brother and his girlfriend are here."

Kara finished photographing the table with the trio of women before moving to the front of the classroom by the older couple. Danny leaned on the drink table in the back, watching the two of them, turning his gaze away every time Ben looked back at him.

"What do you say we get out of here and get a bite to eat?"

Tracy's shoulders sank in relief. "Yes, please."

"Come on." He grabbed her hand in his and led her out of the classroom. It wasn't planned. It felt natural to hold her soft fingers in his, the touch somewhere between innocently warm and sizzling.

Danny stood straighter, off the table. "Where are you two going?"

"We're calling it a night," Ben said. "Nice to see you again."

"Same."

Ben guided Tracy out the studio, their hands separating as they walked out the front door. Instinct urged him to grab it again, to feel her touch surprisingly delicate underneath her bravado exterior. He fended off the urge.

"Where to?" he asked.

"Hmm." Tracy looked up and down the street. "How do you feel about tacos?"

"Hard or soft?"

"Does it matter?"

She could've asked how he felt about eating tires, and he would've gone along. He relished their time together, and anything to prolong it this evening was relished. "Not at all."

Tracy laughed. Every time she did felt like a reward, a prize earned for getting to know her a little better.

"There's an amazing food truck at the park. If we hurry, we can catch it before it closes up for the evening."

"Let's do it."

Tracy headed east, toward the square. Ben walked next to her, enjoying the cold evening, the sun long gone over the highest peaks of the Appalachian Mountains to the west. Even though the mountain range blocked off direct sunlight for the last hour or two of daylight, it created an ombre effect of colors, from peach and gold to lavender and amaranth.

"Sorry about those two." Tracy slowed, the pace more conducive to hearing one another. The square and town center were still surprisingly busy for the evening. The busiest he'd seen, other than last night's meeting, since his return.

"Danny and Kara? It's okay. I enjoy meeting your family."

She took the next few steps in silence before responding. "I bet Kara will officially be family soon."

"You think Danny's going to propose?"

"I kinda hope so."

"That's good, right? That you like her enough to be a part of the family?"

Tracy smiled. "I guess I didn't think about it that way. I just see how perfect Kara is for Danny. If anyone can be perfect for someone else. What I don't know is if Danny would take that leap again."

"He's been married before?"

Tracy nodded. "Hannah's mom. She left right around the time Hannah was showing the first signs of ASD—autism spectrum disorder."

"You think she left because of it?" Mom and Dad left him parentless, but it was all an accident. To purposely put a child through growing up without a parent, it was downright unimaginable. Disdain for this unnamed ex-wife grew as tension in his muscles.

"I can't say what was going on in her head. What I do know is that she was never right for Danny, or Hannah. She left, and I thought the divorce had shattered Danny's heart for good."

"That's terrible. For Danny and Hannah."

"Tell me about it. It was rough there for a while. Danny had moved in with my parents, and as much as I love them for helping as they could, they didn't understand Hannah's situation." She stuck a hand up to stop his response. "They're getting a lot better about educating themselves, going to meetings, really understanding the full spectrum of what autism means and how to accommodate

Hannah. I think Kara helped both Danny and my parents to see each other better."

Ben absorbed the story as they reached the other side of the square and walked past Pearson's Wharf.

"I like hearing about your family. Gives me a little more insight as to who Tracy Bennett really is."

"Oh really?" She chuckled. "What insight does Danny give you to my personality?"

He instinctively raised his shoulders closer to his ears, the breeze drying the sweat he had built up in the art studio around his neck. He'd liked to blame it all on the studio temperature, but he knew better. He did get a little nervous when Kara and Danny came, more self-conscious about being there with Tracy.

"Despite the teasing on the surface, you two really love each other and appreciate family."

"That could be said about any siblings."

"That's not true. Not all families get along the way you do."

"Is that your way of saying you don't get along with yours?"

She hadn't meant it to hurt. She didn't know being reminded of his family's tragedy carried with it a sting.

"You haven't really told me about your family, where you come from."

"That's because there's not much to tell." He took in a deep breath, giving him an extra second to think over his words. "If you had known my parents, you'd realize they were very much like yours. But they're gone, have been for a while."

"I'm so sorry. I didn't know."

"It's okay. You couldn't have known." Unless Aunt Dee gave up her promise, which would be against her nature.

They walked in silence until Tracy held his arm at the elbow, as if he escorted her across town. "So is that all my family tells you about me?"

He struggled with saying what was really on his mind. But when else could he talk about it if not now? The conversation had turned more serious than he ever imagined already. "It seems like

Danny is content in finding someone, having a family and settling down, here in Waverly Lake. The way I see it, you're not that different from your brother. Maybe you'd also find yourself happy staying here."

She turned her head, looking off somewhere in the distance and releasing her grasp. Had he assumed too much? Or touched a sore spot for her?

"What Danny and Kara have is special, yes. I just don't know if I'm cut out for that lifestyle. I want adventure, to see and do all I can while I can."

"I understand that," Ben said. "Heck, I've been all over the country, sometimes by force and other times by choice. There definitely are perks to being out in the world by yourself. No one else has control over your decisions. You don't have to change your plans to accommodate anyone else."

"So you do get it." They traversed a parking lot and into a grassy open space, the entrance to Lakeshore Park.

"I do," he said. "But I also know how lonely of an existence that can be. It seems ironic, but the more you wander the earth, seeing different cultures and ways of life, you lose track of what is important in your own life. It's why I decided to stop roaming for a while and stay in one place."

"And you chose Waverly Lake of all places." Tracy shook her head. "That still baffles me." They stopped in front of a food truck, a giant upside-down taco shell painted on the side. A fork rose out of the shell as a mast with Taco Velero in fiery red letters on its sail.

"What's good here?" he asked.

"Do you trust me to order?"

He smiled. "Go for it."

"We'll take four crunchy tacos with extra hot sauce." She turned to him. "Sorry, do you like spice?"

"Is there any other way to eat a taco?"

She turned to the vendor. "See, there's a reason I hang around this guy."

They received their order, and Tracy led him to a picnic table by a pavilion, one of the closer ones to the lake. Tracy stepped on the bench and sat on the tabletop, facing the lake.

Ben followed suit, taking a seat next to her. "It's an amazing view from here."

"It is. And there's some comfort in knowing it'll never be turned into a parking lot." She looked at him. "That I know of."

He bit into the taco, the warm meat melting the cheddar cheese, mixing with the cool avocado. The tangy hot sauce was the last part of the bite to hit his senses. "This is why I chose Waverly Lake."

"For the view?" Tracy crunched into her taco, trying to catch the delicious messiness on the paper lying on her lap.

"The tacos." He grinned, knowing he probably had as much green and orange in his teeth as he had on his face in paint.

"I can't take you anywhere," she joked, handing him a napkin. "They are good, I'll give you that."

He wiped his mouth. "Seriously though. In staying here for a while, I can go back to that same food truck and try everything else on their menu. I wouldn't get to do that otherwise."

"I guess."

"I'm just saying that being somewhere long enough to try all the dishes, there's a joy in that."

Her lips grew to a smile. "Does that mean you're planning on being in Waverly Lake long enough to do that?"

He looked out at the lake, a blue blackness of water that lapped the sandy beach ahead. It was the question he'd been asking himself the more he grew comfortable being here. He turned to Tracy, the lighter golden ringlets around her face dancing in the wind.

"I wasn't so sure how long I'd stay when I first got here."

"And now?"

"Now...it seems I'm finding reasons to stay." He analyzed her chestnut eyes, until she shied away and scrunched up the paper from her taco.

"You know what's really crazy?" he asked.

"What?"

"That we ordered some of the spiciest tacos I've ever had, without getting a drink."

She laughed and hopped off the table. "Come on. I got a place for that too."

They walked back through the park, making their way across town to the truck. They stopped by Nichols and Dimes and grabbed two Cokes, the kind in the old glass bottles Ben had only seen in commercials. The pharmacy itself was out of an old commercial.

They reached the truck, nightfall having fully set in and parking spots emptying. Tracy drove again, Ben not minding not having to focus on the road, enjoying watching her face, listening to the radio and following the curves of the road.

They were as comfortable in the background noise as they were conversing. Tracy had told him anecdotes about a few properties they passed, but other than that, he savored their time being together in the same truck. There was no forcing of conversation to break silence. No awkwardness.

They arrived at the lodge near ten o'clock. Aunt Dee was nowhere to be seen, most likely asleep in her bedroom off the lobby. She did leave a note for the two of them, highlighting the jobs she wanted each to complete for tomorrow.

"Even when she's not around she's managing us," Tracy whispered.

Ben read through the note. "Looks like our next date is tomorrow." The thought excited him, sending a zing of delight up his spine. He would've been happy if Aunt Dee assigned them a chore to do together. But another date was a super bonus.

"It's my pick." Her eyes widened, a sly smile forming.

"Should I be concerned?" He wasn't really concerned. No, what was extraordinary was that she hadn't corrected him in calling it a date.

"I guess you'll have to wait and see." She headed to the stairs, and he set the note down, following her.

His stomach did backflips as they crept up the stairs. He didn't want the night to end. He wanted to stop her on the landing and kiss her pink lips and talk about everything and nothing.

But this was Tracy Bennett. The odds she considered him in that way were nil, yet he couldn't help feeling drawn to her, wanting to touch her skin, even if just her hand to feel closer. They reached the top of the stairs, facing each other in front of their rooms.

Ben nervously shoved his hands in his pockets. "I guess I'll see you tomorrow then."

"Yeah." She tucked a strand behind her ear, the edge of her teeth biting her bottom lip. "Aunt Dee will make sure of that."

Could he not pause this moment? To savor it a second longer? Instead, he nodded, turning to his door.

"Not that I meant we're forced to. I mean, it's not entirely terrible."

Ben paused, catching her fidgetiness.

She closed her eyes, squishing up her nose. "I'm so sorry, that came out wrong." She turned around and unlocked her door.

He controlled his delight in her stumbling. Was he, Ben Walker, making Tracy Bennett fumble with her words?

She opened the door and again faced him. "What I mean is, even if she hadn't scheduled tomorrow, I'd still want to..."

Ben stood in the hallway. He stood there like a statue until he processed what she said. *I'd still want to.* She wanted to be with him.

He unlocked his door and pushed it open.

"Good night." She smiled and shut her door before he could answer.

He stood in his doorway, staring at her door. His grin grew across his face.

"Good night."

Chapter Seventeen

Thursday, October 13

TRACY IMMERSED HERSELF IN PULLING UP THE remaining floor staples in Aunt Dee's office. She had briefly seen Ben in the morning, while pouring herself a cup of coffee. She didn't know how to behave after what she had said last night.

She worked on the flooring, her hands cramping from gripping the pliers. The two of them had another date tonight, and well, it was silly to not call it a date now, wasn't it? She had such a good time with him, and wanted to be around him, and she'd confessed as much. Was that so wrong?

She just needed to see him, speak with him, to clear the air. The foggy air of mixing a business relationship with a personal one.

Her back-and-forth argument of what to call her relationship with Ben was broken by Aunt Dee.

"Phone call for you, Tracy." She stood in the doorway to the office. "It's long distance, so you'd better hurry."

"Okay." Tracy set down the pliers, her knees and ankles aching from crawling and crouching all afternoon.

She walked to the front desk and picked up the phone. "Hello?"

"Tracy! It's Sara."

Tracy recognized the Aussie accent she had grown fond of during her stay months ago. It definitely was a long-distance call. It had to be nine or ten in the morning where Sara was. "Hey Sara. If you're calling about the New Zealand trip, I've got my eye on a flight that leaves right after Thanksgiving here in The States. That should give me a day or two with you in Sydney before we head out to Auckland."

"That's why I'm calling, honey. Amelia found out her dad needs surgery, and it's scheduled for February. Me and the girls are trying to move the trip up a month's time so we'd be back in time."

"Bump it up a month?" The ten-week trip across New Zealand and nearby islands was the end goal of working for Aunt Dee. "That puts me there at the end of October." She processed the timeline. "I'd need to leave in two weeks."

"I know, it's short notice. We realize that and promise to pitch in. We could each lend you a few pineapples while you're here, if you can cover the cost of the ticket."

Tracy did the math of how many Australian fifty dollars she'd need to last ten weeks. She shook her head. This was crazy. She'd have to leave Aunt Dee without her help, help she promised. But then again, Aunt Dee had Ben.

Oh no. Ben.

"Tracy, you there?"

She sighed. "I'm here. I'm gonna need some time to think over this."

"I understand. But we need to know, like yesterday."

"I get it. I'll let you know ASAP."

"All right, Sheila. Miss you."

"Miss you too." Tracy hung up the phone, the weight of the decision on her shoulders. The trip had dictated what she needed to do all summer and fall. She had stuck to the plan, to earn the money needed, but what happened now that the trip had changed?

"Everything okay?" Aunt Dee approached from the kitchen. "Sounded urgent, and expensive."

"Yes, to both things." She was all for spontaneity and adventure, but such a trip took planning and preparation. To cut her time in Waverly Lake short meant less travel money, and she'd also miss Thanksgiving with her family. That was all in addition to hurting Aunt Dee. Of course Aunt Dee would pretend she was okay with it, but does that mean it was the right thing to do?

Tracy half-smiled. "It's fine. Sara has a way with drama."

"Not to add to it, but you'd better get yourself ready for tonight if you're going to make it on time."

Tracy checked the time on her work cell phone. "Shoot. You're right."

"I think Ben is already raring to go. Poor guy. Doesn't know what he's in for tonight."

Tracy tried not to think about all the possible meanings of what Aunt Dee said. She had meant in terms of the actual date, but Tracy couldn't help thinking he didn't know what he was in for in meeting Tracy. If he was falling for her the way she was for him, then she'd have to stop it. It wasn't fair to Ben to make such a connection, to let him in, only to be off literally halfway around the world. Sooner than she had planned.

It was one thing for her to hurt. It was another hurting someone else. Someone as good-hearted as Ben.

She splashed water on her face and pinned back her front curls along the sides of her head. She slipped on a cream sweater and black leggings and zipped up her leather boots. She left her room, fanning her sweater. Her body sweated, half flustered by the phone call and half hating being late. It was the event planner in her—if one thing is thrown off-schedule it cascades down the line.

She rushed down the stairs and grabbed a brown scarf hanging on a coat hook. Ben stood outside on the porch, looking out over the parking lot, the lake peeking between the trees. She paused, catching her breath. From what she knew of him, Ben was a good person. Yes, it had only been a handful of days, but she generally was a good judge of character. He deserved someone who kept both feet in one spot, or both feet on the same path he walked. She could see herself with him, but what she wasn't certain of was whether she could stay put long enough to try.

"There she is." Ben turned around as Tracy exited the front door. "Ready?"

She smiled. His handsome face had a way of calming her jitters, the ones that ran through her body right now as if she had five cups of coffee. "The question is, are *you* ready?"

"You want to drive?" He held out the truck keys. She appreciated the offer. In fact, she couldn't think of anyone in all her dates across the globe—albeit limited in number—who had made the offer.

"You go ahead."

They stepped down to the truck. She tugged at the tough passenger door and buckled up.

Ben got comfortable in the driver's seat. "Where to?"

"Just head into town. Do you know where the library is?"

"Are we checking out books?"

She chuckled. "Of all the possible dates I could've picked, you think I picked the library?"

"Hey, what do I know? There could be some abandoned basement there."

He certainly did get her. "No, not the library. But you're getting close on the activity." She winked and he shook his head while laughing.

The fear she had built up during the day over her tiny confession last night had immediately vanished upon seeing his face. She questioned why she was so worried about it in the first place.

"You know, with all these dates in town, you'd think it would've been better for us to have stayed in town instead of at the lodge."

"Very true," she said. "But then Aunt Dee wouldn't have us at her disposal early in the morning."

"You make a good point."

"Plus, I heard the next one is closer to the lodge."

"I can't believe after tonight we're three down, two to go."

She mulled over his words. Their discussion subsided, the air heavy once again, pressing her to think about her future, his future. Their future? With two dates left after this one, what did that mean for them? What did he plan on doing after finishing up with Aunt Dee? Maybe it'd be best if she just brought it up, let it out in the open. Or maybe forget anything happened between them all together. This was so unlike her it was frustrating.

They made small talk, the surface kind that came easily and didn't dare flirt with anything serious. As they approached town from the east, Tracy pointed at a street sign. "Turn left here."

Ben obliged, and they crept south, passing the library and its large grassy field on their right. It was where they'd play old black-and-white movies in the summer, an activity her niece Hannah loved.

Tracy's heart pounded. She had grown closer to Hannah these past few months in town. It would be harder to say goodbye to her this time around. And Danny. Now there was Kara to say goodbye to as well.

"Just up here, on the left."

Ben turned, the long gravel driveway taking them back into the woods. The trees cleared at the end of the road, into a parking lot in front of a three-story building. At its core, its crisp white paint and black shutters were impeccable, with intricate posts along its front porch like delicate hors d'oeuvre forks holding up the roof. On the surface, purple spotlights cast menacing shadows along its facade, with fake netting of spiderwebs clustered in its nooks and crannies. A projector shone a ghostly woman figure across a second-story window. A tarp hung over the permanent sign, the letters running down the sign like wet ink. *Waverly Lake Dead and Breakfast.*

"Oh no." Ben eyed her.

"Oh yes." She nodded slowly, with satisfaction.

"I'm not sure how I feel about haunted houses."

Ben parked in a spot at the edge of the lot. Tracy got out of the truck and waited outside for him to follow. He shut the door, hesitant to walk toward her.

"Seems like you know exactly how you feel about haunted

houses. Come on, I'll protect you." She grabbed his arm and rested her hand in the crook of his elbow. He didn't shoo it away or flinch. He simply accepted it as if they had done it fifty times over.

The closer they got to the entrance, the louder the music sounded. It was a combination of eerie music and spooky sounds, like squeaky doors slowly opening, old floorboards creaking, and maniacal laughter.

Ben surveyed the group of people waiting in line. "I think we're the oldest people here."

Tracy eyed the groups of teenagers and couples chatting in line. "Nonsense. Everyone likes a good scare."

"I'm not so sure about that."

"I imagine you'd get some excitement out of things people see as scary."

"You're going to have to give me an example because I'm not buying what you're selling."

She scoffed and tapped his arm with her free hand. "For instance, when you're out hiking, wouldn't it be both scary and exciting to encounter a bear?"

He shrugged. "Bears scary? Not the black bears around here. They're just as happy to be on their way and not bothered by us humans."

"You know what I mean. Not everyone would feel that way. I'd probably be scared if I saw a bear."

"Now a chainsaw wielding clown?" Ben pointed to the newest noise maker, a red-nosed clown with a mouthful of fangs, waving around a chainless saw by a cluster of teenagers. The girls screamed, cowering behind the boys, all of them laughing when the clown moved to scare the next group. "That would be utterly terrifying."

Tracy laughed. "I guess if one of those showed up on the trail, then I agree. It would be terrifying."

They moved up in the line, creeping closer to the entrance. "I don't want to offend you, since I know this is your pick." Ben adjusted his collar, a new denim jacket she hadn't seen yet in his repertoire. "But I'm not so sure this would be a very...romantic date for a blind date?"

"What? How can you say such a thing?"

"It all seems a little much. It's loud, and people are screaming. Just doesn't exude romance."

A figure in all black with a sickle jumped out from the nearby bushes. Ben startled and aimed his back at Tracy, blocking the ghoul from reaching her.

She touched his shoulders gently, savoring his feat of bravery. Teenagers behind them laughed at the scare, and the grim reaper figure moved back into its hiding spot.

Ben turned around, shaking his head. Tracy stared into her hero's eyes. He stared back, reading her eyes like he read her desire.

She could've kissed him right then.

"See," she said. "Romantic."

Chapter Eighteen

IT TOOK EVERY OUNCE OF BEN WALKER'S WILL TO NOT whisk Tracy away from this place. He wasn't a scaredy cat by any means. Like Tracy had said, he'd seen some things on the trail that most people would find disconcerting, even scary—animals behaving aggressively, storms rolling in at breakneck speed. A haunted house was nothing compared to those.

Rather it was the darkness, the lurking being he knew would be there around the corner. It was the anticipation of the jump, the scare, that he didn't like. Why would anyone want to purposely be made to scream?

But this was Tracy's pick. It was her idea of fun, and she truly reveled in bringing him here. He didn't want to let her down by leaving. He also didn't want to leave her behind. All day he had looked forward to this date, whatever it was going to be. He wanted to see her round face and dimples when she smiled. He wanted to talk to her about anything and everything. If that was asking for too much, he'd be content being in her presence.

He'd never been connected to someone like this. When he lost his parents in the accident, he had been young. He'd felt the pain, and it grew as he aged, knowing they wouldn't be around for any milestone big or small. That sense of loss would never go away. But this connection with Tracy was different. Being around her energized and calmed him at the same time. There were no expectations or need to be perfect. He had never felt more himself than he did around her.

"Are you certain this is a good idea?" He stepped closer to the entrance where a bouncer dressed as a ghoulish butler roped them off at the bottom of the porch stairs. A group of four ahead of them went inside, vanishing behind the front door, the dark hole of a mouth to this beast of a house.

"What do they do with this place the rest of the year?" He continued facing forward, anxious for the bouncer to unclip the rope for their turn.

"It's a real bed and breakfast."

"You're kidding." He looked up, examining the ornate gables and spired roof.

"Nope. I think they determined it's more profitable to do this in October than to house guests."

"You know, for all Waverly Lake has to offer this time of year, I don't get it. Aunt Dee said as much about the lodge too."

"That's why she's trying Lovetoberfest. It's not just about the lodge. If more people knew just how gorgeous it is here in the fall, and about the local activities, it could be a fall hot spot."

The bouncer butler unclipped the red rope. "Enter if you dare."

Tracy's face lit up with delight. "Here we go."

"Ladies first."

He heard her giggle as he followed her up the stairs through the dark corridor. "I see what you did there," she said. "Make me go first."

"It's just the gentlemanly thing to do." He continued walking and bumped into the back of Tracy. "Why'd we stop?"

"There's nowhere to go ahead."

He stretched out a hand while Tracy moved to his side. There was no evidence of a handle or knob. "Now what?"

The wall slid open, revealing flashing strobe lights. A labyrinth of tall black panels blocked off parts of the house and guided them through the first story. Unlike the corn maze, traffic only moved one way, and there weren't any wrong turns to take. Around every corner was a themed room. They were cliched and campy, not overly gruesome like the signs he'd seen for ones in Charlotte or Richmond. He nearly laughed at the production, appreciative of their efforts, especially in transforming the historical house.

"I think you're liking this more than you thought you would," Tracy said. They walked along, examining the crazed dentist's office scene.

"It's not over yet." Ben yelped when a hand grabbed his ankle. He nearly stepped on it as it retreated.

Tracy laughed. "Doesn't that excite you? Get the heart pumping?"

"It certainly gets the heart pumping. I'm not sure excite is the correct word." They moved on to the next themed room, a haunted carnival. "Is that what this is for you? An adrenaline rush?"

Tracy's face turned to him, the black light illuminating the streaks of blond in her ponytail. "Sure. That's part of it."

"And all that traveling and adventure...you're always seeking that adrenaline, aren't you?" He knew well enough how much she longed to be doing something else, somewhere else. How she had the eternal itch to keep her feet moving. It's part of what attracted him so strongly to her. "I bet you've been bungee jumping."

"Yep. While I was in Chile."

"Heli-skiing?"

"When in the Alps."

"Seriously?"

"I grew up with a ski resort thirty minutes away. It was the logical next step."

"Wow. We'll save the discussion on what is logical for another time." He caught her shaking her head, the ponytail swaying side to side in the dim light. "Okay. Skydiving."

"Uh huh."

"Hmm. I thought I had you on that one. I can't think of anything more extreme than that."

She waved her finger in the air and continued to walk. "That's the problem with skydiving. It's hard to top that once you've done it."

"You're just always seeking the next big rush." If that was the case, would she ever be satisfied? Is that why she left Waverly Lake so much? Searching for a feeling she'd never be able to hold onto no matter where she was?

He didn't want to accept it. No one could find happiness that way, if that was what they thought made them happy. What were the odds she'd find happiness right here?

"And the other?" he asked.

"The other what?"

"You said the adrenaline is part of what you like about this. What's the other?"

She grinned, her teeth bright white in the black light. "Seeing you squirm."

"You know, I bet most people would think you're cruel for saying that."

"But you don't."

"Don't I?"

Tracy stopped and fully turned around. "No. Because you understand me." Her face turned from amused to serious, her teeth hiding behind the straight mouth.

I understand how you never want to appear weak in front of others. Or how you use humor to mask your true feelings or discomfort. He also knew, somehow, that it meant she cared about him. It was like she had her own language, and he was one of the few people on the planet gifted with the ability to interpret it.

"I do understand you."

Her breathing looked rushed, as if he had upset her. "You'd tell me if I was being too harsh, right? If I'm being insensitive?"

His mouth sat slightly agape. It was like witnessing the armored plates cracking in front of him. She did care about what people thought of her, and how she made others feel. He knew that already, but it didn't hurt to see it in raw form. In fact, he had never felt more attracted to her than in this moment.

He stroked her cheek with the back of his hand. He couldn't help it. "You don't have to worry about that with me."

She clasped his wrist. "I'm serious. Danny, my parents... sometimes they make me feel like I have to change who I am to fit in. That I have to lessen my personality."

He shook his head, his arm now free of her hold. "You're Tracy Bennett. Always have been, always will be. Anyone who expects you to change to 'fit in' doesn't realize they'd lose the absolute best parts of you."

Screams and laughter came from behind them.

"I think the next group is catching up to us." Tracy's voice was soft.

For as much as he didn't want to be here, he didn't want their private moment to end. "We'd better get moving then. I think we're near the end."

They entered a walkway through a tunnel, an illusion of lights spinning around, knocking them off balance. Tracy hit the railing, catching her footing. Ben reached out, holding her shoulder as they stumbled to the other side.

A turn to the right, through a curtain, and the room was dark. He had been out in the woods on the darkest of nights. But this was the darkest dark he had ever experienced. He couldn't see the walls around him, but felt they had opened, that they were no longer walking through a narrow hallway. The room felt massive, yet he had no way of knowing how big it really was.

"Ben?" Tracy's voice came from across the room. She had been right in front of him a second ago. "Where are you?"

"Tracy?" He extended his arms, feeling the space around him. He blinked more than usual, as if his eyes would evolve rapidly with each flicker of the eyelids to see in pitch black.

Tracy screamed a short cry.

"Tracy?"

"Something grazed me."

He moved his arms faster, shifting his position in the room by shuffling his feet. "Keep talking."

"It's starting to freak me out."

"I'm here," he said. "Keep talking, I'll find you." A growl snarled past him, a shoe bumping his foot. *Sweet Jesus.* Okay, he was wrong. This did scare him.

"Ben?" Her voice sounded closer.

Their arms crisscrossed, and he gripped her elbows. Her hands wrapped his upper arms, and he pulled her in close.

"It is you, right?"

"It's me."

Something brushed by them, and Tracy gripped his arms tighter. Ben moved his hands around her shoulders, pressing her closer to him. Her hands moved to his chest, beneath his jacket. Even through the T-shirt, he felt their warmth.

Her breath grew closer, his pull to her strengthening.

"Okay, now can we agree this is the worst date idea ever?"

A figure sounded an eerie cackle. Tracy buried her head in his chest. He held onto her tight. Even though he couldn't see a thing, her presence in his arms was stronger than ever. The flowery hyacinth of her hair, the faintest strawberry of her lip gloss. He swore he heard her heart pounding, or was that his beating in his ears?

"Ideas to get out of here?" Her voice muffled, face still shielded by him.

He wanted to go, but he didn't. He wanted her to stay in his arms.

The lights flicked on. The masked ghouls and demons that had worked the room retreated to the walls.

Ben looked down at the beautiful, strong, scared, and stubborn woman in his arms. She looked up, her eyes penetrating his soul.

A recording played over speakers. "Please exit to the right. We hope you enjoyed your scare." A maniacal laugh followed.

A normal, present voice sounded. "We need y'all to leave." A grim reaper waved his scythe to the exit door.

"Death is telling us to go." Tracy pulled away from him, his arms screaming for one more second of her body in them. "Don't want to tick him off."

Ben woefully retreated his hands back to his pockets. "I thought you enjoyed flirting with death."

He smiled, and they both broke out in laughter. They exited as the crew turned off the lights behind them, ready for the next group.

The outside greeted them, the air fresh and night growing darker. Even so, the moon and stars along with the exterior lighting made it feel like daylight compared to the inside of the house.

He looked at Tracy. He had connected with this woman, in both mind and soul. It felt too good to be true.

"Tell me the truth," she said, strolling next to him on the way to the truck. "Did you really hate it?"

He looked back at the house, the line even longer to get in, then back at Tracy. "It was the best worst date I've ever been on."

Chapter Nineteen

Friday, October 14

"Good morning."

"Morning." Tracy sipped her coffee, leaning against the kitchen counter in Woodsman's Lodge. Aunt Dee poured herself a cup of coffee out of the hot pot. Tracy had ongoing jobs to work on over her stay, but Aunt Dee usually filled her in on the day's more pressing needs in the morning. Tracy braced for the list.

"So tell me," Aunt Dee added creamer to her mug, "how's it been going, these date prospects?"

"I thought you didn't want to hear about them until we finished all five."

"A lady can be curious." She sipped the coffee, staring at Tracy over the rim of the mug. "I do have a lot at stake here. If we blow Lovetoberfest this first year, it may be the *only* year."

"Well, I'm going to keep my word on giving all five a shot."

Aunt Dee's shoulders dropped, and she stared at her drink.

"What I can do is promise you that Lovetoberfest will be all you want it to be."

"You really think so?"

Tracy nodded. "If it doesn't work out for anyone, it'll be

because of not finding the right match, not because the dating event was a bust." Tracy approached Aunt Dee and rubbed her shoulder. "You're just going to have to trust me on this one."

Aunt Dee raised an eyebrow. "I'm not so sure I like the sound of that."

Tracy winked, and Ben walked through the kitchen door.

"Oh hey." He ran his hand through his rusty brown hair.

"Good morning," Aunt Dee said.

Ben walked to Tracy, who thought he was about to hug her with his arm spread out. He stopped short, smiling right at her. "Wanted to get some coffee." He pointed to the pot behind her.

Tracy snapped out of her trance. "Oh right." She moved left, and he moved right, her chin bumping his shoulder. "Sorry."

"My fault."

"You go ahead." Tracy side-stepped out of his way. She caught Aunt Dee's sly eye, which never meant anything good.

"You two have another date tonight, right?"

"Yeah." Ben cleared his throat and spooned sugar into his coffee. "It's actually this afternoon." He checked his watch. "Which means I'd better get started on that list you left me, Aunt Dee."

"Don't let me stop you." She winked at Ben.

He nodded at Aunt Dee in goodbye and turned to Tracy. It wasn't a nod but a glance, one that connected them for a second and made Tracy's lips curl into a smile. She saw it in him too, in the growing crinkles around his eyes. He stepped out through the door into the lobby.

"Am I right in thinking that you no longer are upset with Ben's presence here?" Aunt Dee crossed her arms, supporting the mug in the bend of her elbow.

"I was never upset."

Aunt Dee's face read skepticism.

"It was more...frustration. In fact, I'm still frustrated not knowing how the two of you know each other. It's like this big secret neither of you want to share." They both had brushed off her inquiries regarding their past. If they really had a past at all.

She wouldn't put it past Dee to pretend to have known Ben just so Tracy would be more comfortable with him working at the lodge.

"You like him, though, don't you?"

Tracy stumbled with her words. "I...don't *dis*like him."

"I see how you watch out for him when you're working inside with me, waiting to see if he'll cross your path."

Tracy scoffed. "I do not."

"Do too." Aunt Dee chuckled. "And how you look at each other."

Tracy placed a hand on her hip. "Just how do we look at each other?"

Aunt Dee put down her mug and straightened her posture, addressing Tracy straight on. "As if your world belonged in each other's eyes."

It was prophetic and romantic and mushy. "That's ridiculous." Her face reddened from more than just the hot coffee.

"If you say so."

"I do say so."

The kitchen door opened again, Tracy standing at attention, holding her breath at the sight of Ben.

Instead, it was Miranda, the forty-five-year-old head housekeeper for Woodsman's Lodge. In the summer, Miranda had a full day's work every day with the steady flow of guests. Currently, she came around in the mornings, switching out guest sheets and doing laundry. "Good morning, ladies."

"Good morning." Aunt Dee kept her smugness in her smile.

Tracy took a deep breath. "If you don't have anything to add to my chores, I'd better go get started."

Aunt Dee held a hand out, touching Tracy's shoulder. "I need you to go to Weeping Wares and order the arrangements for Lovetoberfest."

"Arrangements?"

"I want to spruce up the fall decorations in here. Get some garlands and fall flowers for the rooms."

"You do know you can order flowers online or through the phone, right?"

"And you can get yourself a job elsewhere if you don't like it." It was a half-joke with Aunt Dee. She loved to tease, but she also took employing someone, and their work, very seriously.

"All right. Give me a list of what you need."

"Good."

Aunt Dee jotted down the pre-order items, and Tracy took *Tin Can* across the lake. She had that date to make this afternoon, which meant getting out and back as quickly as possible. Every time she set foot on the boat, she was reminded of Ben. The poor guy did not fare well that first day. She chuckled, picturing him gripping the railing. Maybe if he stuck around longer, she'd work on getting him more comfortable with it.

What was she thinking? It was the same back-and-forth she had done all night. They were two people who had no business being in a relationship. There was no guarantee he even felt the same way.

But he had to have felt *something*.

It didn't slip her mind she had to give Sara an answer about the New Zealand trip. Who knew what Ben had planned beyond next week, let alone next month? What was she to do? Hope he felt something?

She docked the boat at Pearson's Wharf. Danny's truck sat empty in the parking lot, indicating he was working, but she hadn't seen him on deck near the vessels she had passed. He could've had the day off and gone out on *Kare Bear*, the sailing vessel he bought off Kara's dad this summer.

Being in the clear from Danny was only half the battle. Weeping Wares was just down the street from Pearson's Wharf, on the north side of Dowager. If Kara wasn't out sailing with Danny, she'd be working at Portside Portrait. Which meant Tracy was in danger of being seen as she walked by the photography studio to the flower shop. She briskly walked past the storefront and entered Weeping Wares unscathed. She did love Kara, but after Aunt Dee's inquisition about Ben this morning, she didn't want to have to deal with a second one.

"Tracy." Her friend George, the owner, wore a hunter green apron, straightening flowerpots on the display shelves a straight shot to the back of the store. He brushed his hands together. The moist air resembled that of a greenhouse, with the sour, yet fresh, smell of dirt and fertilizer and aromatic flowers.

"What brings you in today?"

She pulled the folded sheet of paper out of her jeans. "Aunt Dee has an order for you."

"Did you tell her we accept online orders? We have photos of everything too, so it's real easy."

Tracy placed a hand on his shoulder and shook her head. "I'm surprised she's not sending it by telegram."

"I understand. The internet is not for everyone."

Tracy recalled telling Ben the downward spiral of her internet search the other day. It did have its drawbacks; one being sucking the time out of one's life.

"She wants these ready for Lovetoberfest near the end of the month. I guess it's to spruce up the rooms and add to the romance of the weekend."

George examined the list. "I don't think that should be a problem. I'll go ahead and work on entering this in the system."

"Thanks, George. Just give me a call if you have questions or can't get something here in time." She scribbled her cell phone number down on the paper for him.

"Tracy Bennett has a cell phone now? Wait until I tell Sebastian we have a direct way to reach you."

Tracy held up a finger. "Not so fast. It's a business phone. Aunt Dee made that very clear."

"Yes, ma'am. I will guard it with my life." He folded it into his apron pocket. "Everything else okay? How's our new friend Ben doing? Still coming out with us on Saturday?"

"As far as I know. Though I'm not sure if he's going to like going out with us Saturday."

"Why not?" George stood in defiance. "Are you saying Sebastian and I embarrass you?"

"What? No. It's not that—"

"Why hello! I expected to see George here, but not Tracy Bennett."

Tracy blinked hard before giving George a look of annoyance. "It's Carly Fletcher, isn't it?" she whispered.

He tapped his nose with his index finger then headed off to place the order.

Tracy turned around on her heels. "Carly."

"Good morning, Tracy." She scanned the store, rising on her tiptoes. "Here by yourself? I thought you'd be with—" she clicked her fingers.

Carly Fletcher darn well knew what his name was. It took everything in Tracy's power not to roll her eyes.

"Ben. Yes, Ben Walker."

"He's busy working at the lodge. You know that's what he's here for."

"Is he, though?" Carly touched Tracy's wrist. Tracy resisted flinching, trying not to react as if gossip was a communicable disease. "I'd say from that showing the other night at the town meeting, that man has his sights on something other than Woodsman's Lodge."

Even though Tracy thought the same thing, she wasn't about to tell Carly that.

"You know, he came in for a haircut and shave last weekend, and I swear to you, I thought I recognized those eyes of his. I felt like we had met long ago, but I couldn't pinpoint it. Just how does Aunt Dee know him?"

Tracy shrugged. Even if she knew, she wouldn't tell the gossip queen of Waverly Lake. The fact was, it bothered her inwardly as much as it bothered Carly outwardly. Something he had said last night—*You're Tracy Bennett. Always have been. Always will be.* He had said *always have been.* Did that mean he knew her at some point in the past? Or was she reading too much into it? Her mind was swirling in circles. It kept going back to the original question of how he and Aunt Dee knew each other. Even Carly Fletcher knew that much.

"I swear I'm going to figure it out one of these days. You know, sometimes these things come to me at the oddest times. I'll wake up from a dream and poof, a name is in my head." She laughed, one that took all the high nasally parts of her voice and amplified them. "If I do ever figure it out, you'll be the first to know."

As much as the gossip mill irritated her, Tracy really did want to know the truth. For the first time, she found herself rooting for Carly Fletcher's nosiness to win out. She took a breath, calming the nerves Carly had frazzled. "Thanks, Carly. I'd appreciate that."

"You do the same for me, all right? If you figure it out, let old Carly know. You know how exhausted I get when I can't figure something out."

Tracy didn't, but it didn't take much imagination to picture it.

"Now Carly, what can I do for you?" George rushed over to them, giving Tracy the quickest form of a wink.

He was saving her from the hairdresser's chat, but the damage had already been done. Tracy's hesitations and questions about Ben were pushed up to the surface, after all the work Tracy had done to push them deep down to her core.

She had tossed and turned all night, considering what to do about New Zealand. Her reasoning through it not only had to do with going back on her promise to Aunt Dee, but wanting to stay to have more time with Ben. But how could she even consider someone else, when she didn't know the entire truth of who he really was?

Chapter Twenty

Ben sat in the clunker of a truck, running the heat on high. It wasn't super cold this midday, but last night dipped into the twenties. The sun hadn't warmed up the inside of the vehicle a whole lot, and he didn't want Tracy to freeze.

He started to sweat, but knew it was his nerves more than the air temperature. Why did he do this himself? Every single time they had a planned date, his stomach rolled, head swirled, and hands shook. Yet within minutes of Tracy arriving, perhaps seconds, his shaken insides settled, and they had a great time. There was no reason to be nervous around her, except for the fact she didn't know who he really was.

A minor detail.

"I'm a bad person." He faintly saw his breath in the air. It was a constant struggle, a pull between being truthful with Tracy and avoiding drama with the town. Lately the scale leaned to Tracy. The closer they got, the heavier the weight on his conscience.

Tracy pulled on the passenger door handle, and he gave the door a kick. She hopped into the seat and rubbed her hands together. "Yikes. It's like a metal refrigerator."

"I know. I've been running the heat for a good five minutes."

She smiled. "I appreciate the sentiment."

He pretended surprise. "Oh, right. Yeah. I did that for you of course. Had nothing to do with me not feeling my fingers and toes in here."

Tracy lightly slapped his leg. "Shut up." She chuckled.

"Luckily, it won't be for long. We've got a shorter drive for this one."

"Where are we headed? Or are you keeping it a secret since it's your pick?"

"I'd say *pick* is an appropriate word."

"Hmm." Tracy's grin grew. "There are so many ways I could go with that. Am I at least dressed appropriately?" She clutched the tan checked scarf over her beige turtleneck and brown leather jacket. She wore the boots again, the ones he liked seeing on her because they reminded him of their time in the mud at the farm.

"Dressed perfectly." He caught her eyes for a second then refocused on the road. "What did Aunt Dee have you up to this morning?"

"Going into town to George's place. Did you know he owned a flower shop?"

"I did." He glanced at Tracy. "Only because he told me as much the night of the town meeting."

"Aunt Dee had me order flowers for the lodge for Lovetoberfest. Lucky me, I ran into Carly Fletcher when I was there."

Ben's throat tightened. Had Carly figured out who he was? Between the hair salon visit and his town meeting outburst, she might've put the pieces together. There was no question if she had figured it out, she would've blabbed about it, especially to Tracy.

"You really left an impression on her." Tracy smirked. "I think she's convinced herself she knows you."

Ben cleared his dry throat. "In this life or a past one?"

Tracy laughed. "I could totally see Carly Fletcher convinced she had a past life that crossed one of yours."

"It's just up here." He was all too content to veer off the subject of Carly Fletcher as he turned left, the road taking them for a climb up the mountainside. Even such a short altitude gain revealed the changing world around them, the foliage almost over-ripe in burnt colors, and more leaves splashed on the ground. The truck puttered, battling the climb, probably scaring away the squirrels and birds preparing for the oncoming winter.

He pulled into a parking lot, the clearing affording a view of the water. They sat at the far northern end of the reverse L of Waverly Lake.

"Offshore Orchard." Tracy read the sign as she slammed the finicky truck door shut. "I don't know if I've ever been here."

"Well good." Ben smiled. *It'll be new to us both*, is what he would've said if he wanted to continue lying. But he had been here before, as a kid, picking apples with Mom. "I thought it'd be nice to do something outside again."

Tracy shrugged. "I'm down for something new. Show me what you have planned."

"I will." He led her through the entrance, a neat wooden post-and-rail fence separating the lush fertile ground from the firm dirt parking lot. They made their way to a stone building sitting atop a soft hill to the right. It had a front porch with rocking chairs and a wide chimney emanating smoke. They entered, the smell of blueberry and cinnamon floating through the warm air as they approached a tall counter.

"Mm. Donuts." Tracy eyed the mini bakery in the corner. "Did you take me on a donut date? Because I can't say I'd complain."

Ben chuckled. "No, but we certainly can change it to that if you want."

A woman at the counter greeted them. "How can I help you?"

"Yes, we have reservations for the one o'clock tasting."

"Name?"

"It's under Ph—Walker." What the heck was the matter with him? That was one surefire way of blowing his secret, not remembering his fake last name. Maybe subconsciously he wanted to sabotage it, force him to face the truth with Tracy. It wouldn't be that farfetched. He certainly was tired of the head games he played with himself.

"Yes. It's about to start any minute. Go ahead and line up with the others by the door over there. Here's a sticker for each of you, just place it on your clothing so we know you're a part of the group."

"Thank you." He handed Tracy the sticker, a red apple with the word *Taster* across it in black letters.

"Oh, my goodness, if this is a donut tasting I may just have to put this at the top of the list for Aunt Dee."

Ben laughed. "What is it with you and donuts?"

She held up her hands in a shrug. "I'm pretty sure every human likes donuts. It's science."

They joined the rest of the tour group at the door marked *Employees Only*, who introduced themselves as a retired bank branch manager and his wife, and three middle-aged women on a long girls' weekend away from their families.

The door opened and their tour guide appeared, wearing a gray fleece vest with a permanent plastic pin version of the apple sticker. His read *Cidermaker*.

"Good"—he checked his watch—"afternoon now, already. Sheesh. Welcome to you all and thanks for coming out today. My name is Adam, and I'm a craft cidermaker here for Offshore Orchard."

"Ah, cider tasting?" Tracy asked.

Ben nodded.

They followed Adam through the doorway, into the back section of the building. To the left was a set of plastic flaps, leading to outside. Apples rolled down a slanted chute, and workers separated them by hand.

"We serve many purposes here at Offshore Orchard. We sell our apples locally, and you can even pick them by hand here. And of course, we use them in our baked goods, which we also distribute throughout western North Carolina."

"Donuts." Tracy said it like a zombie, and Ben nudged her.

"But a large portion of our harvest is processed into drinks, which is what you all want to hear about, right?"

There were slight nods. Ben hoped he wasn't one of those guides who expected audience participation.

"Oh wow, nobody had their coffee today?"

Tracy turned to Ben and rolled her eyes.

"How about it?" Adam kicked up the enthusiasm. "We want to see how cider is made?"

"Hell yeah!" Tracy raised a fist in the air, a la Breakfast Club. The others turned around, staring.

Ben didn't know whether to hide or join in with Tracy.

"There we go," Adam said. "Watch the language though."

Ben shook his head, and Tracy smiled. "What? No one else was going to do anything. Think about Adam." She pointed to the tour guide as he led them through another door. "He has to be chipper every time he does this. That takes some patience."

Ben watched the guide, who anxiously waited for them to find their standing spots by a giant vat. "You're right."

Adam talked them through the boiling, grinding—called scratting—and filtering of the apples into cider. For the size of the building and orchard, they pumped out a surprising amount of cider each year.

"When the owners established Offshore Orchard fifty-nine years ago, they had to contend with the fact that the original plot of land sat in a dry county and still does today."

"It's a dry county here?" Ben whispered in Tracy's ear. "What about the wine at the art studio?"

She leaned closer to him, that same strawberry ChapStick smell getting his pulse racing. "You can serve and drink alcohol in the county, you just can't sell it."

"Why was that an issue?" The wife of the retiree asked.

"We make our cider fresh, without preservatives," Adam said. "That means if you keep it long enough in your fridge, the fermentation process sets in, and you'll have a jug of fizzy spiked cider."

The girls weekend women laughed. "That's the best kind!"

"Luckily, they proved that their product was alcohol-free upon the point of sale, so they were able to continue the business. When you walk out into our orchard, you'll see that the north end crosses county lines. But that's another tour." Adam winked.

They sat at two picnic tables, each table with glasses of cider out for the tourists. Ben and Tracy sat side by side, the other couple across from them. The three women took up the other table.

"I hope you enjoyed your tour today. In front of you is a sample of our traditional apple cider, served chilled. The other is our hot, spiced apple cider. If you love them as much as all the employees here do, feel free to pick up a jug or two at the store on your way out."

Ben sipped on the hot cider, the glass warming his fingertips and soothing his throat. "What'd you think?"

Tracy sipped on hers and nodded. "It was...nice."

Ben chuckled. "You didn't find it interesting? That they started this with almost nothing, that this all came from seeds and saplings, and grew over decades to make what we are sipping on now?"

Tracy side-eyed him. "When you put it that way, I guess it is pretty amazing."

"See." He bumped shoulders with her. "You just need to see it through different eyes. Then maybe what you see as mundane or boring won't be so much."

"Maybe." She took another sip.

He laughed. At best, he thought she'd tolerate the tour and tasting. He wanted to take her through something slow and methodical, the complete opposite of what she'd put him through on their haunted house date. But the date wasn't over.

"Don't fill up too much."

"Because we're doing donuts?" She raised and lowered her eyebrows several times over.

"We will buy some donuts on our way out, I promise. But we've only begun the date."

"What?"

"Did you honestly think that I'd take Tracy Bennett on a date that only consisted of a historical and factual tour of a manufacturing process?"

She nearly sprayed her cider, and she coughed. "They should put that in the brochure."

He chuckled. "See, I may have only been in Waverly Lake a week, but I know you, Tracy. I'd be a fool to not have something up my sleeve to surprise you with."

She gained her composure again and dried her eyes that had teared up. "Of all the words I could choose from to describe you, surprising is definitely up there."

"That's a good thing, right?"

She winced. "Eh—"

He nudged her again, and she smiled.

"You two are just so precious." The woman across from them cradled the arm of her husband.

Ben's face burned, hot like the spiced cider. "Oh, uh we're—"

"Thank you." Tracy slipped her arm around his, mimicking the woman's gesture. "We're actually high school sweethearts." She eyed him, playfulness beaming from her face.

"Oh. Yes, right." He patted her hand resting on her arm. "When I saw her that day in advanced organic chemistry two, wearing that lab coat and those safety goggles—"

"That was his weakness, those goggles," Tracy added. "He walked in wearing that Katy Perry T-shirt he got at the concert the night before. I mean, how can you resist?"

He fought to keep a straight face.

"Well, you certainly are cute." She smiled, and her husband helped her off the picnic bench. "Enjoy the rest of your afternoon."

"You too." Tracy smiled.

Ben let out the held-back laughter. "See. I don't think it's the place or the activity that matters with you."

"What do you mean?"

She kept him on his toes. He had never worked harder at pleasing someone. It wasn't laborious, as if she demanded to be made happy. He enjoyed the challenge, and the reward. Her happiness was better than any payment he could imagine. But he wasn't going to say all that out loud.

"You know how to make anything an adventure."

She smiled, her fake grip on his arm loosening. She slowed the movement, her fingertips grazing his bicep, her eyes fixated on his. His muscle, his arm, his whole body ached to have the simple touch back.

"Okay, Ben Walker. Just what adventure have you kept up your sleeve?"

Chapter Twenty-One

Tracy still couldn't get over not knowing Offshore Orchard existed. Although if she had known, the chance she would purposely visit on her own accord was slim. After finishing the tour and tasting with Ben, she wondered *why*. It definitely was something different from the usual goings on and things to do in Waverly Lake. Was it because it didn't offer thrills? Did she really seek out over-the-top excitement, passing up on places and experiences that otherwise she would've enjoyed?

"Just where are you taking me? A tour of the orchard?" They walked side by side along a grassy trail, a wide road cutting through the orchard somewhere in the middle. The pathway was marked off, upright metal posts holding a thin rope the entire length of the path.

"I guess they don't want people touching all the fruit," she said.

"They do have an area they allow you to pick apples, if you want to bring some back with you."

"But that's not where we're going?"

Ben shook his head. He enjoyed this secrecy a little too much.

They passed rows and rows of trees, bushy and lush with the season's harvest. Adam the tour guide had said something about the varieties they grew; red and golden delicious and gala, which wasn't the norm for the region. She may not be the best at identifying the types, but the fruits were distinct among the rows, some deep maroon, others a yellow green, another red mottled with yellow.

Two signs, cut out in the shape of the county, stood on wooden posts in succession.

Leaving us high and dry!

Goodbye!

A third and fourth, in a different shape than the other two, greeted them.

Hello!

Rise and shine!

"We just crossed county lines," Ben said. "Remember Adam said they couldn't sell alcohol there?"

She nodded as they approached another building, this one a red barn. Rather, a building painted to look like a red barn, as opposed to an actual wooden red barn.

Ben held open the front door. "Well in this county, they can."

As they entered, a warm burst of air carried with it the sour smell of yeast. Folks gathered around a table to the right, the sign above reading *Tasting Station*. Ahead, a man stood behind a stand, like a maître d' readied to seat them. Instead, he checked their IDs and told them to enjoy responsibly.

They moved past the check-in, and Ben moved aside. "Wait right here."

"Where are you going?"

He headed to the left side of the room, where two employees stood behind a bar, with a few occupied bar stools and bar-height round tables and chairs scattered in the space. The back wall was glass from waist-height to ceiling, large stainless-steel vats occupying most of the visible space. She stepped closer to the window, peeking through the pipes and tubing, trying to glimpse into the large pool of apple product in the large cylinder about as tall as she was.

"All set."

She turned around, and Ben held a wicker basket in one hand with a red plaid blanket draped over his shoulder.

"What's all this?"

"Your surprise." He smiled and nodded for her to follow. He led her back outside, past the barn, and up the hillside. The pathway once again roped them off from entering the heart of the orchard but allowed the public to make the climb. Tracy's breathing quickened, and she wondered if it was from the steepness of the climb or if the air could be thinner at this altitude. It did carry with it an aromatic crispness, a sense of cleanliness as if no one had breathed this air before. She laughed it off, chalking up being winded to not having hiked uphill in a while. Not everyone could be an Aunt Dee.

About three-quarters of the way up, Ben stopped in a grassy clearing. Below sat the soft slope of the orchard, the red barn building halfway down. Beyond that lie the green valley, before the earth rose up into another mountain.

Ben set down the basket and unfolded the blanket. Tracy took one end and helped set it down on the grass. Another group enjoyed the same on the other side of the path and waved to her as she looked over. She waved briefly with a smile and sat on the blanket.

Ben opened the basket and laid out the goodies. There was an assortment of crackers, cheese, sweet sausage, a mini French loaf, three kinds of preserves, and more fruit than any two people could consume in one sitting.

Tracy eyed it all with hungry eyes. "This *is* a surprise."

"And to top it all off." He pulled out four twenty-ounce glass bottles and placed them in a row. "Their signature hard ciders, from sweetest to driest, for our own private tasting."

He handed her a place setting, wrapped neatly in a black cloth napkin, and a clear glass.

"Which one would you like to try first?"

She pointed to the one on the far left. "I'm a dry fan." She smirked. "Like my humor."

Ben shook his head and poured her a glass.

"What?

"Nothing." He poured himself a taste of the cider to match hers.

"Go on. Out with it."

He took a sip and sighed. "Very well."

Tracy wriggled her bottom on the blanket, making herself more stable with her crisscrossed legs, as if bracing for impact.

"I think you like to have the appearance of being dry. I mean, outwardly you can be quite blunt and stern and stubborn. But as I've gotten to know you, I think deep down..." He tapped the top of the bottle on the right end.

She chuckled. "I've been called a lot of things, Ben Walker. I'm not sure sweet is one of them."

"I daresay I call you it now."

She diverted her attention to the spread, not wanting him to read her mind through her eyes like he had the knack of doing.

"You may not see it, but it's there. Through all the surface teasing, you're kind to Aunt Dee. I can tell you love her very much. Same goes for your brother and your niece. When you talk about Hannah, your eyes light up, your face glows. You'd think she was your own daughter the way you gush pride in her achievements."

"Everybody has a soft spot for family." She waved a hand. "That's nothing special."

He caught her hand brushing it off and held it in his. Her playful smile eroded. "Just take a look at your two best friends. Now, I don't know a whole lot about this town, but I do know about this area, and the way people think and perceive things. I can only imagine how hard it has been for George and Sebastian to be open about who they are. I know they consider themselves lucky to have you as a friend. Knowing you, as little as I do, I'm sure you're a fierce advocate for them."

She wasn't used to someone praising her. For anything. She'd made good grades—minus the one failing class in college—but that was expected of a Bennett, according to her parents. She didn't play sports or an instrument and hadn't held a job for longer than a few months at a time.

She was uncomfortable with praise, which caused an internal conflict she hadn't dealt with before. She took pride in being confident, in being herself. Also, it was more than okay to be kind to people. In fact, she wished more people would be, and just the sound of George and Sebastian's names struck a chord, wanting to defend them if anything negative came out of his lips. It was the source of her hatred for gossip because it usually led down the path of insensitivity to downright cruelty. If both things were true, why couldn't she be proud of being kind?

Or was it that Ben looked at her now as if she were the most beautiful creature on earth, with loving eyes and a soft voice speaking his truth, that got her off kilter? How does one respond to that kind of attention?

With diversion. "Tell me, how did you hear about this place?" Tracy popped a grape in her mouth, the juiciness cold yet satisfying.

"Okay, I get it." He slowly backed away. "Enough talk about kind Tracy." He smiled, a painful one to look at because she wanted to smooch that face of his when he did it. "My mom took me here before."

"You...you're from Waverly Lake?" That would explain a lot. Like how Aunt Dee knew him before last week. Yet how would *she* not know him, or anyone else in the town outside of Aunt Dee?

"Oh, well, you know, we'd drive by here, on the way to Aunt Dee's." He took a swig of the cider and a bite of a cracker, smothered in apricot preserves. "My mother's mom and Aunt Dee were good friends." The dry cracker crumbs sprayed out of his mouth, even though he hid his mouth behind his hand.

"You're a right mess." Tracy chuckled.

"Don't make me laugh." He chewed more and took another sip. "Better?"

Ben swallowed again. "Yeah."

"You were saying your grandmother and Aunt Dee were friends?"

"Right. And when my grandmother passed, my mom kept the friendship going. Aunt Dee would even baby—"

"Sorry to interrupt." A woman stood over them, clenching a shawl around her shoulders. "I was wondering if you had any spare napkins? My friend over there had a bit of an accident."

Tracy looked across the path at the other group. One of the women held her arms out, shaking them over the grass. An amber patch splotched her white sweater.

"I don't think so." Ben rifled through the basket.

Tracy unraveled her place setting. "Here, take mine. I haven't used it yet."

"Oh, thank you. You sure?"

She nodded. "Looks like she needs it more than I do."

"Oh, bless your heart." The woman retreated to her picnic, and the women chuckled and chatted over the spill.

Ben stared at her, not doing a good job at concealing the smile.

"What?" But as she asked it, she knew what he thought.

"Deep down." He tapped the sweetest bottle of cider again.

"How about we drink that instead of the whole metaphor-for-Tracy thing?"

"Can't argue with that. I'll need some more food in my stomach though."

They made quite a team in preparing a fancy lunch. Tracy sliced bread and handed Ben crackers as he slathered on jams and cheeses and slices of sausage. Tracy divvied the fruit to make each of them a medley on their plates and they worked through two of the samplers of hard cider.

When they had more than enough—at least Tracy thought it was a sinful amount of food to eat in one sitting—she lie on her stomach, face in her hands, staring out over the orchard and valley. The sun was blocked by a thin layer of white, wispy clouds, yet the trees still cast shadows down the hill. With the uniform distance between them, they made a checkerboard of dark, shadowy spots and lighter daylight spots.

"It really is beautiful here." It wouldn't take much to close her eyes and take a nap, with nothing but the birds, and the apple tree leaves, rustling in the wind. "I think it may be one of the prettiest places around here."

"I'd have to say Waverly Lake has a lot going for it in terms of views. The lake, the mountains, trees, Carolina sky. What's not to like?"

Tracy would normally think of a list of things not to like about Waverly Lake, and promptly share them. Instead, she focused on the things of beauty he had mentioned. Views she had taken for granted most of her life. There were very few places she'd been to that rivaled her own hometown. Ben had a way of making her pause and taste the apples.

"This is up there in my books," Ben continued. "But it's not my absolute favorite spot here."

Tracy sat up, interest piqued. "You've been here a week, and you have a favorite spot?" She eyed him suspiciously.

"I sure do."

"And where is this magical spot that beats all this?" She held out her arms, presenting the postcard view.

"How about we pack up, and I'll show you?"

Chapter Twenty-Two

BEN PARKED THE TRUCK AT WOODSMAN'S LODGE. THE date had gone more smoothly than he could have ever imagined. Except for that near slip-up. He had almost revealed Aunt Dee babysat him from time to time, a fact that surely would've given Tracy pause, if not a direct line between the dots she tried to connect.

Here amongst the shadow of the hillside forest, the air was cool and damp. While the orchard sat on the eastern leeward side, sheltered from wind, Woodman's Lodge faced south, not entirely protected, yet not as bad as it could've been.

Tracy closed her jacket tighter. "If this is some roundabout way to say the lodge is your favorite place, you could've said so back there and saved me the time wondering."

He grinned, shaking his head. "No. Not exactly. Come on."

He walked to the left of the cabin, heading west. Tracy followed, examining the trees and pathway as if for the first time. While she obviously enjoyed the bigger, more fantastical events for excitement, Ben wondered if she appreciated what he put her through right now. The anticipation, the anxiety of figuring out the secret he possessed. It had been the same at Offshore Orchard. She just couldn't wait to hear what surprise he had around the next corner.

They joined the established and well-trodden Truelove Trail, traipsing over the same path he had arrived on last week. It was hard to imagine he'd only been back that long. So much had happened, between the long working days with Aunt Dee, to the dates he'd had with Tracy, not to mention the clothes-buying outings and meetings in town.

As quickly as the leaves of the Appalachian woods burned through all the colors of fire, he too sensed he was different. The future of Phillips Manor clung to his thoughts as readily as the Virginia creeper around its decaying columns. At first, he was sure he wanted to stay out of it. But now? How could he let it go to waste? For what, a parking lot? Because he didn't have the courage to claim it? Claiming it meant admitting his name. It meant walking around town as a different person, and not an hour went by that he didn't consider taking the leap.

Then there was Tracy. If time spent in Waverly Lake increased his propensity to stick around, Tracy damn near sealed the deal. She had an outward beauty all to her own. If she didn't already know everyone in town, she'd turn heads. It made him think of the places she'd visited, the adventures she had taken. What did that mean for her dating life? Did she date at all?

"You're being awfully quiet." Tracy followed his steps along the trail, eventually reaching his side as the trail widened.

"Sorry. I get in my head when I'm out here."

"No apologies necessary. Sometimes I say too much and don't get in my head enough." She flashed a smile.

"What? You? I can't imagine." He winked.

"Why do you think they call this Truelove Trail? I've never really thought about it until now."

Ben shrugged. "Maybe because it's wide enough to hike side by side? A lot of the AT isn't. Or maybe it's the site of some famous settlers falling in love?" He snapped his fingers. "I know. It's a test for couples—if they complete the trail intact, then they must truly be in love."

"All right. Maybe going back to quiet wouldn't be a bad idea." She giggled.

He pointed to a path branching off Truelove Trail. "This way."

"What is this?" She examined the trail, her look almost apprehensive.

"Something I've been working on." His shoes sunk a little deeper on the freshly cleared path, although the fallen leaves had already made a go at blending it with the rest of the forest floor. "Whenever Aunt Dee isn't sending me off on an errand, and I've finished her daily tasks, I come out here. I've moved most of the larger stones out of the way and had to trim the extended limbs, but for the most part it is clear."

"Where does it go?"

"Right here." He stepped into the clearing, about a hundred square feet of flat mountain floor, half-covered in dirt and leaves, the further half the top of a smooth rock formation.

"I trimmed a few of the branches on the edges here to help with the view." He turned around, smiling. "But this right here—this is my favorite spot."

Tracy bit her lip. He extended a hand to her, compelling her to step closer to the edge, but not too close, where a good portion of Waverly Lake could be seen for one hundred eighty degrees.

Her eyes fixated on the lake, oblivious to his extended hand.

"Are you all right? It's nothing to be scared of. We're only a few meters above water level. It's solid and not slippery, at least not today. Maybe when it rains it wouldn't be wise to walk on the stone, but—"

"I'm sorry." Tracy shook out of her trance. She accepted his hand and joined him in the center of the clearing. "It's not that."

"What is it?"

Her lips quivered and her face had lost its usual fiery glow. "I remember this place."

"It's still technically on Aunt Dee's property. I checked."

"No, I mean, from a long time ago. I didn't really remember it until seeing it now." She shook her head and sat on the ground, arms wrapped around her bent legs.

"Oh?" With each rock he had cleared and muddy step sucking his shoes, he wondered if Tracy would remember. Not just remember, but feel about it the way he felt about it.

"Remember I told you about the Phillips family, when we were by the house?"

Ben took a seat next to Tracy, the stone floor colder than the air.

"Their son, Hunter...he and I used to come here. We'd play in the woods all afternoon and sneak out here. I'd jump into the water."

"Always the daredevil, huh?"

She smiled, though her attention was twenty years away. "I'd try to get Hunter to jump, but he wasn't that confident in swimming yet. The water would be so cold in early summer that I'd run through the woods for a good ten, twenty minutes to get hot enough to accept it. Then we'd just lie out in the sun, on this rock."

She extended her legs and leaned back, lying flat on her back. She held her head and stared up at the sky. "I can't believe I almost forgot about it."

"You were just a young kid." His worry gave a jolt of adrenaline. "Right? I mean, that's what it sounds like."

"Yeah," she said. "Just a young, stupid kid." She sat up again, as if propelled back into the present. "You know, Hunter was my best friend back then. I thought we'd be best friends forever, that's how stupid I was."

She did remember. Everything.

"I don't think it's farfetched to think a friendship could last a lifetime," he said.

"It's naive," she said. "I mean, I make friends now, everywhere I go, and we stay connected. But it's not like what I had with Hunter. Not what I thought I'd have with him. I guess children are overly optimistic over just about everything."

He wanted to defend her five-year-old thinking, but she continued, a passion in her that had to come out.

"I wonder if that little kid—well, adult now—knew how heartbroken I was when he left." She met his eyes, fervor in every fiber of her being. "We promised that no matter what, we'd write to each other until we could be together again."

A knot formed in Ben's throat. "What happened?"

"I kept my end of the bargain. I wrote letters, about what was going on here, in my house, at school. About anything and everything. At first, I got a few of his in return, but then after some time...my letters came back. He had moved on to somewhere else, and we lost contact. I guess what hurt me the most was that I hadn't moved." She looked up at him. "He could've still written to me, here in Waverly Lake. But I guess he didn't see our friendship the way I had seen it."

You couldn't be more wrong. He wanted to hold her, grab her in his arms and say a thousand sorrys. He did stop writing letters, but not because of forgetting her. He had moved several times, but she was right, he could've continued. But that was during a time he'd

wanted to be forgotten, wanted his last name to mean nothing to the people around him. He didn't want to be sought after and make decisions his dead parents had placed upon him.

Was it really so different now? He had a chance to correct his wrongdoings. Tell her everything, make her feel better. Then maybe, just maybe, he could hold her in an embrace and be forgiven.

"Enough of me being a downer." She sat, legs crisscrossed. "How'd you find this place? What made you put in the work on the trail? I can't imagine it was easy."

"It was..." He contemplated making light of it, but knew better. "Pretty agonizing."

She chuckled. Yep, honesty paid off.

"You can't see the lake much from the cabin. But, with this piece of land still being part of the property, I figured it wouldn't hurt to have a way for guests to enjoy the lake. It's not that far of a walk, nor is it a difficult one. Maybe we could set up a few Adirondack chairs out here, secure them to the ground."

It was impossible to miss the anguish in Tracy's face. "You don't like the idea?"

She looked out at the lake. "It's not that." She stood and slipped her hands in her back pockets. "This was a special place for us—me and Hunter. It was our own secret place that no one else ever came to."

His heart ached for her, for them as children. They didn't know what adult life was like in their infinite optimism. He longed for it again, so they could be together as the two of them against the world, without the worries of reality.

And she really had loved him. It was all he cared about knowing. She had loved their friendship, and it meant as much to her as it did to him.

"Okay, Ben Walker. You won me over."

If he had been drinking, he would've choked. "Excuse me?"

"Set my sentimentality aside. I think you have a great idea."

"Really?" he said, skeptical of the change of heart and embarrassed he misinterpreted winning her affection.

"Yes, really. It's a special place, and it should be available for anyone who stays at Aunt Dee's. This is a view to be seen, not a view to hide." She walked in a circle, intermittently looking at the ground and lake. "You can fit four chairs. Maybe arrange them in a semicircle around a firepit. We'd have to see what the regulations are for that around here, but wouldn't it be a great spot for sunset drinks, or even to have a hot cup of coffee in the morning?"

"It sounds perfect."

At that, her face beamed. She stared at him for a second longer than he was comfortable with. "What?" He fidgeted with his hands and shuffled his position until leaning on his left foot and holding his hips. "Are you scheming something?"

She shook her head, amused. "No. You just keep coming up with the surprises this afternoon. First with the apple orchard, then the cider picnic. You know, when you told me you had a favorite spot in Waverly Lake, I had assumed it would be one of the common touristy areas, like Lakeshore Park, or even one of the islands." She scanned the view one more time. "I never imagined it was something like this."

He shrugged, abashedly. "I'm a simple man. Just give me a bit of nature and I'm happy."

She smirked, an impish delight across her face. "That second part may be true."

He held his mouth agape, mind whirring to understand her meaning.

"But a simple man?" She waved her finger. "That part I'm not so sure."

Chapter Twenty-Three

Saturday, October 15

"Don't feel obligated to go. I know how you are on the water." Tracy stood next to Ben at the dock, *Tin Can* bobbing ever so slightly in the lake's wavelets. Her leather jacket didn't hold in warmth as well as insulated coats, but it did wonders to block the wind, a more important feat on the water.

"Is that your way of telling me you don't want me to go?" He slipped his hands into his puffy navy vest. He had declined the offer of a life vest, and Tracy wondered if he wore the down vest as a psychological life preserver. She had reassured him George and Sebastian had plenty onboard anyway.

"Not at all. I don't mean it like that." With the way he had acted that first day out on the water, heading to town, she didn't want to put him through another anxiety-ridden outing. But she did want to spend time with him. At this point, she'd rather stay behind with him, if that's what he wanted. "I mean, I want you to go come along, if that's what you want." With how much her mind was an open book, why was it so hard for her to articulate what she really thought? Anything she said sounded just shy of indifference.

"George and Sebastian go all out for these dinner cruises. And I do mean dinner cruises. You'd think they ran a professional side hustle the way they treat them. I just didn't want you to be in the position of not being able to eat out there, or feel you had to even if you didn't feel well." It was a little clearer and more convincing. The bottom line was she didn't want him sick and miserable and feeling obligated to hide it out of politeness.

"Oh, I don't get seasickness, if that's what you mean." He took a deep breath and looked out over the water. "If my stomach is in knots, it's because I'm worried of falling overboard, or the ship sinking. Not because of motion sickness."

"Okay. I guess that's better than seasickness." She shrugged, unsure of it.

George and Sebastian arrived with a blast of the boat horn, startling Ben. George stood at the wheel, focusing on docking while Sebastian waved in greeting.

Tracy caught the line from Sebastian and helped secure the boat to the short dock. *Milady* was everything *Tin Can* wasn't— wooden, sleek, shiny, and well-maintained. With a royal-blue hull and white trim that popped in contrast with the rich, mahogany stain finish, the motorboat was something out of Kennedy-esque mid-twentieth-century Cape Cod. A flagpole off the stern held the American flag, and just below it, a rainbow flag.

"You should learn how to *pahk*," she said in her best accent.

"Okay, I've been to Massachusetts, and not once did I hear anyone speak like that." Sebastian offered her a hand onto the deck.

"Must not have been in the right *yahd*."

He closed his eyes. "Just stop." He wasn't truly disgusted by her stereotyped accent, judging by the giggle he broke into. It wasn't often Sebastian laughed, but Tracy did manage to make him giggle. Which, coming from Sebastian, was infectious. Sometimes her cheeks hurt spending an evening out with him.

She offered her hand to Ben, who took it, and hobbled onto the deck. She grabbed his elbow with her other hand, stabilizing him. "You okay?" She said it softly enough for only Ben to hear. He nodded.

"Good to see you again." George put out his hand, and Ben shook it.

"You too. Thanks for having me. I hear it's a privilege to be invited." He nearly winked a twinkling eye at Tracy.

"I don't know about a privilege, but I do hope you came hungry."

Sebastian took his place standing next to George by the wheel. "You'd think we're feeding half of Waverly with the amount of food we brought."

"Shall we?" George checked the passengers for the okay, and Tracy untied and brought in the line.

Ben grappled with his footing as they set away from Woodsman's Lodge, out into the open water of Waverly Lake. *Milady* rode smoothly over the water, with no motor vibration under Tracy's feet or fumes pumped through the air. It cut through the water, the surface of which looked covered in tiny rivulets from the low-lying breeze. They sparkled with the reflection of the remaining golden sunlight.

Tracy took Ben's hand. "Come on."

She brought him forward, and they sat in the two seats positioned in front of the helm. The captain's chair was tall enough, despite George's short stature, to afford him full view ahead without Tracy or Ben getting in the way.

"You doing okay?"

Ben had yet to let go of her hand. He stared at the water, biting his lip, then looked at the grip he held. "Sorry." He let go and grappled onto the arm rest.

"It's okay. I can have George slow down if you're not comfortable."

He simply shook his head, as if speaking would disrupt whatever psychological equilibrium he had achieved.

They rode in silence, the boat picking up speed, and Sebastian and George chatting behind them in shouts now and then. They approached an island, a smaller one situated in the western branch of the lake, not too far off from Danny's house on the outskirts of town.

George anchored them some ten meters from shore. "I thought we could cook dinner here and watch the sun set."

It had to have been the best spot to see the sun set over the western mountains. They were west enough to be clear of other islands and most of the main boat traffic. It was quieter than in the corner of the lake by Pearson's. Plus, the houses were scarcer, further apart and set back from the water. It didn't feel like people were watching them from their back decks.

George attached a metal grill to a post along the stern near the starboard side. Sebastian dragged the overstuffed cooler and helped him with dinner. It took only a matter of minutes before the burgers were on the hot grill. Tracy caught whiffs of the grilled beef and peppers and onions when the slight breeze let up.

"Are you all right?" She stood over Ben, who hadn't moved from his seat.

"Yeah. You don't have to keep checking up on me you know."

She sat next to him. "I'm sorry. I just want you to go have a good time."

"Here we are." Sebastian handed each of them a filled wine glass. "I hope you like red. I told George I'll be damned if we serve white wine with beef."

Ben took a sip. "It's very good. Thank you."

Sebastian walked away, seemingly pleased with the wine verdict.

Ben looked at her, smiling with a tinge of red stain on his lips. He held up the glass. "It can only help, right?"

She smiled and clinked glasses with him. "To it helping."

They both chuckled and sipped on the wine.

"I promise to stop asking you for the rest of the night." Tracy turned to him. "From now on, if you're not okay, it's up to you to tell me."

"Fair enough." He took another sip and turned his gaze to the pink sky over the mountain ridges. "You know, if I'm going to be around Waverly Lake longer, I'd better get over my fear of the water."

She heavily gulped down the mouthful of wine and set the glass in a holder. "Is that the plan? Staying in Waverly Lake longer?" For a second, she had forgotten her unknown future. It was just him and her, sitting out on the lake, watching the sun set, in this moment. And she wanted his answer to be yes.

"Honestly, I wasn't sure what life was going to bring me, coming here. I didn't really know what I'd do, or how long I'd stay." He handed her his glass to put next to hers.

"But now that you're here?" She suppressed the creeping thoughts of leaving Aunt Dee's for New Zealand, Sara needing an answer soon—as in yesterday. She clung to the hope that Ben would be here, and he'd be here when she got back, or dare she even think it? That she'd not go at all and stay here. With him.

"I think I'm starting to see what I want in life. What I'm meant to do."

She bit her lip and sunk back in her chair, taking in the gradient of colors to the west and at the same time not processing them at all. "Which is?"

He smiled, a soft smile that melted the chill of the breeze on her face. She reached over and touched her cool fingertips to his cheek, grazing his face, feeling the coarse stubble of beard that had grown in the last day or two.

She wasn't sure what his answer was going to be, but she sensed it had something to do with her. With them. And she couldn't help letting him know she felt the same way. That she wanted him to be a part of her future, that the connection they'd made this past week was more than that of two coworkers, or even two friends. Deep down she was attached to this man, connected in a way she had never been with any other man.

Whether it was the red wine, or the lulling of the boat on the water, or the fiery painted sky ending this day, she wanted to savor this moment. This man. Nothing else mattered.

He touched her back, his fingertips playing with hers until he wrapped them around her hand. He lowered her hand from his cheek and gently tugged, pulling her closer. With his other, he stroked her forehead, tucking away the loose strands of hair behind her ear. His hand worked down and caressed the back of her neck. His warm breath tickled her lips, and she closed her eyes, shutting out George and Sebastian, the boat, the water, the world.

She tugged at his vest and pulled him in, meeting his lips. The warm, soft lips tasted of wine and longing. She wanted to laugh in delight and cry in agony, the craving to kiss his lips, to lock her soul with his, one she hadn't realized she wanted this badly until it finally happened. He tasted her back, pressing her neck closer into him. She didn't want to break for air. This man was her oxygen, her energy.

"Who's ready for—Oh." Sebastian's voice traveled across the boat, but it took Tracy an eon to actually listen. Ben stopped at the same time she did, breaking their embrace apart. Her chest rose and fell heavily, as if she now breathed new air, air that Ben also shared.

Tracy finally looked back at Sebastian standing by George and the grill.

"We can keep it warm for a while if you like." George nudged Sebastian.

Tracy and Ben both looked down as if there was something magical to see between them. She touched her cheek, as flushed as the wine she now longed for to fill the void.

"Well, I'm famished." Ben shouted back to them. He kept his gaze on Tracy for a few more seconds, intertwining his fingers with hers on the seat where the other two couldn't see. "What do you say? Grab some dinner?"

She smirked, the smile impossible to wash off. She pulled her hand away from him and investigated him slyly.

"What?"

"You never answered my question."

"What question?"

"You were saying you were starting to see what you wanted in life, and I asked what that was."

He stood and offered his hand. She took it, standing to meet him face to face. Now he was the one with the sly look.

"Are you going to answer it?"

He leaned closer, his cheek so near to hers it felt hot. His breath tickled her ear and neck as he whispered.

"I already have."

Chapter Twenty-Four

Sunday, October 16

"Regulations state we can manage a fire pit as long as there is a certain amount of clearance, which works if we place it here." Tracy pointed at the schematic of the rock outcropping.

"That leaves ample room for four chairs out there, and we can even put a little side table here." Ben traced his finger on the paper, crossing his arm over Tracy's. They briefly met eyes, and Ben read the giddiness in hers.

Aunt Dee looked over the two of them. "I don't know. What if someone gets too close to the edge, or, heaven forbid, a child falls into the lake? Seems like we'd need a guardrail."

"We looked into that as well." Ben rolled out another sheet of paper on top of the original. Of course, he had thought of that. As someone who couldn't swim, it was something on his mind since he had rediscovered the place upon his return. Heck, it was on his mind as a kid hanging out there with Tracy.

"There are plenty of spots along Truelove Trail and others around the lake that don't have protection," Tracy said. "It's not required, but most of those are on public lands. Since this would be on your privately-owned property, it's probably best to have it."

"We can have one like this, so it doesn't obstruct the view." Ben awaited Aunt Dee's verdict. The spot held a special place for him and Tracy, although at first he didn't know if Tracy had remembered. But Tracy's enthusiasm only grew the past few days as they worked together on the proposal. Aunt Dee had the final say and could squash the whole project with one word.

Aunt Dee eyed him, scrutinizing his hair or shaven face for all he knew, looking for a sign—something—to find as an excuse to shut it down. She turned to Tracy, whose eyes softened. She gave a gentle nod and waited, likely as anxious as he was.

"Give me a detailed budget and timeline to complete it. Then we'll talk."

Tracy looked at him and they relaxed, as if they had held their breath for the last minute. It wasn't a no, which was as close to a yes as they could get for now.

"Now that's enough standing around. Tracy, you'd better go pick up the doors Howie repainted. He's expecting you this morning and can help you load."

"Yes, ma'am." Unfazed by Aunt Dee, Tracy winked at Ben, grabbed the truck keys, and headed out the door.

Ben rolled up the crude drawings. He could work on itemizing a budget for her this morning and still have time to complete his work by the end of the day.

"You two seem to be getting along okay." Aunt Dee rested her elbow on the counter, chin in hand.

"Yeah." He looked at Aunt Dee, the lines near her eyes multiplying as she grinned. "Okay, fine. More than okay."

"You know I care about you, right?"

He nodded, awaiting the Tracy-won't-be-pinned-down speech everyone in town seemed to want to give him.

"But that's my great-niece. I've spent more time with her than most great-aunts do. Have you thought about what you're doing after all of this? Not to mention who you really are. I know my Tracy, and I can see it in her eyes. She's falling for you."

It wasn't exactly news to him. They had kissed, a deep magnetic melt-into-a-puddle kiss on the boat yesterday. One that signaled she felt for him as he did for her. The rest of the evening was bliss, wrapping his arm over her shoulder, Tracy resting her hand on his knee, slapping it playfully when Sebastian made her laugh. They acted like a couple, and it felt genuine. Still, it was nice to hear it from someone else who knew her. That he hadn't been deluded to think she cared for him.

"Except she's falling for a version of you that isn't all of you." Aunt Dee eroded his euphoric memory of holding Tracy, of tasting her lips, and feeling her curls in his fingertips.

"So, as I see it, you have more than one problem on your hands." Aunt Dee raised her eyebrows high on her forehead with her scolding. "That's why you should find it as no surprise I spoke with Steve Albertson."

"What?" It was a surprise, even if Aunt Dee somewhat justified her actions.

"By my calculations you still have five days to claim the property, Ben. I have it on good word that after the last town meeting, the council has decided to put the property up for auction once it's in their hands."

"What? As in, anyone with the right amount of money can buy it?"

"And do with it what they want with it, as long as it's legal. They've already filed to change the zoning to mixed, in order to attract commercial investors. Which means it could very well end up being a parking lot."

Ben closed his eyes, picturing the house demolished to rubble.

"Now I know it might be tricky with the taxes and sorting out the financials, but don't you think it's worth trying?" She looked at the front door, as if Tracy's ghost watched them. "Is there nothing here you find worth staying for?"

He backed away from the counter. "It's not that simple."

"Sure it is. The way I see it, you can leave, find a life elsewhere, and forget about Tracy. Or you can stay and perpetuate the lie you've been living. Or stay and be who you are. All of you. And taking care of that property, whether you keep it or sign it right over to someone else, is mandatory if you choose the honest route."

"I've thought about it, Aunt Dee. Trust me. It's most of what I think about in my waking hours. It even infiltrates my sleeping hours. My heart is pulling me here. I can't help but want to stay. I just don't know if I'm ready for what that means. Dad was one of the most notorious surgeons in the state and donated an entire library wing. I heard the county community center has a memoriam plaque for Mom after all her hours she devoted." His voice cracked, which didn't help his eyes dry the water collecting in them. But how good it felt, relieving, to talk to someone else about it, someone who knew the truth about everything. "How could I possibly be ready to fill those shoes?"

"Oh honey." She took his hands, Ben letting go of the rolled-up papers, letting them fall to the floor. "You're not filling their shoes. That's not what they wanted for you, nor does anyone else in this town. Your parents wanted you to have your own shoes, pursue your own dreams. If that meant selling the house to do so, they were for it."

"Really?"

"Yes, of course." She chuckled softly. "Besides, no one could fill your father's shoes."

"I know. He was the perfect man—doctor, loving husband, wonderful father."

"I meant he had enormously large feet." She laughed, and it helped clear the aching in his heart. "Oh, your father had his flaws."

"That's hard to believe."

"Everybody does, and if you don't believe that, then that's one of your flaws." She sighed. "Come here." She wrapped her arms around him, holding him tight. She smelled of menthol and lemon from her vapor rub, and baby powder infused her sweater from her dryer sheets. She smelled like home.

She let go only after he motioned for it to happen. He wiped his eyes and picked up the proposal plans off the floor.

"Maybe if you choose to stay, I'll tell you a bit about your father's flaws."

He smiled. "I'd like that."

"It's a deal then. Now, what about Tracy?"

"You just get right to it, don't you?"

Aunt Dee looked half amused and half eager to hear his answer.

"I'll tell her tomorrow night. It's our final date to scope out." She deserved to know the truth, whether he stayed or not. After the past week, the great dates they had, he was fooling himself in thinking he wouldn't give them a chance to be a *them*. The kiss yesterday—oh how it made his mind spin and toes tingle just thinking about it—was that next step. One he didn't think Tracy took lightly, and he wasn't going to throw that all away over his fear of who he was. It was time for the truth, time to move toward the future. Together.

Aunt Dee hesitated, staring him down. He never knew if she was critiquing him or fishing for her next words. But her response was simple. "Good." She patted his arm and made for the kitchen.

The phone rang at the front desk, and Aunt Dee turned around.

"I got it." Ben picked up, setting down the papers on the desk. "Woodsman's Lodge, how may I help you?"

"G'day, I'm trying to reach Tracy." The accent on the line was thick.

Ben peeked through the front window, the pickup truck nowhere in sight. "She is out right now. Can I take a message?"

"Just tell her Sara called. She has my number, but she doesn't have to call me back. I've emailed her the itinerary for the rescheduled flight. It heads out Tuesday—"

"Um..." He cleared his dry throat. "The flight to?" What right did he have in asking? Other than the person he was falling in love with was leaving and didn't tell him. His insides twisted, and he scrambled for a lie. "And from? She may need to buy a bus ticket to the airport right away, but I don't know when she'll be back to get this message."

"Oh, right. That's awfully good of ya. Her flight is out of Charlotte, Tuesday at eleven a.m., and it's to Sydney via Los Angeles. I told her already she can stay with me, and we'll fly together to Auckland. Tell her this was the only option that fit all our schedules, with Amelia having to be back for February."

His heart had to be heard through the phone. He grasped for words, for air. "Okay, I'll give her the message."

"Thanks for that. I'll call again—"

Ben hung up the phone and stared at the receiver.

Tracy was going to New Zealand.

That wasn't a simple weekend trip. Or a week-long trip. What had the woman—Susan? Sara?—said? *To be back for February.*

She had planned a trip to New Zealand and would be gone for months. *Months.* Yet hadn't said a word about it.

Did Aunt Dee know about it? No, she couldn't have. Why would Aunt Dee push him to stay if she knew Tracy would be gone for months, halfway around the world?

How could they start a relationship that way? Not that he was one hundred percent sure Tracy wanted a full-blown relationship, but...he had felt something more than a whim, more than fun, yesterday. He had felt it all week, building up in him and bursting to come out. To connect with her.

Even if she did feel the same way he did, and they could make it through the first months being apart...she hadn't told him about it. Sure, he had a secret of his own to tell her, one that plagued him all week. But he had made up his mind to tell her. He vowed to Aunt Dee he would tell her tomorrow night. There was always the risk Tracy would turn away from him once she found out, but he was willing to take that risk now. Could they start a relationship with this secret Tracy had kept from him?

What he needed was time to process this. The one thing he just found out he was running in short supply of.

"Who was that?" Aunt Dee appeared from the kitchen.

Ben stared at her, not really distinguishing any features. Rather he registered a blurry figure that emanated noises from somewhere atop its body.

"Ben?" Aunt Dee approached and tapped the reception counter.

He snapped out of his stupor. "What?"

"The phone call? Was it for a reservation?"

"Oh. No." He shook his head. What if he hadn't been the one to answer? Was Tracy ever going to tell him, or was she just going to leave Tuesday for him to find out on his own? There was only one way to find out.

"It was a friend of Tracy's. Told her she was out for the morning."

Aunt Dee shook her head. "I can't say I like her friends calling on the business line. But at least Tracy's sticking to the rules of the cell phone."

"Yeah." He pulled forth a twinge of a smile.

He had promised Aunt Dee to tell Tracy the truth tomorrow night at their last date. He meant to keep his promise. But now he had another secret to address, one that may disrupt his plans after all.

Chapter Twenty-Five

Monday, October 17

S*ARA CALLED.* C*HECK YOUR EMAIL.*

Aunt Dee had said Ben answered the phone and took down the message. That's all the information she could give out. Was there any way Ben heard what the email was about?

She had to tell Aunt Dee about the New Zealand trip. By the time she got the message, she had less than forty-eight hours until her flight out of Charlotte, and she couldn't wait any longer to let Dee know.

With the sky overcast and breeze steady from the west, Tracy maneuvered *Tin Can* across the lake to Pearson's. She wanted to arrive early before the evening's date in the hopes Danny was working. As much as Tracy was an open book about most of her life, there weren't a whole lot of people she was comfortable enough with to talk about relationships. To be honest, she'd never really had to talk about a relationship because her life was so up in the air she had never considered any serious enough to do what she was about to do. If she did date, it was for fun, knowing full-well—and stating it clearly—that it wouldn't go from dates to *dating*.

She docked the boat, tying the bow and stern lines to the cleats.

The last time she was on a boat was on *Milady*. Just thinking about it made her blush. The kissing happened naturally, along with the hand holding, caressing, and laughter of a perfect evening where they didn't care what to label this beautiful thing of theirs.

With morning came care. They couldn't avoid talking about it forever, although they were doing a heck of a job at it in the meantime.

"Tracy!" Danny waved from *Kare Bear*, sitting at the tiller. Kara bundled up with a scarf and hat near the bow, waving to Tracy.

Tracy reached the end of the dock as the sailboat slowly drifted her way. "I was hoping to catch you here. Wanted to chat."

"Oh? Everything okay?"

It was a loaded question—one she couldn't answer before they slipped by her.

"Hop on and we'll talk."

"I have to be back in half an hour."

"We'll drop you back off. Right, Kara?"

Kara nodded and waved Tracy on.

Tracy had to think fast. If she didn't jump on board not only would she have time to kill, but she'd miss the opportunity to talk over her thoughts before seeing Ben. Even though she didn't expect to share her feelings with Kara, she *had* to talk.

"Okay."

Danny nodded to Kara, who moved midship and threw out the line. Tracy caught it, quickly wrapping it around a corner pylon, slowing down *Kare Bear*. With line in hand, reaching out for Kara with the other, she hopped on board. Kara secured her landing and helped retrieve the line.

"Sorry to crash your evening. You were heading out now?"

"We had an early dinner," Danny said. "Thought we'd go out on the water. The original plan was to watch the sunset, but not much to see in this weather."

Kara bit her lip, thinking over her sunset cruise for the five-hundredth time. They had made such a connection, breaking through the barrier of friendship into a relationship. The next morning had gone well, talking over the plans on the property, but then it was like Aunt Dee had assigned them jobs that kept them apart. When Tracy did have a minute to pop by Ben's room last night either he was out somewhere or already asleep. Which, with the way Aunt Dee worked her yesterday, had not been too disappointing, since it meant she could hit her pillow sooner.

"Judging by your quietness, you *do* have something to talk about." Danny sat at the stern, leaning back, making himself comfortable to hear a long story. As if the boat needed no guidance in its drift away from Pearson's.

She wanted to talk, but now that she had the opportunity, why was it so hard to come out with it? "Where's Hannah this evening?"

"That's what you wanted to talk about?"

"Danny." Kara shot him a look.

"Mom and Dad are watching her at my place."

"Wow. That's a big step." Usually Hannah's nanny, Mrs. Warren, or Tracy when she was in town, babysat Hannah. Their parents, especially Mom, found it difficult to be with Hannah by herself. Mom had made leaps and bounds over the past months. "How do you feel about it?"

"Trying not to think about it, thanks." Danny switched back to being attentive with the tiller, looking ahead at the sparsely occupied lake.

"Everyone will be fine," Kara said. "They have both our cell phone numbers, and Mrs. Warren's and—"

"I know, I know," Danny said, stopping her. "Doesn't mean it's not a little hard for me to leave her."

Kara smiled and walked back to Danny. She sat beside him, rubbing his arm and resting her head on his shoulder.

Tracy shook her head. "You two are disgustingly cute."

Danny gave a toothy smile, reveling in her back-handed compliment.

"Speaking of." Kara lifted her head, straightening up. "What's going on with you and Ben? Last time I saw you together at the art studio, it seemed like things were going rather well."

Tracy let out a deep breath. It was the reason she asked to talk in the first place. *So just do it then.*

"Can I ask you two something? In all seriousness."

"Depends. Are you avoiding Kara's question about you and Ben?"

"No, I'm actually addressing it." She avoided the temptation to roll her eyes at her brother. "How did you two know that what you felt for each other was..." She searched for the words. "The real thing? That you knew you had to be with each other?"

"Okay." Danny's half-joking face turned serious. He looked at Kara, who still had her arms holding onto his. "I guess you can say that before Kara returned to Waverly Lake, I was in a rut. I had my routine and went through the motions of my life, taking care of Hannah, putting in my mechanic hours. I wasn't necessarily unhappy. But when Kara showed up..." He looked at her again, as if conveying his thoughts to her head without words. "I didn't know I could love home as much as I do."

Kara grinned ear to ear and rubbed his knee. "It's the same with me. I honestly was dreading coming back here, but then, I saw Danny."

"It wasn't exactly that fast," he joked.

She chuckled. "No, I was reluctant, but eventually—" she turned her gaze to Tracy, "—you see the world through a different lens. I saw the town through Danny's eyes. I even saw New York differently. Everything with Danny was right, and without Danny was wrong."

Danny kissed her cheek and Kara blushed.

"I appreciate your honesty," Tracy said. "Even if it's obnoxiously sweet."

"Is that what you're feeling about Ben?" Kara said it matter-of-factly, without kidding behind it.

"We...kissed. The other day. And up until then—no, who am I kidding?"

Danny and Kara looked about as confused as she was emotionally distraught.

"As much as I wanted to keep my distance from him, we've just grown closer and closer. It feels right with him, you know? I don't know how else to explain it. I've never connected with someone like this before. Somehow, he knows me. He understands everything I stand for and what I don't."

"How did it feel?" Kara asked. "Kissing him? Did it feel right?"

Tracy tussled her curls. "It felt more than right. I know this sounds cheesy, but it felt magical. Like something in the universe connected, or was aligned, or something." She felt so stupid for saying it out loud.

"Let me ask you this," Danny said. "What is it that you need our opinion for? It sounds like what you have with Ben is amazing."

"It is amazing. But...at the same time, I also don't know him. Like there's some unknown about him that I can't reach."

"Maybe that part will take time," Kara said.

"I'm not sure if we have time." Tracy folded her arms, tucking her hands underneath to warm them from the chill.

"What do you mean?" Danny asked.

"I had it planned for after the fall."

"What planned?"

"A trip to New Zealand. I was going with some friends I met back in Australia. But stuff came up, and they pushed it earlier."

"How early?" Danny shuffled in his seat. "I can't believe you were going to New Zealand and didn't tell me."

"I didn't tell anyone. That's part of the problem. The other part is that I'd fly out tomorrow morning."

"Oh, my goodness, Tracy! I can't believe you. What about Aunt Dee?"

"Just calm down." Tracy stuck out her hand, as if pushing a button. "I needed to talk to someone about all this because I plan on telling Ben tonight. Everything. I'm going to tell him how I feel about him."

"Does that mean you're not going? What are you saying?"

"I mean, I don't know what his plans are. I don't know if he's going back on the trail after this, or if he's staying, or moving somewhere else. I just need to talk to him. If, in fact, he feels for me the way I do for him, and there's a chance he'd stay to stick it out with me."

"Then you'll stay?" Kara said.

Tracy nodded. "I'd cancel the flight, the trip, the whole thing."

"Wow." Danny ran his hand through his jet-black locks. "I never thought I'd see the day."

"Okay, okay." Tracy shook her head and smiled.

"I'm happy for you, sis."

"Me too," Kara said. "I think it's wonderful."

"Thanks."

"There is one thing, though." Danny held up a finger. "I mean, if you are okay with me giving advice."

Tracy nodded. "Please. I need it from someone here. Uncharted territory and all."

"If you're really serious about this, about being with Ben, then why not go for it one hundred percent?"

"What do you mean?"

"I mean, it sounds to me like you still have a Plan B. A backup plan in case something doesn't go right tonight."

"You mean cancel the flight, period?"

Danny nodded.

"I don't know..."

"Can I say something?" Kara unlocked her arms from Danny's. "There was a point where I had to decide between here and New York. And I chose to go to New York. I thought that if I hadn't given myself the chance to do it, I'd regret it. So I went to New York, and it wasn't right."

"Are you saying I'll regret not going to New Zealand?"

"No. What I'm saying is, if I was being completely honest with myself, if I really dug deep and listened to how I was feeling, I wouldn't have gone to New York in the first place. I knew that I wanted to be with Danny. But I also knew that Waverly Lake was right for me, with or without Danny. I hoped it would be with." She glanced at Danny before returning her gaze to Tracy. "But I knew all the same where I belonged. If I can help you in any way, then ask yourself, not whether Ben wants to be with you, or if you are meant to be together. But rather, where in your heart do you feel you belong?"

It could've been the romance of being on the water again, or the fact she had opened up about Ben, or simply hearing it come from other people's mouths. Tracy had known what the right thing to do was before this conversation. It was the extra boost she needed to really feel it, really see what she wanted her future to be.

Danny had turned the boat around, the three of them sitting in silence. Danny and Kara worked together as a cohesive unit, tacking smoothly as if second nature, knowing their roles, and connecting with each other with little communication.

They approached Pearson's Wharf, Tracy anxious to get on the dock. She had a few minutes before their scheduled date and she didn't want to waste any of them.

She turned to Danny. "Do you think you could let me inside?"

Danny looked puzzled. "Right now? Inside the building?"

"Into Pearson's office."

"I do have a key, but I'm going to need to know what for."

She smiled, the joy of knowing her future better than any daredevil thing she had done in the past. "I have a phone call to make."

Chapter Twenty-Six

BEN SAT ON A STOOL AT A TABLE IN THE CAKE ZONE, Waverly Lake's downtown bakery. With about three minutes to spare until the start of class, there was no sign of Tracy. Sure, he had purposely tried not to be cornered by her in the past twenty-four hours. Sara's phone call had been a lot to process, and he didn't want an argument to break out with Tracy before they had the opportunity to complete their fifth date. Perhaps their last date, fake or real.

Aunt Dee did a fantastic job of keeping them on separate schedules, in different locations. Whether it was on purpose, he didn't know. But he wouldn't put it past Aunt Dee to sense the tension after the phone call and deliberately give him time to cool off.

Whether she was going to tell him about New Zealand or not, he had to tell her his truth. Although he preferred Tracy to be up front. For goodness sakes, if she truly was going away that meant she was leaving tomorrow morning. Possibly even tonight.

As much as he was nervous in making his confession, he still had bundling nerves of giddiness. The last time they were together for longer than a few minutes, they had been on the water. Having one of the best nights of his life.

"I'm so sorry." Tracy arrived, taking off her jacket and hanging it over the back of the open stool at the table. "They didn't start yet, did they?"

"No. The instructor said there were two more we were waiting on. I guess one more, now that you're here."

"Good." She grabbed his face in her hands, and before he could register what was happening, she pressed her lips against his.

He pulled away. "Tracy, what—?" But he looked into her eyes, brown irises hungry. The pure joy on her face—her rosy cheeks, unbridled ringlets bouncing over her forehead, her smile a deadly combination of sweet and sexy—tossed out any tension or anger or hesitation he felt. He caressed her cheek, warm to his fingertips. Her plump, red lips called out his name.

"Ben—"

He surprised her, stealing away one more kiss, one that blurred all memory of what he had planned to say. There was only this moment, parting her lips, tasting the soft wetness of her mouth.

"Class." The instructor rang a bell for their attention.

Tracy pulled away from Ben, the vacant space between them taking a piece of his soul. He smiled, and she chuckled, covering her lips abashedly with her hand. She was precious, and beautiful, and how could he ever be mad at this woman?

Because she was leaving the country. For months. And who knew where she'd be after that. Or if she'd even want to talk to him after what he had to tell her.

The dread of reality returned.

"There's something I want to talk to you about," he said. The instructor shot him a look as she introduced the reason why each of their tables had a large, round hot plate device, to make pumpkin cream cheese crepes. He lowered his voice to a whisper. "Maybe after class?"

"I also have something to tell you, but I don't think it can wait."

This was it. She was going to tell him she was leaving for New Zealand. He braced himself for the emotional impact.

She looked him in the eyes before facing the front of the baking class and continued whispering. "I know I can be flighty sometimes. Everyone in town will tell you that if they haven't already. It's hard for me to establish roots anywhere because that means taking on responsibility for more than a few months at a time."

She was breaking up with him before they were even technically a couple to be broken up.

"But this is different. I'm different." She turned to him again, and damn if her cute face didn't beg to be kissed. "I can see this working out."

She touched his arm and leaned in closer. "I can see *us* working out. I just had to tell you tonight because—"

Because you're leaving.

"Because I don't know what your future plans are. I understand if you didn't intend to stay in Waverly Lake, and wanted to go back out on the trail. Heck, you've given me a better understanding and appreciation of nature. It's like you've opened my eyes to the world around me that I never bothered to look at. I see it all differently— outside, Waverly Lake, my future."

"What are you saying?" He clearly heard the words she had spoken. But his deciphering couldn't possibly be correct.

"I don't want to ask you to change your plans, is what I'm saying. But I am asking..." She shook her head and grabbed his hand in hers. "I want to be with you. Be together. Do you think, maybe, that could happen?"

"I..." *Want to be with you. Want to make this work. Want to hold you in my arms like no one else is in the world.* "Yes."

"Yes?" She let out a half sigh and half laugh. "You mean, yes, you want to make a go of it?"

His smile grew until it hurt. "Yes, I do."

She kissed him, a brief one that only created longing for more.

"There's something I still need to talk to you about."

"Sorry I'm late!" The high-pitched low-country accent of Carly Fletcher ground the instructor's words to a halt. "I tell you, more parking downtown wouldn't be such a bad idea after all." She plopped her purse on the front row table and laid her jacket over it.

"Maybe we should start thinking about underground parking garages." She carried on as if the instructor had been merely warming up her vocal cords and not telling the class which ingredients to mix.

Carly scanned the room, and her eyebrows jumped to attention at the site of Ben and Tracy. "Oh, hey you two." She gave a silly wave like fingers playing floating piano keys and walked over.

"Excuse me miss," the instructor said, "but I'm trying to conduct a class here."

"I'm so sorry. It'll only be a minute." Carly rolled up her sleeves and turned, facing the instructor. "Actually, go ahead, I'll just watch what these two are doing."

The instructor shook her head in annoyance and refocused on the ingredients.

"What are you doing here?" Tracy whispered.

"I'm taking a baking class, what does it look like I'm doing?"

Tracy closed her eyes, keeping her composure. "I mean, why are you at our table?"

Carly snapped her fingers. "It's because of him." She pointed to Ben. "I didn't know you two were going to be here, but since you are, I can't keep it in."

"Keep what in?" Tracy asked.

Carly poked a finger in Ben's shoulder. "I knew from the moment you walked into my salon that I had known you. Somehow, you were familiar. Then I saw you at the town meeting about the Phillips Manor, where you delivered that grand soliloquy, and it got me thinking even more."

Ben's breathing all but ceased. "We were in the middle of a conversation here."

"It was those gorgeous"—she squeezed his cheeks—"eyes of yours. It took me a few days, but I figured it out."

"Figured out what?" Tracy placed one hand on her hip.

"Tracy, we need to talk." Ben's heart forgot how to lub-dub and went straight to hard lubs.

"I went through some old pictures I had in salon storage. Lo and behold, I found some of Ellie Phillips. She was a regular customer of mine, you know. On one such occasion I had taken a Polaroid when she arrived, and after I had done her hair, you know, to show the before and after. It just so happens on that occasion she had her son with her."

Tracy shook her head. "What does any of this have to do with Ben."

"Honey." Carly held Tracy's wrist. "This isn't Ben Walker. This is Hunter Phillips. As in Hunter B. Phillips. As in Hunter Benjamin Phillips." Carly clapped her hands together.

Tracy's forced polite smile vanished. Her face turned white, and she looked up at Ben. "No. That's not true."

"Tracy." Ben reached for her shoulder, and Tracy stepped back.

"It can't be true. You would've said something."

"I wanted to tell you."

"All this time." She looked at him in horror. It was worse than being stabbed with a knife. "I opened up to you, about him. About our friendship. How I loved him. Our favorite spot." She grabbed her forehead, chest heaving in disbelief or anger, or both.

"You don't understand. I don't want my parents' life. I didn't want the pressure of the town on me, about the house, about their legacy. I wanted people—I wanted you, especially—to get to know me outside of my history here."

"Oh, I know you, all right. You're a liar is what you are."

"I promise, that's what I was going to tell you tonight."

"Oh really?" She pressed her hands into fists and held them by her side. "Why tell me at all, huh? If it weren't for Carly here, I may have carried on thinking I loved a man who didn't even tell me who he really was."

She loves me. Those were words to be excited to hear coming from someone for the first time, but they couldn't have injured him more. "I wanted to tell you. Especially if you were leaving for New Zealand tomorrow."

"What? I—"

Carly's eyes widened, and she backed away from the couple.

Even she sensed this was a lot to handle. "How about the class take a five-minute breather, yeah?" She reached for the nearest student and led them out into the customer space of the bakery. The others stared along with the instructor, wide-eyed.

"Well don't dilly-dally. Everybody out!" Carly fanned them out of the room, as if guiding a swarm of flies out a window.

Their departure left them in a bubble of quiet.

"Looks like we both had secrets we were keeping from each other." Ben looked at his feet. "Your friend Sara told me, on the phone."

Tracy's breathing quickened. "You have no right to bring that up right now."

"I'm just saying that if we want this to have a fighting chance, we need to clear out all the secrets. That's what I wanted to do tonight."

"Well, the secrets certainly have come out, haven't they?" Tracy pulled her jacket off the back, knocking the stool onto the floor with a loud clap. The evacuated class startled in chatter at the sound through the doorway.

"Look, don't go." He followed her, and she turned around in the doorway. "Let's talk this through. Yes, the secrets came out, not exactly as I had planned, but—"

"That's the thing, isn't it? You had control over this whole relationship the entire time. Like you were buttering me up to talk about him—talk about *you*—through all of it. What kind of narcissistic behavior is that? One that I've had my fill of, thank you. Now if you'll excuse me. Wait, no. I don't need any kind of approval from you to leave."

She turned away and scrambled through the bakery, the crowd moving out of her way as she left through the front door.

Carly walked over to him. "I'm sorry, Ben. Hunter. I'm not sure what you want to be called."

He held up a hand to silence her, a motion that had no effect on the town gossip.

"I didn't know she'd take it like that," Carly said. "Honest."

"Well, I did." He huffed, hands on his hips. "Why do you think I didn't tell her for so long? Why I didn't tell anyone in this town? Now the woman I love is probably gone for good."

He wiped his face with one hand and made for the front door. "And I am too."

Chapter Twenty-Seven

Tuesday, October 18

Tracy watched her parents' coffee pot fill with caffeinated goodness, the dripping noise temporarily blocking out the noise of reality jumping around in her head.

"I don't get too many of these mornings." Beverly Bennett appeared in the kitchen, wearing a full face of makeup, a wrinkle-free blouse, long skirt, and low-heel dress shoes.

Tracy looked over her mother, then at the red clock lights on the coffee maker. *7:14.* "Do you go to bed in all that? Is that how this happens so early?"

"Oh how I miss having you in the house." Mom retrieved a mug and poured herself coffee before Tracy registered it was done brewing.

Tracy sighed. It was always a dance being in the same room with Mom. She had to side-step issues, backtrack the words that flung out of her mouth in reaction to whatever insensitive thing Beverly had to say that day, all while generally moving the conversation forward to be done with it.

"Thank you for letting me stay last night." If it stung to say it, Tracy couldn't feel it. Not after the blow received from Ben. Or

Hunter. Or whatever she was supposed to call him. Besides, she was thankful to have somewhere to go other than Woodsman's Lodge. She couldn't bear staying in her room, knowing he occupied the one across the hall.

"Want to talk about it?" Mom looked over the brim of the mug, hiding her full facial expression of curiosity with a tinge of satisfaction. It's not that Mom rooted for Tracy's failure. She reveled in the fact that Tracy had come to the house, to her company, when something was so clearly wrong.

No. I don't want to talk about it. But that's not what came out of her mouth. Maybe it was because she hadn't slept much last night, and she didn't have the energy to hold her ground. Or perhaps, deep down, a part of her, did want to let it all out to Mom.

"I was scheduled to be on a flight in a few hours, out of Charlotte."

Mom perked up in her chair at the kitchen table. "Today?"

Tracy nodded and joined her at the table with her oversized mug of coffee. "I had planned a trip with my Sidney friends."

"As in, Australia?"

"We were going to take a big trip out to New Zealand together, in the winter. Well, our winter. There it'd be heading into summer weather." She sipped on the coffee, not caring that it was a touch too hot to enjoy it. "But a situation came up, and they had to bump it earlier. To today."

"You're headed out of the country, today? What about Aunt Dee? Didn't you think about—"

"Mom, just stop. Please. Last night I canceled the flight."

"Hm. I'd be lying if I said I'm sorry you aren't going." Mom looked at her, and Tracy expected to read gloating in her eyes. Instead, there was something else—compassion, even empathy. "May I ask if this has something to do with that new friend of yours? Ben?"

Just hearing the name pierced the wound again, and she shuffled in her chair as if the emotional wound manifested into a physical one.

"I'm going to take that as a yes." Mom's gaze veered to the kitchen window, and she bit her lip.

Danny walked into the kitchen, decked out in jeans and a puffy jacket. Was Tracy the only one in the family not an early bird?

"What are you doing here?" Tracy asked.

"I was about to ask you the same thing." Danny reached for a bakery box on the counter and stole a donut, holding it in his mouth as he poured himself a cup of coffee.

"You first." Tracy leaned back, appreciative of the break, however brief, in the morning confessional.

He pulled the donut out of his mouth, chewing on the bite left behind. "Kara's taking Hannah to school this morning."

"That still puts you being here in question." Tracy smirked, the first hint of a smile in the past twelve hours.

"Mom and I are going to Asheville today. There's a regional conference for ASD doctors, educators, and such going on this week. Families are encouraged to attend, and this was the day we both could go."

"Oh wow." Tracy was both proud of her brother and Mom for taking the initiative in supporting Hannah and the ASD community, and also a little wounded she wasn't asked to go.

"I would've asked you to join. I just figured—"

Tracy held up a hand. "It's okay." She knew what he figured. She knew what everyone thought of her. She'd have other plans. She wouldn't stick around town long enough anyway so why make the effort to support her family, or get to know other families? And they wouldn't have been wrong. She had planned on getting out, to fly halfway around the world.

"Your turn." Danny took a seat, forming a Bennett-family triangle at the table.

"Tracy was just telling me how she canceled her flight to Australia," Mom said.

"Ah!" Danny grinned. "So it went well then, after we talked?"

"You knew about Australia?" Mom shot Danny a glance.

He shrugged back. "Only recently." It was hard not to be in self-defense mode around Mom. "By the way, her cancellation may have had a little to do with me, and Kara, so you're welcome."

"Would someone please fill me in on what's happening?"

"Yes, Tracy," Danny said. "Please fill us in."

The two nosy family members awaited her words. She sighed. Sometimes it was better to say nothing, and other times saying it all better served everyone. Unfortunately, this fit the latter scenario. "I spoke with Danny and Kara yesterday, about Ben." She looked at Mom, waiting to see if the spark of hope reignited in her eyes. "I... cared about him and was asking for advice. Which led me to cancel the flight to Sidney."

She put up a hand before Danny could say anything. "I had already considered canceling. I think I just needed an extra boost of confidence to actually do it."

"And to tell Ben how you feel." Generally, Danny would've revealed that info just to make her feel uncomfortable around Mom. But Tracy saw it in his eyes, on his face, that there was no malice in it.

"Yes." The coffee did little to overcome the hoarseness overtaking her throat. "I opened up and told him everything. How I felt and wanted to make a go of it—of us being an us."

"Oh no." Danny leaned back in his chair. "You stayed the night here, didn't you? That means...he didn't feel the same way?"

Tracy opened her mouth to speak. The question was a simple yes or no, but she realized she didn't know the answer. "I'm not sure, actually. I mean, he said yes at first, but that was all negated afterwards with the lies."

"I'm confused," Mom said. "He was lying about how he felt for you?"

Was that part real, or a lie too? She shook her head. It didn't matter, because he was a liar, which meant she'd question him just like that over everything. "Carly Fletcher had barged in—"

"Carly Fletcher interrupted your date?" Mom scoffed. "That woman has no boundaries."

"I'll agree with you there," Tracy said. "Our date was at a

cooking class, but that's beside the point. Carly said she had recognized Ben, from long ago and couldn't place him. Couldn't understand how she knew him, and she figured it out."

"What's that have to do with how you two feel about each other?" Mom was now riveted, coffee mug clenched with both hands and bottom scooted to the edge of her chair.

"Turns out Ben isn't actually Ben Walker." Tracy looked up at Danny and Mom. "He's Hunter Phillips. Technically, Hunter Benjamin Phillips."

Mom reacted with a dropped jaw and wide eyes. She turned to Danny, whose look of confusion was almost amusing.

"You mean the Phillips boy?" Danny asked. "The one from years ago that moved when his parents—"

Tracy nodded.

"Your best friend when you were a child?" Mom asked.

"Her only friend when she was a child." Danny winced from Mom's elbow in his side. "Sorry. I know, it's serious." He straightened his goofy smile and then shook his head. "No, I'm not understanding. Are you saying you're upset to find out the man you've fallen for is actually a former best friend? Isn't that a good thing? I'm sure Kara would agree with me that it is."

"He lied about it." It came out louder than she expected and startled Mom and Danny. "He didn't tell me. All this time, talking about Phillips Manor, at the town meeting, and..." She thought about their afternoon at their special spot. Him showing her that place may have just been the moment she had realized she loved him. Her eyes watered, in anger, in hurt. "He deceived me from day one. He's deceived us all."

She looked at her family through blurred eyes. "How do I trust someone who couldn't even tell me who he was?"

Danny sighed and stared at Mom, who only had a head shake and dropped shoulders to respond with.

"So what now?" Danny asked.

Tracy shrugged. "I think there's still time to reschedule my flight out of Charlotte for tomorrow. I canceled less than twenty-four hours ago, and it hasn't been refunded yet. It wouldn't disrupt the group's travel plans that much—"

Mom abruptly rose from the table. She walked to the sink and set down her mug with a clang. She stared out the window, arms stiff on the countertop. When she swung around, Tracy knew to be quiet.

"Are you telling me that you're now going to run off to Australia or New Zealand or wherever, just because Ben lied about his name?"

"It's not just his name. It's who he is. And it wouldn't be running off—"

"Oh please." There it was. That same attitude Tracy possessed and forgot she had indeed inherited from her mother. "You can't keep running away every time there is conflict in your life."

"Is that what you think I do?"

"No." Mom folded her arms over her chest. "I don't think you do. I *know* you do."

"That's just not true."

Danny stood, setting his mug far down the counter and working his way out of the room. Out of what was about to happen.

"You put on this big act that it's boredom you run from. What happened when you failed your first class in event planning? You blamed it on your professor and ran off to Chile the next semester."

"The university put him on probation for grading bias!"

"Or when you applied for an internship at Biltmore Estate, but didn't get in? That's when you took your cross-country road trip with Sebastian.

"I had nothing else going on. Why not take a road trip?"

"You're always making excuses, instead of trying harder and facing your problems." Mom delivered it with stern sincerity.

"That's not true." Tracy's voice quaked, and tears welled in her eyes. "Danny, tell her that's not true."

Danny stood with one foot out of the room, anxious to get out of the dose of reality Mom dished out. The pity on his face said it all. He agreed with Mom.

Mom unfolded her arms and softened her posture. "Maybe it's time you stand your ground and face conflict. Because if you don't, you'll always be this way, Tracy. You'll always be on the run. Escaping. Never getting a chance at having what you truly want in life."

The tears escaped, despite her efforts to thwart them. "I was standing my ground. I made the choice to stay. I poured out my heart in front of him." She broke in sobs. It was over. The facade of strength, of being okay, cracked into ashes. She laid her head on her arms on the table and let it out.

A hand gently rubbed her back, and she slowly lifted her head. Mom stood next to her as she wiped her eyes.

She grabbed Tracy's hand and squeezed it, eyes tender and loving. "So stay."

Chapter Twenty-Eight

Wednesday, October 19

BEN OPENED HIS EYES, GROGGY AND NOT REFRESHED IN the least bit, to the sound of rustling sleeping bags and clanging pots. Two other men had stayed the night in the shelter, a surprise to Ben as the season was late and the overnight temps dipped below freezing.

Between the hard "bunk," which was more of a shelf along the three solid walls of the shelter, and his sleeping bag being underrated for the weather, made for a rough sleep. Perhaps worse was the fact that his past finally had caught up with him. Carly Fletcher had no business spewing out his real identity. He had been seconds away from telling Tracy himself.

Tracy's reaction was exactly what he had worried about.

But it was over.

Tracy hadn't returned to Woodsman's Lodge that night, or in the morning, probably on her way to Charlotte. By this time, she roamed thousands of miles away. His secret pushed the woman he loved to be as far away as possible from him.

But other than that, he was doing great.

"Sorry to wake you," one of the pair said. "We need to get an early start with the foul weather coming this afternoon."

"You're fine," Ben said. "It's probably best I get going too." The forecast called for rain, which in and of itself wasn't a deal breaker when it came to hiking. Yes, it made for mud and slippery rocks along the trail and could make the experience downright miserable. But wind was more concerning. The next shelter wasn't for another thirty miles, which meant he'd have to tent camp. The wind forecast coupled with the onslaught of rain meant falling branches or worse — whole trees. No one wanted to be in a tent below when one gave out.

"We're hoping it stays up here and doesn't reach too much further south," the man said.

"I hear ya." Ben readied his pot for boiling water. A simple breakfast of coffee and peanut butter and trail mix would have to do. He wasn't hungry much anyway.

The crunching of leaves in rhythmic steps indicated another hiker approaching. The hiker could've given up just shy of reaching the shelter last night or was just joining the trail. The nearest trailhead parking lay about a ten-minute walk north.

Ben rolled up the sleeping bag into his compression sack and tightened the bands.

"Thought I'd find you here."

He knew the voice, but didn't believe it until he turned around. Aunt Dee stood outside the shelter, wearing a down vest and hiking boots that made her already skinny legs look like toothpicks.

"When I saw yesterday that not only had you skipped breakfast, but your belongings were missing, I figured you high-tailed it out of Waverly Lake. I guessed you were headed south, which, thankfully, I was right. And seeing as this shelter is conveniently twelve miles or so from the lodge, suspected you'd stay for the night."

"That's some impressive deducing."

"Well, I may also have given Roger Dornan a call. I know you don't go off without telling one person where you're headed, and I just so happen to know that person."

The last thing he wanted was to talk to Aunt Dee about any of this, and to hear she had called Roger made it worse. "What do you want?"

"I thought I'd give you this back." She threw an envelope on the ground before him. "I don't accept written goodbyes. Only ones in person."

He had written the note when he returned that night, after Tracy walked out on him at the baking class. He couldn't justify staying any longer at the lodge, yet didn't want Aunt Dee convincing him otherwise. Some good that did. "I just thought it'd be easier."

"For who? You?"

"For everyone."

"Hunter, I wish you could see this is the hardest route for you, not the easiest."

He secured the compression sack in his backpack. The other two hikers waved as they hit the trail.

"The name is Ben. And I have to get going. Supposed to be bad weather later today."

"That's the story of your life, isn't it? No matter what name you go by."

"What are you talking about?" For all the chores and grueling jobs Aunt Dee assigned to him, he never once had gotten mad at her. He had appreciated her hospitality and the chance she gave him to earn his keep. But right now, she was walking a narrow line.

"You know a storm is coming, and you try to stay ahead of it. You're always running ahead. And when it does catch up to you, instead of enduring it, you continue running. One of these days you're going to have to accept who you are, Hunter Benjamin. You're going to get tired of running, but when you do, no one will be there to help you through the storm."

"That's a bit ironic, don't you think, considering Tracy, according to anyone in Waverly Lake, is the one who doesn't know how to face anything."

"Whatever is happening, has happened, or will happen with you and Tracy is another issue. What I'm talking about is you. If you can't accept who you are, what your place is in the world, you'll never be happy. With or without Tracy."

He sat on the ground, next to his backpack, boots grinding the loose dirt. "She found out. Before I could tell her."

Aunt Dee sighed. "I figured as much."

"I mean, say I do come back. The town knows who I am, and I take care of the house, whatever that ends up meaning. Then what? I'll pass by all the spots we've been. I'll see her brother working at Pearson's. I'll smell her when I buy more of those soaps you two like for the lodge." He shook his head. "I'd be surrounded by the memory of her."

Aunt Dee faintly smiled and worked her way to the ground.

"No, I'll get up."

"Don't you dare," she said, completing her transition. Her years of morning walks paid off in the agility department. "You know, it's funny what even a week's time can do to a person."

"I certainly didn't mean to fall in love with someone."

"Well, that's just it, isn't it? When you arrived, you were worried about being surrounded by the memory of your parents. Is that what happened in reality?"

He thought back at his arrival, that first day with Tracy walking through town, over to Phillips Manor. "At first, a little."

"Then what?"

All his other memories, joyful, warm memories, were filled with Tracy. Not with the sorrow he had expected of being back in town, without his parents alive. He looked at Aunt Dee, her eyes aged with wisdom and too much insight to handle.

She held up a hand. "I know. Not everyone likes it when I'm right." She smiled.

"Even if you're right—"

"Which I am." She nudged him.

Ben grinned. "Who's to say I can do it again? That I can carry on in town and forget about Tracy? I know it all sounds ridiculous that we have only known each other for a week."

"Ah, but you're wrong again. You've known Tracy since she was a girl, and she's known you since you were a boy. As kids, we are who we are. When we grow up, we learn ways to magnify our good traits and diminish the bad ones. One could say you know each other better than anyone else ever could because of your past. Just think, you've had the opportunity to know all of her."

He did know Tracy. But in his mind, he knew two separate Tracys — the girl and the woman. He had never thought of it the way Aunt Dee described, as both making up the whole.

"Why are we talking about this anyway, like Tracy's dead for goodness sakes?" Aunt Dee wriggled her way up to her feet.

Ben jumped up and offered her a hand. "You're right. I guess I'd have some time to process it all before she came back from New Zealand." *If she came back from New Zealand.*

"You don't know?" Aunt Dee shook her head. "Tracy didn't go anywhere. She's still in Waverly Lake."

"What?"

"Are you telling me you high-tailed it out of my place, with a lousy goodbye note, all because you thought Tracy had left overseas?"

"It wasn't only that. I mean, she didn't want to talk to me after finding out who I am."

"Good grief. You two belong together, I'll tell you that." She pulled a folded piece of paper from her vest pocket. "One more thing to give to you, then I'll leave you alone." She put it in his hand and then grabbed his shoulders. "If you continue down this path, that is your decision to make. But I want you to know you're always welcome at the lodge. Into my home. For as long or as short as you need."

She hugged him, a solid squeeze, and he returned it. She was a tough woman, but a loving one, and with the few people he had in his life, he was forever grateful for her.

She stepped back and pointed her finger. "Just as long as you say goodbye to my face and not in another one of those dumb letters." She winked and headed north, off to where she had likely parked.

Ben lifted the pack onto his back and stared down the trail. He'd have to get in a good ten miles to hit a big bluff on a hilltop. Although he'd be out in the open to get pelted by rain, he'd be safe from the trees.

He looked down at his hand, folded paper still in his grasp. Somehow he knew if he opened it, his path for the day, for his life, could change. It would be physically easy to take it over to the animal-proof trash bin at the shelter and throw it away and stay on course. But he couldn't do that to Aunt Dee.

She had come all this way. For him. The orphaned boy she barely knew and the confused adult she knew even less. Yet she came.

He unfolded the paper. It was a printed spreadsheet, with three columns. The first was labeled *Activity*, the other two *Contact Info* and *Comments*. A fourth column had an added sentence. *Top three indicated by an asterisk.*

The first filled line under *Activity* read *Honeysuckle Farm, corn maze.* He skimmed past the contact information and read the comments. *The corn maze was better than anticipated. Definitely do the Pumpkin Pitch. Prepare to get muddy and have a blast.*

He read the next line. *Breakwater Art Studio, arts and craft. Great activity to test the inner child in each other—who doesn't love a little paint battle?* The listing had an asterisk.

As he read on down the list of dates, the more certain he was reading Tracy's work, her thoughts on each date spelled out for him on paper.

The second asterisk was by the line for Offshore Orchard. *One of the best-kept secrets around, and most romantic afternoons I've ever had.*

The words tugged at his soul. It was raw Tracy, an open book that didn't care what the person reading thought. If only she had told him in person what she thought about that date. Or any of them.

But she had. In other ways. In her willingness to try new things, in her laughter, in simply being there in the moment with him.

He scanned the paper, only seeing two asterisks.

At the very bottom was the third. A series of five asterisks. She had written it by hand on the paper. *Sunset Cruise. Highly recommend adding this. The perfect date for a first kiss and realizing how much you're in love.*

He held the paper, staring at the last sentence. The rush of guilt returned, the guilt of lying to her, of not telling her the first moment they met who he was.

Even with the weight of that guilt the words confirmed—no, reminded—him of what he knew.

She loved him.

For a second, he regretted ever unfolding that paper.

Chapter Twenty-Nine

Thursday, October 20

"Good morning." Aunt Dee leaned on the kitchen counter, sipping coffee.

"Morning." Tracy wiped her eyes, the sleeplessness catching up to her. She had never taken a sleeping aid, but now understood why someone would. Lack of sleep dulled some senses while heightening others. The faint pitter-patter of rain remnants from the storm seemed loud, every light excruciatingly bright. Yet her sense of giving a darn about anything had all but vanished. That was going to change today.

"I mean, good morning." She straightened her posture and contrived a smile.

"That wasn't even close to being convincing." Aunt Dee eyed her.

"Have to start somewhere." She grabbed a mug and poured herself coffee. "I figured if I put the effort into looking and sounding the part, then maybe eventually I'll convince myself it's true."

Aunt Dee patted Tracy's shoulder. "Give it time, honey. You'll be back to normal in your own time."

"No, I won't." Tracy gulped the hot brew. "That's what I've decided. Today starts my new life."

"A new normal?"

"Whatever that ends up being."

Aunt Dee rubbed her shoulder before stepping away. "Are you sure you want to continue working here through the winter?"

Tracy nodded. "As much as I hate to say it, Mom was right. I need a dose of facing problems. And I have to stop leaving people I care about for the next place, the next thing I take on for a short while, and then do it all over again. I really am sorry for even considering leaving you hanging—"

"You already apologized. Several times."

"I know. I just want to be clear."

"You're crystal."

Tracy tried not to think too much about the oncoming winter. She tended to stay away from the cold and working for Aunt Dee would either be grueling outdoors or confined to housework inside. It still beat staying at Mom and Dad's, even if Mom had been right. No, especially since Mom had been right. Tracy would see and hear the hints of gloating every time she shared a room with that woman.

Tracy moved to a seat at the small kitchen table. "What should I take care of today?" It would've been nice to have another special event to plan. Perhaps something over Thanksgiving week or leading up to Christmas. Of course, it would be a nice distraction. More importantly, it would give her more experience, both in helping her better her craft, but also in beefing up her resume.

Aunt Dee moved closer, holding on to the back of a chair at the table. "We have our Lovetoberfest guests arriving tomorrow. We need to match up who gets to go on what date and with whom, then give the names to the vendors so they know who to expect."

"I already matched them up based on their answers to the questionnaire. I'll call the vendors this morning."

"Look at you. Little Miss Organization."

"I did pick my college degree for a purpose. Maybe it's time I take it seriously, starting with Lovetoberfest." Tracy closed her eyes, tipping her head back. "I'm grateful for the work. If I'm being honest, though, I'm not looking forward to this. Seeing people eager to find love, having that happy euphoria of connecting with someone." She stuck out her tongue as if nauseated.

"Yeah, your 'new you' needs a lot of work."

Tracy smirked.

"You mean, you don't want to see what I had to see this past week?" Aunt Dee raised her eyebrows.

"I don't know what you're talking about." Tracy kept her gaze on the dark brew in her mug.

"Don't kid yourself, Tracy."

"It's hard to say you've connected with someone when you find out they'd been lying about themselves the entire time."

"Had he really been lying?

"Um, yes." She shifted in her chair. The wound was still too fresh to press again. "For starters, he gave all of us the wrong name."

"Just because the name he called himself was different doesn't mean there wasn't truth in everything else."

Her pulse intensified. "He knew me, from before. And I knew him."

Aunt Dee sat in the chair and leaned toward Tracy, as fired up as her great-niece. "How would you have reacted if he told you that, up front? I mean, the day he walked in here."

Tracy shrugged. "I don't know. I probably would've been happy to see him again. Happy to hear about his life and get to know him again."

"Well, guess what? You did get to know him again."

Aunt Dee and her button pushing. Tracy took a breath, reeling in the growing irritation. "It's not the same. We could've shared memories about our past."

"Which you did. You said you talked about your special place down the trail, and your memories of him at the house as you lived next door."

"*I* did. *He* didn't. It's not the same thing."

"Let me review here."

"Can we please just drop this?"

"No, I want to wrap my head around your logic. You're telling me that you got to know him as an adult and share your childhood history from your point of view, and you fell in love with each other. Are you saying if you knew about his past and he shared that with you, it would've torn you apart?"

"No." Tracy rubbed her forehead. "I'm saying the opposite. If anything, it would've brought us closer together. I wouldn't have put up such a wall with him at the beginning if I knew then what I know now."

"Yet he still managed to tear it down and win you over." She rose again from her chair. "Sounds to me like you were going to love him no matter what. And if he came to that front door right now and you two talked it out, you'd only grow that love."

Aunt Dee played word tricks. That was all this was. Sure, the way she had broken it down made Tracy look nuts. He lied and broke her trust. That had to factor into it, didn't it? But...she had fallen in love with him, independent of their past. And she had loved him as a friend as a child. Why would knowing the truth do anything but strengthen that love?

"I think it's finally sinking in." Aunt Dee patted her shoulder again. "I'll leave it at that."

Now that Aunt Dee finally quit talking about him, all Tracy wanted to do was continue the conversation. Explain herself better, about the importance of trust in a relationship. Not that she had noteworthy experience with relationships. Ben leaving town when the truth hit was no different to what she had done in the past to people here, across the country, across the globe. Even though she walked out on him that night, it hurt not to talk it through with him after calming down. It was painful knowing he was out there, each minute further away from this place, further from her.

The pain came paired with the guilt of remembering how many people she had done the same thing to. She deserved to hurt, as Ben deserved to move on away from her and live his life. It was the penance she had to live out in order for her new start. She couldn't start fresh if she didn't process the emotions of the past.

Aunt Dee placed her mug in the sink and moved toward the door. "Are you okay matching people up and calling the vendors?"

It snapped Tracy out of her spiral of thoughts. "Yeah. I'll take care of it this morning."

"Good. Let me know the result. I'm still not sure how to arrange who gets what room. Maybe you can help me with that too."

Tracy nodded. "Let me take care of it. Finally put my degree to some use." And prevent her from going down that hole of Ben thoughts. "By the way, I seemed to have misplaced my list. Have you seen it?"

"Seen what, dear?"

"My list of dates that we went on. I made some notes for myself. Figured I'd write a brief paragraph about each one for the guests to have some idea what to expect, what to wear, that sort of thing. I printed it off before..." *Before I walked away from Ben. Before he left.*

"If I see it, I'll let you know. I hope there wasn't anything important on it?"

Tracy's eyebrow furled. Aunt Dee gave a smile that looked like worry on the surface. But in Tracy's bones lie suspicion. "No. Don't worry about it. I can print off another one. Sorry I can't really give an objective opinion about the baking class." They hadn't really started the actual date before it ended. Yet somehow, she had the time to pour her guts out to him.

Tracy stood, hoping physical movement would wash away the emotional embarrassment of the memory. She placed her mug in the sink by Aunt Dee's and turned around, catching Aunt Dee stepping outside the kitchen. "If you really want an opinion on the baking class, there is one person I can ask."

"Oh? Who would that be?"

"Carly Fletcher." Tracy's smirk grew into a smile, which turned into a chuckle. Aunt Dee looked at her wide-eyed and broke into laughter. It was the first full-hearted laugh Tracy had since Monday.

Hopefully for new Tracy, the first of many.

Chapter Thirty

Friday, October 21

"How soon can I go on the property?" Ben sat in the dark cave of the office of Steve Albertson.

"Since you called me yesterday, I was able to retrieve the keys." Steve handed Ben a stuffed manilla envelope. "They're in there with all the paperwork. I'm sure no one in town would object to you going right now if you really wanted. The council seemed relieved when I told them you made contact and were taking responsibility. Even if it was down to the wire."

"I'm sorry it took so long to come to my senses."

"Hey, you had to do what felt right for you."

"I actually feel relief too, now that it's in my hands." If he had known just how good it felt, perhaps he would've done it sooner. But he wasn't ready to back then. Plus, he wouldn't have had the opportunity to plan Lovetoberfest with Tracy. Whether she wanted anything to do with him now or not.

"I know you and I don't know each other well, but I know Frank Letts would've celebrated this occasion if he were here."

"I'm sorry he couldn't see it in person."

Steve nodded, a nostalgic memory fleeting with a smile. "Well, I'm looking forward to seeing your vision come to fruition. On that note, make sure to have the utilities transferred over to your name. I wouldn't want you staying there on these cold nights with no heat."

"Will do." Ben peeked through the open top of the envelope. He certainly had a lot of reading ahead of him. "That brings me to something else I wanted to discuss with you."

"What's that?"

"My name." He had mulled over what to do about his name. Officially he was Hunter Benjamin Phillips. Mom and Dad had called him Hunter, Tracy and other kids and the town called him Hunter. Back then. But ever since using his middle name, he felt reinvented. It wasn't exactly a fake name. Just a different part of his name. It emphasized he was the same person, yet different. Going back to Hunter didn't sit right.

"Hm. I think you're going to find it more tedious to use Ben Walker. We're talking officially changing your name—"

Ben shook his head and held up a hand. "No, not Ben Walker. I was thinking Ben Phillips."

Steve rubbed his jaw before nodding. "I don't think that will be a problem."

Ben smiled and waved the manilla folder in the air. "Thanks for this. For everything."

"You're welcome. Ben Phillips." Steve smiled and waved him off.

Ben left the law office, his belongings on his back, and headed west on Dowager Street. He had headed back to town instead of Woodman's Lodge two days ago and considered camping along the outskirts. It was a last resort, one he didn't want to execute considering the downpour of rain that met up with him. Luckily, he had bumped into Danny, who was on his way to Pearson's. He explained the situation, and Danny let him stay the past two nights at his house, promising not to say a word to Tracy.

He stood on the sidewalk, eyeing the storefronts of the main strip through Waverly Lake. There was something that brewed in his mind since the debacle on his last date with Tracy.

He walked to Dye Happy Salon, peering through the front windows. He couldn't imagine there'd be a time the place operated without Carly Fletcher's presence, but he checked for her just the same. He opened the door and set down his things in the corner. A hair dryer stopped blowing, and he eyed the blond-haired woman holding it.

"Excuse me a minute." Carly Fletcher dropped a stack of magazines on her client's lap and walked to the front of the salon. The vibrant pink of her sweater stood out against the sleek gray interior. "I wasn't sure if we'd see your face around here again."

Ben ran his hand through his hair. "I wasn't sure either."

"You know, when I finally realized how I knew you, who you really were, there was nothing but happiness about it. The long-lost Phillips son? How amazing is it that he's alive and well, and came back to Waverly Lake? I didn't mean for it to—"

Ben stopped her with a hand in the air. "I know you didn't. I don't expect an apology, or explanation, from you."

"It'll make me feel better if you know I didn't mean to come between you and Tracy."

"If I can make you feel better, then know you didn't. It was my fault." He pointed to the two lounge seats, and they sat, both sitting near the edge of their seat. "I wanted to apologize to you."

"That's not necessary."

"Please. I should've told Tracy—everyone—who I was. It wasn't right deceiving the town like that. If anything came between me and Tracy it was my own stubbornness. I didn't want the town knowing who I was because I wasn't ready to be who I am. I wasn't ready to be—how'd you put it? The long-lost Phillips son. I wanted to be Ben Walker, a no-name here who could start fresh. Although it may have tasted good for a while, reality weighed on me, and I just got deeper and deeper into hiding behind the lie."

Carly's head sunk and she placed a hand on his knee. "I

understand why you did it. I really do. Your parents were some of the best, kindest people to have lived in this town, and while at first revelation I thought you'd embrace that, I can see how that puts pressure on you."

He nodded. "I should've handled it differently."

"Well all there is now is what you do from now on." She smiled and withdrew her hand. "I want you to know we'll all accept you with open arms, Ben." She closed her eyes and shook her head. "Hunter."

"It's Ben," he said. "Ben Phillips."

Carly's lips curled up in a delighted smile. "Okay then." She stood up and he followed. "That sounds right."

He nodded and picked up his backpack.

"I'll be seeing you around, then?" Carly asked.

"Only if you're planning on staying here in Waverly Lake." Ben smirked.

"Is there anywhere else?" She winked and returned to her customer.

Ben exited and trekked down the street. His memories of Waverly Lake when he was a kid ran fuzzy. Now that he had spent the past week in town, his memories started to meld together, not knowing if some parts were actual remembrances or just his current experiences superseding them.

Either way, walking the main strip today had a different feeling than when he first returned. The hesitance and unease were replaced by hopefulness and calm. Perhaps calm wasn't the right word. More like peace. He wasn't entirely calm, knowing what lie ahead. Aunt Dee would understand his actions and welcome him in return, but what about Tracy? The most important relationship he had cultivated during his time here, what helped lead him back home, was in jeopardy. Whatever her reaction would be, he had to deal with it. Because not having a life with Tracy in it, even if she didn't want something more, was as bad as not having a place to call home.

He knew how crazy it sounded, knowing someone for a week.

But Aunt Dee had been right. He and Tracy knew each other all their lives. The years of separation disappeared when they were together. It was impossible to think he could feel that way while she didn't. That was the one thing that kept up his hope.

He stopped at the wrought iron gate of Phillips Manor. He dropped the backpack and pulled out the manilla envelope, grabbing the keys attached to a simple ring. With the lock in hand, he jiggled the smallest key into it, freeing the chain. The swing of the gate sounded off a creek, the moanings of an estate that had slept for years and needed to stretch. He grabbed his bag and plopped it on the front porch. Looking out over the yard, he ran through the work needed on the exterior and grounds. Paint on the columns and rails, bricks in the stairs replaced, landscaping beds torn up and re-soiled, the lawn mowed and seeded.

He braced himself for the condition of the interior as he tried out the remaining two keys on the chain on the front door. The door complained less than the gate, but the transition manifested not in noise but lack of it. The house hadn't felt heat or air conditioning in years. The cold inside felt deeper, crisper than the chill outside. A thick layer of dust covered what little furniture remained in the property, covered up haphazardly by plastic tarps. The giant crystal chandelier still hung above, cobwebs overtaking it, as if the glass prisms themselves were intricate pieces of the spider's trap.

Time had stood still, and he broke its bubble.

His boots felt the grit on the marble as he walked into the foyer, the double staircase still a grand sight despite the lackluster condition of the interior. There were so many possibilities of what the place could be—a bed and breakfast, a museum for Waverly Lake, a historical home that offered tours. Steve Albertson had said as much. Heck, the town had said more, including the horrible idea of demolishing it and turning it into a parking lot.

But there was one thing he had in mind for it. Steve Albertson not only approved, but stated the whole town would appreciate his vision. Whether that vision would come true or not, it was going to be his home.

For how much work it was going to take, he had one more thing to do before he could get started.

He had to face the woman he loved, no matter the consequences.

Chapter Thirty-One

"Here are the keys, and your room is number six. Just take the stairs over there and you'll see your door on the left." Tracy caught Aunt Dee watching her, forcing her smile to artificially grow, which probably looked more like a scary, toothy grin to the guest. She wasn't the one about to go on a bunch of dates this weekend, but she was serious about treating the job professionally. That meant dressing more formal in pants and a blouse, while also trying her hardest to hide her heartbreak.

Aunt Dee, with a more successfully convincing smile, greeted the guest and got out of his way as he carried his bag to the stairs. She made her way to the front counter. "Don't get me wrong. I am grateful that you're staying here with me through the holidays, especially for this event you helped to set up. But would it pain you to at least act like you are happy?"

Tracy tipped her head back. "I'm sorry. I really am trying. It's just they're coming in here, so eager to find love. It's almost unbearable how optimistic they are."

"They're hopeful." Aunt Dee kept her tone compassionate, obviously aware of how wounded Tracy felt. "As they should be. Everyone deserves love, and who's to say they won't find it here today, or tomorrow? Maybe they won't, but maybe they will."

"I know, I know." Tracy stared at her hand as Aunt Dee patted it. "It's just hard to get out of this funk and move on while that romantic optimism is everywhere you look."

As if on cue, two of the guests bumped into each other on the stairs.

"I don't know if being around all these meet-cutes is the best thing for me right now."

"Maybe not," Aunt Dee agreed. "But work has always helped me to keep focus on something else when I'm trying to forget whatever else is going on in my life."

"I generally would agree. The problem is that my work is a constant reminder of *him*, and what we had. This place, these people going on the dates we had gone on. Have I actually chosen the best path to torture myself?"

Aunt Dee shrugged. "It may be the hardest way, but perhaps it's the fastest way? Like ripping off a band-aid."

Tracy returned the pat on Aunt Dee's hand. "You keep telling yourself that to justify keeping me here."

Aunt Dee swatted her hand away. "Don't you be throwing guilt at me."

"I'm just kidding. A little."

"I can't help it that you two spent your time everywhere. I send you to Bleary Hardware, you think of him. I send you anywhere downtown for that matter, you think of him. Just the journey to town has you thinking of him. So why not work the day here?"

Tracy took a deep breath. "You're right."

"I know I am. And outside of being glum, you're doing a fantastic job." Aunt Dee smiled and winked, moving out of the way as another guest entered the lodge and approached the counter.

"Hi, welcome to Woodsman's Lodge." Aunt Dee pointed at her smiling lips in the background, and Tracy forced a bigger one. "Do you have a reservation with us for Lovetoberfest?"

"Yes." The woman fumbled for a paper in her purse. Her hands shook and her ears turned redder than her blushing face. "Here's my confirmation."

"No problem"—Tracy unfolded the paper for the name and reservation—"Miss Cartwright." She logged the woman's arrival in the computer and retrieved the room key.

"I can't really believe I'm here and doing this." The young woman oozed with nerves.

Tracy handed back the paper, along with the room key. "Don't be so nervous. Just think, everyone else here for Lovetoberfest is in the same boat."

The woman nodded. The front door opened, and Miss Cartwright startled. The man turned his back to the counter, taking in the room.

Aunt Dee was right. All these guests wanted was to find that special someone to spend their time with, someone they could potentially spend the rest of their lives with.

Tracy turned away from the computer and looked at Miss Cartwright directly. "Look, I personally tried out all the dates. The absolute worst that could happen is that you get to see the best parts of Waverly Lake, without having to be by yourself, and you don't happen to make a connection."

The woman sighed, and for the first time smiled genuinely. "When you put it like that it's not so bad."

"It's not bad at all." The man behind Miss Cartwright turned around, hands in jacket pockets, distinctive green and brown eyes sending pinpricks along Tracy's arms.

"Oh, are you here for Lovetoberfest?" Miss Cartwright asked, her voice still a little trembling.

Ben shrugged. "Sort of." He met Tracy's shocked gaze and returned to Miss Cartwright. "I didn't mean to overhear, so I apologize. But Tracy is right. You'll have a great time this weekend, whether love is in the cards or not."

The woman smiled and nodded in exit, carrying her bag to the stairs.

Ben stayed put, keeping his distance from the counter. Tracy walked around, still shocked to see him. She had all the time in the world these past few days to think of what to say to him if he ever did return, and now that he was here...

Her mind was hollow, not a word within reach to spew out. She rewound time, to their last encounter, when she walked out of The Cake Zone, and the next day when Aunt Dee told her where he'd gone.

"What are you doing here? I thought you were fifty miles down the AT by now."

"Yeah, well, I quickly learned why few people hike the AT this late in the season."

Tracy squinted, as if that would help in understanding him. "That's why you're back? Because of the weather?"

He nodded. "Not going to lie. It did get bad there in the rain." He stared at his boots before meeting her eyes again. "But that's not the real reason." He nodded towards the table and chairs by the mural, and Tracy followed him, taking a seat.

"I wanted to apologize," he said.

"That's a good start." Tracy kept calm in her face, the opposite of how she felt inside.

"I had meant to tell you that night at the baking class, who I really am."

Tracy started to shake her head.

"Please, hear me out." He shifted in his seat, closer to the edge. "I realize now that even that was wrong. I should've told you much sooner. I should've let the whole town know. But especially, of all people...you were my best friend all those years ago, and I never forgot it. If I had to choose one person to see upon my return last week, it would've been you."

"So why not tell me?" His words were already melting her facade. Damn him. She was supposed to be upset. "It could've been so different."

"I know." He rubbed his face, a labored look in his eyes. "I keep thinking about that. How different would it have been? What would be different? And every time I go down that path, I conclude one thing."

"Which is?"

"I think we would've resumed our friendship right away."

"Would that have been so bad?" Her patience was starting to dwindle.

"Yes." He sat taller and nodded. "Yes, it would have."

Tracy's jaw dropped. "If this is your apology, then I don't accept."

He held up a hand. "I say it would've been bad because we would've been friends and not what we ended up becoming. I think —no, I know—I would've fallen in love with you no matter what you wanted us to be. But I don't know if you would've let yourself love me back if we had that label on us."

Tracy's guts twisted. "That's pretty bold of you to assume."

"That we would've stayed in the friend zone?"

"That I loved you back." She regretted it immediately. She wanted to hurt him as badly as he'd hurt her, and she'd accomplished it. But all it did was make her feel worse, seeing the pain she had inflicted, written on his face.

He crept back in the seat. "Maybe I was wrong about that too."

The disappointment in his face practically brought her to tears. She placed her hands on the table, ready to get up. "If that's all you have to say, I have to get back to work. It's Aunt Dee's big weekend, and I can't let her down."

"Wait." Ben grabbed a hold of her arm on her way up. He stood too, right in front of her. "All the years away from this place, I'd been looking for who I really am, who I want to be. It wasn't until I returned that I realized I had been running from my past, from myself. But I'm here for good. I've taken ownership of the estate, and I'm ready to try to live up to the legacy my parents left."

Tracy loosened from his touch. "I'm happy you figured it all out. I really am."

She walked to the kitchen, just somewhere in another room so she could escape from this, shutting herself off from what she felt compelled to say back.

"The fact is that I can do this without you," he said.

She stopped walking, but didn't turn around.

"But Tracy, I don't *want* to do this without you. I'm not saying I need your help. In fact, I'll do all the work no matter how grueling and dirty, if it means you'll just be there, by my side, in this next phase of my life. Of our lives. I love you, Tracy."

The tears had a mind of their own, leaking out of her eyes worse than the dripping faucet she had discovered yesterday in the upstairs bathroom.

She turned around, not ashamed to show the ugly cry. It didn't matter anymore. "What I want to tell you, is that I did fall in love with you. But that I fell in love with only part of you. I don't know who you are. You lied to me and hid things from me, and I can't trust you. That's what I want to say to you."

He nodded, biting his bottom lip, the tears refusing to cooperate with him. "I understand." He stepped back, towards the front door.

"But I'm not saying those things to you," Tracy said. "I'm not saying them, because I do know you. All of you, kid and adult. As much as my head tells me not to, I *can* trust you. I wouldn't trust my life with anyone else."

He stepped back towards her.

"I am here to stay too," she said.

"For good?"

A smile broke her tears. "Long enough to try all the dishes. With you."

He rushed to her, embracing her as if she was falling and needed his support. She did need it. She needed to feel his hands on her face, his lips on her lips, kissing her with fervor and fire, feeling the warmth of his mouth and taste of his passion.

She cried and giggled with joy, his lips breaking away from hers to kiss her tearful cheeks and finally her forehead before separating from her.

"I think we made our first match of Lovetoberfest." Aunt Dee stood by the two guests at the stairs, who clapped out of both cheer and confusion.

Tracy hid her face on Ben's shoulder. "That's embarrassing."

"Nah." He caressed her curls off her face, and she looked up at him. She meant what she said. She didn't care about his name or the secrets or any of what bothered her the past two days. She was exactly where she wanted to be, in his arms. "That's just love."

She gasped at a thought. "Maybe that's why it's called Truelove Trail. No matter how long you're gone or try to leave, it leads you back to where you're supposed to be. Who you're supposed to be with."

Ben took a step back. "Wait, what happened to cynical, eye-rolling Tracy?" He jokingly looked around the room.

She pushed him playfully.

"Maybe you're onto something there. Or maybe it has nothing to do with the trail, and more to do with Aunt Dee." He slipped something in Tracy's hand. "Aunt Dee came to visit me on the trail. She told me you had canceled your trip overseas."

Tracy nodded, opening the folded paper in her hands. It was the printout of her spreadsheet that had gone missing. "That Aunt Dee." She looked back at her.

Aunt Dee jumped to action with the guests. "How about I give you a tour of the upstairs. There's some good history in these walls." She winked back at Tracy.

Ben pointed to the empty comments cell by the bakery date. "I was wondering if you'd like a redo on that fifth date?" He smiled, his hand rubbing her back.

She pointed to her notes at the bottom about their time on the boat during the sunset cruise. "I had actually considered that one our first date. The first real one."

"Oh?"

"It was the first time we were together because we wanted to be, independent of Aunt Dee's assignment."

He tilted his head. "I guess you're right."

She bit her lip, stopping the desire to taste his again. "So how about we go on a second one?"

Epilogue

Saturday, Five Weeks Later

"ARE YOU SURE THIS PLACE IS GOING TO BE READY BY Christmas?" Tracy stood in the kitchen of Phillips Manor, now The Phillips Community Center of Waverly Lake. In such a short time, Ben—and that was what he asked to be called now, Ben Phillips—had cleaned up most of the first floor of the house. He had salvaged the wallpaper in several of the rooms, replaced some of the tiles in the foyer and kitchen, and changed out the appliances while adding a gas line.

It wasn't the size of a commercial kitchen, but it was close. Enough to be able to prep, cook and store food for dozens of people on whatever occasion was needed. That was Tracy's department. Just the thought of the possibilities throughout the year of Easter egg hunts on the front lawn, or Fourth of July cookouts, arts and crafts for kids—she had too many ideas she couldn't imagine ever getting bored as the official event coordinator.

Not to mention she had the chance to be around the man she loved.

"It's my job to worry about that." Ben wrapped his arm around her waist and pulled her close, kissing her as if stealing a much-needed breath of air. "You just need to worry about getting the word out and filling up the place."

"Don't you worry about that." She tapped his nose and kissed him back. "This place has been the talk of the town for the past month. I just hope we can pull it off. It'd be so great to see this place filled with happiness again. I never realized how many people went without family or Christmas dinner around here, and to give that to people is amazing."

Ben's idea not only honored his parents, especially his mother, but gave him what he missed after his parents died. He explained to Tracy his life as a foster child, spending holidays with temporary family or not celebrating them at all. He missed out on the sense of community between family, friends, and neighbors. He wanted that for everyone in Waverly Lake. A community center right in the heart of the town that everyone could get to, unlike the county community center thirty miles away.

"We'd better stop chatting then and get on with it." Ben winked, and Danny walked through the door.

"Knock, knock." He tapped the frame of the door with one hand, the other carrying a flat box. "Thought I'd bring donuts."

"We've got the coffee." Kara appeared behind him with Hannah.

"You didn't have to do that," Ben said.

"You have to eat sometime," Kara said. "With what Danny has told me, you all have been working day and night on this place."

Tracy eyed the workers outside through the window, one of them on a ladder leaning against the outside wall. "I'm just getting nervous it won't be done in time."

"There you go again. You have to trust me." Ben selected a donut and took a big bite.

"I didn't think I'd ever live to see the day." Danny put the box down and chose a donut for himself.

"Those are for Ben and Tracy and the workers," Kara said.

"I'll sweep up the kitchen when we're through. Does that count as a worker?"

Kara nudged him, and they chuckled.

"You didn't think you'd live to see the day this place would be restored?" Ben blew over the steaming cup of coffee.

"I never thought I'd see Tracy take on such responsibility." This time Tracy elbowed him, and he laughed. "And actually enjoy it."

Tracy handed a glazed donut to Hannah. "Don't you listen to your dad, Hannah. There is another job I love, and that's babysitting you."

"Can't do that forever," Hannah said, her tone as level as the new kitchen countertops.

Tracy scoffed, and Danny and Kara got a good laugh.

"Just what are you teaching my precious Hannah?" Tracy asked. "I didn't know sarcasm was a subject in second grade."

"Yet you excelled in it." Danny grinned.

"Right." Tracy stood up from rustling Hannah's hair. "If it had been a subject, I would've had an easy A."

Kara whispered something to Danny, and his eyes grew.

"Oh yeah, I almost forgot. I also came by to invite you both to Sunday brunch tomorrow."

Tracy eyed Ben, who looked confused. They had attended Sunday brunches since October, when Ben decided to stay for good. And Tracy.

"We'll be there, as usual," Tracy said.

Kara bit her lip and Danny grinned. "It's going to be a little different."

Tracy placed her hand on her hip. "Different how?"

"Think bigger." Danny urged Kara to stick out her hand. A diamond ring shone on her finger.

"Is it—You guys?" Tracy screamed and hugged Kara, then Danny.

"We haven't told Mom and Dad yet, so we thought we'd surprise them tomorrow."

"Do you think that's a good idea, surprising Mom like that?" Tracy met Danny's eyes, and they both nodded in agreement. It was a brilliant idea. Mom was going to be elated.

"All right, we'll leave you guys to it," Danny said. "Come on Hannah, we've got to go."

"Can I have another donut?"

"I think one is enough," her father said.

Tracy grabbed another glazed one and handed it to her with a wink.

Danny wagged a finger. "I'll remember that when you have kids."

Whether by instinct or something else, she met eyes with Ben, who simply grinned. Maybe marriage and children were in their future, but she didn't worry about that.

Danny and his family left, quieting the room as much as could be with the clamoring going on outside. Tracy stared at Ben, breathing slowly, a calmness washing over her.

"What?" Ben asked.

"I was just thinking how we talked about skydiving before, and I realize now I was wrong."

"Wrong how?"

"That there is something that tops skydiving." She wrapped her arms around his waist and pulled him in close. She nuzzled her nose with his, then softly touched her lips to his in a sweet kiss before pulling away.

"This."

***

Thank you for reading! Did you enjoy? Please add your review because nothing helps an author more and encourages readers to take a chance on a book than a review.

And don't miss more in the of the Waverly Lake series with book three, CHRISTMAS ISLAND, coming soon!

Until then read more great books like RESCUE ME, by City Owl Author, Lauren Connolly. Turn the page for a sneak peek!

Also be sure to sign up for the City Owl Press newsletter to receive notice of all book releases!

Sneak Peek of...

RESCUE ME BY LAUREN CONNOLLY

One of these houses is mine. I'm just not exactly sure *which* one.

A sigh pushes out, weighty and exhausted, from deep in my chest. The sun set hours ago, back when I was still on the highway. Trying to read the tiny print on each of these mailboxes isn't easy after staring out the windshield for the past two days. My eyes practically crackle, begging me to close them.

Sleep. Just go to sleep.

"That one! I...I think."

I pull up alongside the curb, letting the heavy engine rumble on as I flip through photos on my phone. Martin sent me a picture two weeks ago, a selfie of him with a large tan house behind him that looks like the one I've stopped in front of. Unfortunately, the homes on either side of it are mirror reflections.

Normally, Martin's preference for uniformity doesn't bother be. Tonight, though, I wish he had picked a weird bungalow with daisies painted on the siding and a turquoise front door. Just so I know, without a hint of a doubt, that I am parking in front of *my* house.

And I am definitely parking because I need to pick one of these clone homes before I drive myself mad puttering around this neighborhood all night.

As I shut down the engine, the whole car settles as if she's ready to sleep for the night.

"Enjoy your rest, Penelope," I mutter to the steering wheel.

I need a bed bad. A pounding started in my temples way before I even crossed the Louisiana/Mississippi border. The headache comes courtesy of long hours in the car paired with my hair being pulled up into a high, messy bun. I'd let the heavy mass down if I wasn't terrified of its condition. Two days' worth of greasiness has built up. I doubt removing my hairband would even do anything. The hair would likely continue sitting on top of my head, permanently reshaped.

My priorities have changed: before a bed, I need a shower. The vision of scrubbing a thick lather of shampoo into my scalp plays in my brain like a porno. I can imagine the transformation of the knotted mess into its normal smooth cascade.

"Butter on bread," my mom always says when she affectionately tugs on a strand.

Not sure I approve of being compared to a boring slice of white bread, but I take comfort in the fact that she's simply referring to my complexion and hair color rather than my personality.

When I push the car door open, the heavy New Orleans air embraces me. It is almost as warm and wet as an actual shower but nowhere near as refreshing. The humidity sits on my skin, weighing me down as I trudge up the front walk of a house that I hope is mine.

The easy solution would've been to just call Martin on Friday night when I decided to change my travel plans. That way my fiancé would be waiting out on the porch, ready to wave me down.

Instead, I chose the surprise method. I'd like to convince myself that this is a romantic gesture.

I just couldn't stay away from you for two more weeks!

In reality, my silence arises from shame. Whenever I let my thumb hover over his number, I couldn't even imagine how the conversation would go.

"Hey, honey! Guess what? I lost my job!" I whisper under my breath and pause with my foot on the bottom step leading up to the elevated porch.

Well, I guess I *could* say that.

Now that I'm here, potentially a few steps away from Martin, the words don't seem so inadequate. Depressing? Yeah sure. But I can clearly envision his face, how his blond brows will dip in the middle as he scowls. Not *at* me but *with* me. I can taste the glass of red wine he'll pour me as he rages over the unfair treatment.

That's when I realize why the need for surprise. I don't actually want to *talk* about how I got fired from my dream job. All I want is to see my anger reflected in the face of my partner. To feel connected to him in a way I haven't in a while.

With the moving plans, and Martin preparing to start his residency down here, and me trying to finish up all my large projects before going remote, we've barely talked. I can't even remember the last time I looked him in the eyes during a conversation. We usually just shout to each other from opposite rooms.

And sex? Well...it's been some time.

As I knock on the mystery door I hope is mine, I make a resolution. Whether I find Martin in this clone house or the one next door or the next street over, when I finally locate my fiancé, the first thing I'm going to do is stare deep into his eyes. I'll hold his gaze until our connection is firmly reestablished. Then—after a shower—I'm going to jump his bones.

Light spills into the dark night from around the edges of the curtains. At least that means whoever lives here, hopefully Martin, is still awake. After the polite taps of my knock ring out, the steady pad of footsteps sound behind the door. I brace myself, ready to stare my fiancé down.

Only, Martin doesn't open the door.

A small slim woman dressed in a robe stands before me. She is adorably petite. I could practically fit her in my pocket. Her bare feet peek out from under the floor-length robe, and her long brown hair lays in a damp mass over her shoulders.

Envy spikes hard through me. Clearly, this woman has just taken a shower. My greasy strands weep in envy.

Also, her appearance makes it clear my navigation skills have failed me. I am no closer to my own glorious shower, having no idea which one of these houses Martin bought for the two of us to live in.

"Sorry. I thought this might be my house. Do you know a blond man? About so tall?" I hold my hand a few inches above my head like the sleep drunk idiot I am.

I'm ready to continue describing my fiancé out of pure desperation when I notice the woman's face. With a stranger knocking on her door at midnight, I would expect confusion or annoyance. But if I had to guess, her slack-jawed, wide-eyed stare is closer to horror.

Apparently, my need for a shower is even direr than I knew.

"I told you I'd get it..." The familiar rusty voice drifts from behind the stranger as my fiancé trots down a set of stairs visible just over her shoulder.

The showered girl shuffles back, so I have a clear view of Martin, clad in only a pair of gym shorts, his hair just as gloriously damp from a recent cleaning as the woman in front of me.

Our eyes meet. His top half stops, but his bottom half doesn't get the memo. Instead, one of his bare feet slips on the wooden step, and he lands hard on his ass, shocked gaze never leaving mine.

So, this *is* the right house.

It's just everything else in the world that is wrong.

Whatever way I might want to interpret this situation is made impossible when I flick my eyes back to the stranger, who I now realize is wearing *my* green, cotton robe. Red splotches scorch along the tops of her cheekbones, and guilty tears pool on her lashes.

Something dark and sickening rolls in my stomach, but I flash freeze it. After one last look at the boy I've loved since my senior year of high school, I turn to the girl he chose to hurt me for.

"You can keep the robe." Reaching out, I clasp the doorknob. "And the man." I wrench the door closed on the most devastating scene of my life and sprint back to my sleeping car.

Penelope revs to life, more dependable than any man could ever be.

I shift into first gear and tear down the street, not caring who I wake up. With the roar of my sweet girl's engine, I can't hear Martin shouting.

But I can see him. In my rearview mirror, he sprints down the street after me. I skid around a corner and lose sight of him.

And he loses me.

I drive in an emotional fog, unable to dislodge the frozen ball of grief in my chest. The devastation sticks to the inside of my skull, blocking my ability to think.

It's only when I almost run a red light that I realize I shouldn't be driving.

Pulling into the next parking lot, I somehow end up in the drive-through lane of a fast-food joint. Functioning on autopilot, I roll down my window when I reach the speaker.

"What do you want?" The woman asks with the complete disinterest that can only be achieved by someone employed for the night shift at a drive-through.

The question hits me hard. Acting as a chisel, it splits the ice in my chest apart.

Grief flows free.

"What do I want?" I laugh, high-pitched and manic. "Oh, I don't know. How about a job? Or a home? Maybe my dignity?"

And now I'm crying.

"Um...we serve chicken."

I've gone insane. Martin's betrayal has turned me into a raving loon who drives around New Orleans in the middle of the night scaring fast-food workers.

This isn't me. I'm not this type of weird.

"Oh. Right. Of course." Swiping away the tears blurring my vision and pulling in a few choking breaths, I attempt to read the glowing menu. "I guess a family meal then."

"Eight, twelve, or sixteen pieces?"

The cracked ice in my chest has given way to a massive aching hole.

"Better make it sixteen."

"You want it with sides?"

I'm not going to be able to manage many more of these questions without the crazy laughing/crying returning.

"Yeah, whatever sides are popular. And biscuits, please. I'm gonna need a whole lot of biscuits." A sob makes the last word come out choked.

She rattles off the total, and I pull around to the window to pay. A short woman wearing a goofy chicken hat gives me a kinder smile than I was expecting after my breakdown.

"I slipped an extra biscuit in there," she whispers while passing me the armload of fried comfort.

"Thank you," I mutter, keeping my eyes to myself and hoping I never run into this lovely woman again.

For a moment, I park and consider consuming the entire order myself.

The idea is tempting.

But I still need a shower and a bed.

Penelope's engine purrs like a comforting embrace, as I pull back out on the road. The headlights point toward my childhood home.

My parents are about to get a late-night visitor, bearing fried chicken and a broken heart.

Don't stop now. Keep reading with your copy of RESCUE ME, by City Owl Author, Lauren Connolly.

And don't miss more in the of the Waverly Lake series with book three, CHRISTMAS ISLAND, coming soon!

Don't miss CHRISTMAS ISLAND, book three of the Waverly Lake series, coming soon, and find more from Mary Shotwell at www.maryshotwell.com

Until then, discover RESCUE ME, by City Owl Author, Lauren Connolly!

Summer Pierce is determined to date only nice guys. But when her latest prospect reveals himself as an alpha jerk in decent clothing, Summer doubts her ability to distinguish good from bad. Especially when her hot, pierced, tattooed library patron with an aloof attitude ends up supporting her on her darkest day. Could trusting a "bad boy" be a huge mistake?

Cole Allemand visits the library for the books, but he stays for the librarian. Summer is as bright and warm as her name, and luckily, she has a hero worship for authors. While Cole works days at a local animal shelter, at night he's putting the finishing touches on his novel. All he needs is a book deal, and the woman he's been crushing on for months will be within reach. Only, Cole finds he can't wait for the publishing world to give him his go ahead, especially when he knows his past may push Summer away.

As the two form a bond outside of the library, Cole works to strengthen the connection with all the tools at his disposal, including serialized fantasy stories, adorable cats, and an in-depth understanding of the Dewey Decimal system. When a mysterious stalker threatens the librarian's safety, trust becomes the element that could turn their tale into a true romance or tear apart the fragile happy ending.

Please sign up for the City Owl Press newsletter for chances to win special subscriber-only contests and giveaways as well as receiving information on upcoming releases and special excerpts.

All reviews are **welcome** and **appreciated**. Please consider leaving one on your favorite social media and book buying sites.

Escape Your World. Get Lost in Ours! City Owl Press at www.cityowlpress.com.

Acknowledgments

Thank you City Owl Press, for giving me the flexibility to expand the stories of characters in Waverly Lake. You're an amazing group of people who stand up for authors and issues you believe in. Thank you to my editor, Tee Tate, who has the gentle patience to put up with my commonly repeated errors with such grace. To my agent, Amy Brewer at Metamorphosis Literary, for support and feedback on this second book in the series.

Thank you to my readers and fans who fell in love with Waverly Lake, and wanted to continue with this setting and cast of characters here in book two. I am grateful for your reviews, support, and interaction on social media.

A special thanks to my husband and friends who have taught me what I know about hiking and backpacking. Matt, even though I complained about blisters, you put up with me and motivated me to finish that section during our honeymoon. I wanted to write a character who loves the outdoors as much as you do, so I hope you like Ben.

About the Author

MARY SHOTWELL is the author of small-town love stories with happily-ever-afters for all seasons. Her debut romance novel *Christmas Catch* (Carina Press, 2018) was a Golden Leaf Finalist and earned a starred review from Library Journal. She loves incorporating her science and nature background into her fiction. When adulting, she's a wife to husband Matt and mother to three children. She currently resides in Tennessee.

Visit her website to her blog about writing, travels and publication news.

www.maryshotwell.com

facebook.com/AuthorMaryShotwell

twitter.com/MaryEShotwell

instagram.com/authormaryshotwell

tiktok.com/@authormaryshotwell

About the Publisher

City Owl Press is a cutting edge indie publishing company, bringing the world of romance and speculative fiction to discerning readers.

Escape Your World. Get Lost in Ours!

www.cityowlpress.com

facebook.com/CityOwlPress

twitter.com/cityowlpress

instagram.com/cityowlbooks

pinterest.com/cityowlpress

tiktok.com/@cityowlpress

Made in United States
Orlando, FL
01 August 2022

20448914R00150